Ballad of the Beanstalk

Amy McNulty

www.patchwork-press.com

COPYRIGHT

To everyone who's ever dreamed of a fantastical world just around the corner.

Chapter 1

The worm Clarion almost impaled with the dibbler poked its long, pale head through the dirt toward her, so straight and taut it was like a dagger someone stabbed up from beneath the soil. At first she thought she'd missed it entirely, but after she instinctively turned the tool and drilled the hole larger, she watched it stretch and fight until it snapped its own tail off.

Clarion stared as it slithered into the upturned earth and gaped at the still-wiggling tail that flopped from beneath the dibbler.

"Clair?" Elena readjusted her bonnet and tucked a strand of auburn hair that'd fallen out of her plaits back inside the fabric. "Have you found something?"

Krea scooted over, the basket full of seeds hanging from the crook of her arm tipping slightly, almost causing the basket's contents to fall. "Oo, is it some crystal? Mum told me to be on the lookout for crystal in the witch's garden, she did. Rocks have healing powers."

"Your mother has more rocks growing in her head than there are rocks in my garden." Jacosa finished scooping water from the little canal that ran through her property and out under the stone wall that protected her garden from rabbits and other varmints. "And there's no such thing as magical healing crystals, and if there were, you wouldn't find them growing in the dirt like common potatoes." She dropped the watering can next to Krea's feet, causing the poor girl to jump back and lose a few of the seeds in her basket. "You'd be wise not to call me a witch within earshot, either, not if you hope to make use of any of my potions and poultices ever again."

Krea mumbled something about there being "nothing wrong with a witch being called a witch" but pressed her lips tightly together when she caught Jacosa eyeing her.

"It's just a worm." Clarion stood and slapped some of the dirt off her skirt. Most of it blended right in with the dust and mud caked on from mucking around with the last two pigs left on her family's small pig farm. "I'm sorry. I... I was just thinking."

"I know we raise them, care for them, and become their surrogate parents, only for them to wind up on our neighbors' supper tables." Clarion's papa didn't mention that they wound up on their own table, too. Or that they became trade for the cows, sheep, and chickens that wound up roasting in their place over the fire. The piglet thrashed under his grip as he tried to slip the tip of the kitchen knife beneath the splinter in the pig's leg. *"But that doesn't mean we don't treat them with kindness while they're with us. Hold it still, Clair."*

Clarion squeezed the pig's little hoof tighter and stretched the leg out as far as it would go. She didn't like being so close to the pigs then, especially when they were squealing and thrashing like they were little monsters.

Her papa twisted the knife and the splinter of wood

popped out. He lay the knife beside him on the ground and picked up a piece of scrap cloth, tying it tightly around the animal's injured leg. His eyes met Clarion's and the corner of his lips twitched up into a smile. "We have a responsibility as the bigger species, no matter what others may say."

He smacked the piglet's hind end and Clarion let go. The piglet scrambled off to join its four siblings at the trough.

"Grab it, then, they're good for the chickens." Krea dropped her basket on the ground and peered into the small hole created by Clarion's dibbler. Clarion snapped back to the present, remembering the worm instead of the piglet. She was sure Krea couldn't have imagined that the sight of an injured worm had conjured up images of Clarion's late father. Krea showed little interest in the work of her own papa, and besides, the town blacksmith had little knowledge he cared to pass on to his daughter when he had four sons from whom to choose to succeed him. Never mind that they were all under the age of six.

Krea's lips puckered. "I don't see no worm."

Elena picked up the watering can. "You don't see *any* worms."

Krea glared at Elena. Clarion wondered if she should say something. She hated when Elena understood what Krea meant but felt the need to "fix" her words anyway. It often led to unnecessary fights between them.

"All right, all right." Jacosa clapped her hands together. "Seeds don't sow themselves." She tapped her index finger against her bottom lip. "Although that would be very convenient, wouldn't it? Maybe I have something that can make an animal to do it for me. Oh—for crying out loud!"

The girls paused in their work to examine the eccentric enchantress. Jacosa kicked at a large rock—about the size of her torso—with her boot. She tossed her hands in the air before crouching down. "Fell off the fence here, I reckon." She grabbed it with both hands and strained to pull it backward, groaning.

Clarion moved to assist her, but Jacosa waved her away. "No, no. Don't trouble yourself. I'll have to do this another way." She stood and shook her head to no one in particular, walking off toward her cottage and slapping her palms together. "Always something, isn't it? Always something." The familiar far-off look in her eye let Clarion know the witch had all but forgotten the girls she left behind. "If only I could boost my magic. If only it weren't so darn hard. And disgusting..."

Clarion wondered at what the witch might do. The older woman didn't like wasting magic. It was why she offered some of her magicked herbs and spices in exchange for the villagers' help in her garden instead of figuring out some other way to do it on her own. Jacosa never wasted any of her most enchanted plants for the trouble, just the little ones that could cure a sprained ankle in two minutes or make a woman having trouble bearing children fertile. (The latter was for Krea's mother. And it worked far too well, to tell the truth.)

Clarion had gotten distracted again, had forgotten to soothe the tension between her two dearest friends. They were still arguing.

"You have a problem with the way I talk, I'll thank you to keep it to yourself." Krea's too-big bonnet slipped down over her eyes. It was a hand-me-down from her mamma because she was too proud to take any of the old ones Elena didn't want.

Elena turned away from Krea, likely because the sun shone so brightly behind her towering friend. She didn't like when her skin got too much sun. It made freckles break out all over her nose, and although Clarion thought she looked adorable with those little flecks of color on her small and elegant nose, Elena thought they made her look rugged and childish. "All right. I'm sorry. You won't have to tell me twice."

"No, I'll have to tell you a dozen times before sundown." Krea scoffed and snatched her seed basket back from where she'd left it. "And you still won't learn your lesson." She tossed a pinch of the seeds unceremoniously at the hole.

Elena's voice lost some of its sweetness as it cracked. "How many times do you expect me to apologize?"

Clarion crouched to cover the seeds with dirt and remove her tool. The piece of the worm left behind had ceased moving. She didn't think until too late to remove the dibbler holding it down, but she wasn't sure if it'd do any more good anyway. Her papa had told her once that when a worm snapped like that, it became two separate beings, but she didn't know if he was teasing her or telling the truth, now that she thought of it. And she'd never have the chance to ask him again.

The dibbler slipped from her fingers. She felt the tears on her cheeks before she even knew they were forming, heard the choke escape her throat before she realized she was about to make a sound.

"Clair!" Elena put her hands on Clarion's shoulders and helped her stand on shaking legs. "Let's get to the shade."

Krea followed the pair to the largest tree in Jacosa's garden, a giant apple tree that was just starting to blossom. Elena spread her skirt out among the white petals that had already fallen, as if she were posing for an artist's portrait. Krea bristled a little as she dropped her seed basket and sat cross-legged on the other side of Clarion, who wiped her eyes with the bottom of her palm.

"Clair? You okay?" Krea reached over to hug her, squishing Clarion's tanned cheek against her own. When Clarion opened her eyes, she found Elena frowning at them.

"Come here," said Elena as Krea loosened her grip. Elena wrapped her arms around Clarion more gracefully, resting her cheek against Clarion's ear. When the two girls drew apart after a moment, Elena kept one arm around Clarion's back and held the other out toward Krea. "You too. I'm sorry. Really, I am."

The three friends, often confused for sisters in their sixteen shared years of life, rocked in their three-way embrace. Krea didn't stop the never-ending chain of arms from swaying until Clarion finally laughed, and her eyes brightened.

"Ah! There you are!" Krea pinched Clarion's cheek, bringing forth a flush of color. "The pig farmer's daughter, as her papa loved to see her."

Elena's arm dropped from Clarion's shoulders slowly, almost reluctantly. She straightened her bonnet and tucked in that loose tendril of hair, which had fallen from her plaits again. "Why don't you sing, Clair?"

"Sing?" asked Clarion. Her head sank into her shoulders. "Here? Now?"

"Why not?" added Krea. "Don't you need to practice for the springtime ball?"

Clarion wove her fingers together. They were cracked and dirty, and calloused from too many plucks of the string. "I don't have Papa's harp."

"*Your* harp," said Elena, but she soon seemed to think better of it. "He wanted you to inherit it. It's the last legacy from your family, from back when they led this village. I mean... Anyway."

Clarion knew why the latter words spilled so quickly from Elena's lips. It was *her* family that had wrested control from the last lord and started calling themselves the "mayors" of the town. Elena was often embarrassed by that fact. But that was half a century ago, and besides, Clarion's papa had had no sons, so there'd have been no one to inherit the position even if he had been lord.

"Well, I don't have the harp with me." Clarion's face glowed when mentioning her most prized possession. "But I'll sing if you sing with me." She took both Krea's and Elena's hands in hers, more to anchor herself in the moment than to encourage them to join her.

Clarion was the first to sing, and her voice, like a breath of air after an exhausting run, rung out over the

6

rustling branches and blossoms and the twittering of the birds in the grasses nearby. *"They told me you had left for the land above. I told them you would never leave me, my love."*

Elena joined in, her voice timid and quiet, her eyes never leaving Clarion's face. *"But when I looked for you, you had gone. I couldn't give up; I searched all over 'til dawn."*

Krea was always less confident about joining her friends, but Clarion smiled at her even as she sang the next verse, and Krea added her own voice, although it was the wrong notes and it sounded like she had a sore throat. *"Were you stolen away by the kings of old? Or did I know ye not, so I've been told?"*

The girls stopped to giggle, even Krea, despite the flush on her neck. But when they continued, a young man's tenor voice broke out from the dirt path along the stone wall surrounding Jacosa's garden.

"I'd like to have faith that I knew ye well. That you love me still, and in the land above you dwell."

"Jackin Mayorsson!" Krea snatched a handful of grass and tossed it at Jackin, ignoring how the blades simply fluttered in the wind. "You ruined a perfectly good ladies' harmony by jumping in there uninvited."

"A perfectly good ladies' harmony?" Leaning forward, Jackin placed both elbows on the top of the small stone wall. "Are your ears as ill-suited for music as your tongue?"

"You know what I mean!" Krea wrinkled her slightly-too-long nose. She gestured at her friends. "These ladies."

Jackin's gaze floated dreamily over Krea's head to Clarion sitting beside her. "Yes, in that case, I'm sorry to have stopped the song."

Elena stood and slapped her skirt for any traces of grass stains and dirt. "Well, out with it. What does Father want?"

"What makes you think our father wants you for anything?" Jackin tore his gaze reluctantly from Clarion. Clarion shifted uncomfortably, remembering that day a few weeks ago he'd told her how perfectly the traces of her brown hair poking out from beneath the bonnet complimented her hazel eyes. "I'm here on other business."

Elena shrugged and picked up her skirt. "I'll get Jacosa then."

"Yeah..." Jackin slouched until his chin nearly touched the stone, completely forgetting to disguise where his eyes were fixed once more.

Clarion didn't have to stare at him long to *feel* his eyes poring over her. She'd noticed it for months now, maybe longer. She hadn't had time to think much about it, not with her papa passing, and the remaining pigs still needing looking after.

Krea cleared her throat. She felt the intensity of Elena's strapping brother's blue-green gaze, but she mistook the intent. "I'm supposing you already have a lady escort for the springtime ball now, Jackin?"

Jackin's head snapped up, the fact that Krea was still present seemingly almost as surprising to him as her question. "Well, no. Actually, I thought... That is, if you—" His eyes seemed determined to catch Clarion's, but Clarion kept darting her gaze back to her hands.

"Yes!" Krea jumped up, tripping over her hem as she snatched both of Jackin's hands in hers. "Yes! I'd love to go with you!"

Jackin's face fell at once. "Krea? I didn't mean... I thought you'd be going with Tenney and—"

Krea dropped just one of Jackin's hands in order to wave at him dismissively. "Pox on Tenney Woolman and all his poxy friends. That fool don't deserve a cow for a date, nor do any of them either."

If Jackin were as cruel as some of those boys, he might have said that Krea was as close to having a cow for a date as one could get, short of putting a bonnet on an actual bovine. Not that Clarion agreed with that assessment at all. Blonde and tall and well-endowed, Krea was fair enough, in her rough way, but Clarion knew the boys in the town, and she knew not a one of them had any eye for beauty. Jackin wrested his hand free of Krea's and ran it through his silver-white curly locks. He stood straighter and cleared his throat. "But I can't let Clarion go without an escort. It wouldn't be right."

Intending to pick up her dibbler, Clarion had already descended the small hill. She heard her name but responded a moment too late, her thoughts still elsewhere. "Me? No, I'm all right. Your father asked me to bring my harp to play."

Jackin frowned. "But you can't play the entire time."

"I'm not much for dancing." Clarion patted the earth back over the holes she'd made now that Krea had filled the voids with seeds. "Besides, your sister asked me to be her escort."

Jackin laughed. Then the smile fell from his face. "You're serious? Two women can't be each other's escorts."

Krea looped her arm through Jackin's. "They can if they intend to keep those toads calling themselves boys away."

Pulling back, Jackin used the excuse of the wall to separate them. "Father won't approve of Elena dancing with a woman."

"Who said anything about dancing?" Krea backed up to give Jackin the space he needed to jump over the fence. "Elena's just going to watch over Clarion as she plays and beat off any suitors with a stick."

Jackin's face soured as he clapped his hands together to shake off some of the dirt.

"Jackin Mayorson, haven't you ever heard of a gate?" Jacosa weaved her way through the seedlings and newly-upturned dirt to shove a small parcel at her unwanted intruder. She kept one red bean in her grip. "I could have sent Elena home with these, you know. What'd you come all this way for?"

His gaze once again catching hold of Clarion, Jackin flushed. "I had nothing better to do."

Jacosa raised her brows. "This is why I say no good comes of a young'un without a family profession."

"We have a family profession," said Elena, catching up with Jacosa. She clutched her skirt high and was careful not to disturb any of the new plantings. "Jackin's going to be the next mayor."

Jacosa turned on her heel. "Well, I suppose doing a whole lot of nothing is proper training to be mayor, that's true."

"*Jacosa!*" Elena gasped.

Jacosa fluffed a hand at her and put the bean between her lips. Her words were hard to make out, and the bean jumped up and down as she spoke through gritted teeth. "Instead of standing here debating whether or not a young man can prove himself useful, why don't you actually start proving it?" She grabbed a piece of the bean and spit the other half out as she made her way to the giant rock. Bending over, she shook the piece over the top of the rock, then smashed the small legume against the fallen piece of fence entirely. "Now I won't need you for any heavy lifting, mind you, but I could stand a helping hand or two when it comes to corralling this, once it—"

A monstrous roar shook the earth. Clarion, crouching, fell back, and both Elena and Jackin swooped in to catch her, but Krea caught hold of Jackin first. Jacosa just planted her feet firmly onto the ground, her hands on her hips, her gaze steadfast on the clouds above.

The shaking stopped as suddenly as it'd started. Jacosa's lips puckered. "I thought they were being awful quiet these days..."

"They?" Jackin stood straight, freeing himself from Krea and tugging on his vest. "Don't tell me you believe the stories."

Jacosa poked one long, spindly finger at the bag Jackin absentmindedly cradled against his chest. "Boy your age wouldn't know the difference between a story and the truth if the truth hit him upside the skull."

As if on cue, the rock that had given Jacosa such trouble coasted through the air past them, clipping Jackin on the back of the head.

"Ack!" Rubbing the place where he'd been struck, Jackin winced as he turned. "What hit me?"

"Useless, even when I give you a task that should require no stretch of that idle mind of yours." Jacosa's face soured as she grabbed hold of her muddy skirts and stepped around Jackin, practically knocking him over, to get to the gate. "After that rock!"

Krea laughed and jumped up, threading her arm through Jackin's. "Yes, ma'am!"

Jackin seemed dazed as he stumbled after the witch and his would-be sweetheart. He didn't even spare a glance for his crush and his sister as he and Krea followed the raving woman and her flying rock down the path to the town.

Clarion watched them go, feeling warm and safe in Elena's arms. The soft tip of Elena's finger ran over Clarion's brow and down her cheek.

"Are you all right now?" asked Elena, squeezing Clarion's shoulder. There was a lot of hope in Elena's eyes, and Clarion couldn't bring herself to disappoint her.

And she was so tired of it all. So tired of explaining why she felt so lost when there were such good things all around her still. She knew that, she *did*, but it wasn't enough to fix her. To make her feel better.

"I am," lied Clarion, burying her head beneath Elena's chin. That way, Elena couldn't see the new tears.
But as she felt Elena's head shift, and the press of the dainty young woman's lips on top of her head, Clarion watched the drops tumble and fall against her sweetheart's lap.

Chapter 2

larion wiped her nose against the cuff of her sleeve for the fifth time since leaving Jacosa's. She was purposely taking the long way home, avoiding the main path for fear of bumping into Elena, Krea, and Jackin once more—and to give her eyes more time to soften and lose their puffiness. She told everyone she had to go, refusing to let anyone walk with her, on account of her mother. But she should have asked Jacosa for something to rub on the skin beneath her eyes to make the bags seem less inflamed. Not that it'd help if she couldn't stop crying.

Clarion knew the tears only made it worse, that her friends would often talk about her like she wasn't even there, like a hug and a song would be enough to make her smile and that would be the end of her gloominess. She wanted so badly to keep the tears to herself, but they kept coming unbidden. They were in the tail end of the worm in the dirt. In the breeze on her cheeks. In the mud caked on her apron. In the sight of her little farmhouse as it edged closer. In every step she took toward the ramshackle cottage that had once housed her papa.

"Welcome home, little one!" Clarion's papa was always covered in dirt and mud. He put another streak of

mud on his cheek as he wiped his nose.

"Clarion! I expected you back hours ago!" Eustace, Clarion's mother, managed to keep the dirt off her face, even if there was always the telltale sign of it on her cuffs and at the hem of her skirt.

Clarion took a deep breath and picked up her pace. She didn't want her mother to know how slowly she'd made her way there. "I was helping at Jacosa's." She dangled the small bag of medicinal herbs that had been her payment.

Her mother snatched it from her as she approached and opened it greedily, frowning at its contents. "That's it?" She stared at Clarion, as if accusing her of eating some on the way back. "You're gone all morning and half the afternoon, and that's all you have to show for it?"

Clarion wove her fingers together. "Jacosa's plants are expensive."

Eustace grunted and tied the pouch closed again, tucking the little bag into the pocket of her apron. "Yes, well, I don't see why, seeing as how she gets half the youth in town to grow it for her. If I still helped, I'd pinch some right into my pocket when the witch was inside her cottage doing whatever nonsense she does to her herbs and seedlings, I'll tell you that much."

"Jacosa told me you *did* do that, and that's why you're not welcome there anymore." Clarion regretted the words as soon as they were out of her mouth, even if they were true.

Eustace glared at her daughter. "She deserved it, too." At least she didn't deny it. She sighed and turned back to the pig pen. "Wonder if we should start our own garden. Beats trading for produce with what scraps we have."

Clarion frowned and swept past her mother. Leaning over the rickety fence her father had constructed to keep their pigs in, she searched high and low for the two remaining pigs they had. "Mother, where're Royse and Randel?"

"Royse and who?"

"*Randel*! The pigs! The last two we saved so we could breed them again."

Slipping a hand on Clarion's shoulder, Eustace sighed. "I sold them. We can't afford to feed ourselves, let alone—"

Clarion turned on her heel and slapped her mother's arm away. "The pigs are *how* we can afford anything! You can't just sell them all off. Those pigs are our livelihood!"

"The pigs *were* our livelihood." Eustace dug into her apron pocket and pulled out a large silver coin. "And people are craving ham and bacon. The butcher gave me a whole silver for the two of them, far more than they were worth."

"And what do we do now?" demanded Clarion. She knew the tears were squeezing out from between her eyelids again, but her rage kept her from wiping them away. "How will we have pigs to sell the butcher in the days to come?"

Eustace dropped the coin back into her pocket and patted it twice. "We do what I've been telling you we're gonna do, and that's the both of us are going to clean houses."

"Papa *entrusted me* with the pigs." Clarion's shoulders slumped and she slid to the ground, not caring if her dress got covered in more mud. "I stood by while you sold swine after swine, thinking so long as you let me keep Royse and Randel..." Her voice grew quieter. "I promised him I'd make him proud of me."

"Oh, hell's bells, that thoughtless father of yours." Eustace sniffed. There were tears forming in her eyes, too, but she seemed determined not to let them fall and flounder. "Expecting his wife and daughter to do the pig work. No. No, I've never had the stomach for it. Foul beasts, better on the table than in the yard."

Clarion stared up through the waves of water covering her sight. "The dirt on Papa's grave hasn't even settled yet, and you'd do this—you'd sell what little I had left of him!"

"You still have that useless harp, don't you?" Eustace

chewed her lip and stared into the house's open window. A silver light danced off a small corner of the harp from the reflection of the late afternoon sun. "You don't know how many times I asked your father if we could get rid of it—"

"No!" Clarion stood, blocking the door inside. "You can't!"

"We'd get far more for it than we would for a couple of pigs. The mayor himself made an offer only yesterday—"

"*No!*" Clarion knew her mother could shove her aside if she truly wanted. But she was determined to keep the harp hers, if only for a moment longer.

"You don't think he deserves it more than you? He has the space in his house for it—it came from his house to begin with."

Clarion stomped her foot, ignoring the droplets of water that glanced off the toe of her boot. "It was *our* house. Papa's family's house."

Eustace crossed her arms and tapped her fingers on her cheek. "Clarion, honestly, you need to stop acting so childish. You're old enough to be a wife and mother now, but I couldn't tell you apart from any of the five-year-old girls in the village, I swear. Especially not with how *distracted* you've been lately..."

Clarion's brows furrowed and she spread her arms wide. If she had already lost Royse and Randel—if she wasn't even able to say goodbye—she would do all that she could to stop her mother from taking the very last thing she had from her papa.

Eustace threw up her hands. "You've already agreed to play at the ball tomorrow. You think it's reasonable to ask the mayor to send a cart to pick up the harp only to lug it back here the next day?"

"We're not selling it!" Clarion ripped open the door and ran inside. The sheet over her harp was askew, like her mother had removed it—perhaps to show it to an eager buyer. She rubbed her forearm over her eyes and sniffed, ripping the sheet to the ground.

"Clarion," began her mother.

But Clarion had already sat down and began to play. She played the tune of the song she'd practiced singing with her friends earlier that day, the song about the man who couldn't find the woman he loved—the woman who may have been taken by those above or who may have run off to live a less unbelievable life without him. Eustace's pinched features softened and she shut the door quietly behind her. She took some logs from the stack beside the fireplace and tossed them into the hearth as her daughter played, grabbing the flint and striking it over and over on a stone, but it wouldn't light so easily. It was frayed almost to a nub. Clarion knew she'd need to use some of that silver to buy a new one. But their pantry needed stocking and Eustace needed more thread to patch the holes in their clothes and make something useful out of her papa's clothing now that he no longer needed it. Eustace tossed the useless flint atop the mantel and leaned against it, breaking into sobs.

Clarion stopped mid-song the third time through, her hand clutched in a gentle fist in the air. "Mother?" She got up quietly, shame flooding her body from the memory of their exchange a few moments before, and reached out to console her mother. She kept one hand on her mother's heaving back and grabbed the flint, examining it. "I can try lighting the fire—"

"It's sold."

Clarion froze.

Eustace stood straighter, letting her daughter's hand fall. "I promised Judd after he took it to his home for the ball, he could just keep it there. He said he'd give me three golden coins for it, Clarion. *Golden coins.*" She gripped Clarion by both of her shoulders. "You don't understand how badly we need the money. When your father was alive, we barely managed to get by, but now that he's gone and those pigs of his proved so useless..."

Clarion stepped back, away from her mother's grip, her hand still clutching the stub of flint. "You didn't..."

Eustace patted at her face with her apron. "I did. But listen, Clarion, Judd said you could come play it there at any time! In fact, he was hoping you would. He'd *pay* you to play it and entertain his family with your 'gentle music.'" She smiled. "That's what he called it. And he said his daughter suggested it."

Clarion shook her head. "She wouldn't. Elena knows how much that harp means to me."

"And she knows how poor we are now, Clair! She knows how we have to struggle just to put what little food we have on the table. Clair—"

But Clarion had already walked out the front door, her quivering palm still gripping the useless flint.

Chapter 3

larion wasn't sure where she was going at first. She ignored all the calls of "good evening" she heard as she walked through town until she remembered what her papa had always instructed.

"You're not the only one who matters, Clair." He tapped the side of her head. *"It's easy to get lost up in here, weighed down by whatever it is that ails you. A little kindness goes a long way."*

Clarion slowed her steps and threw back her shoulders, gripping the worn out flint tightly in her palm and holding her head high. "Good evening."

This worked well for her because it made the townspeople turn back to their own affairs—to their mugs of ale, their shopping, their gossiping, and wrangling their children—and if she'd run straight through them all silently crying, she would have become the next topic on their tongues.

It wasn't until one called her by name that she even thought about where she was and what she was doing and she was finally able to push the thoughts of unfairness and loss out of her mind.

"Whatcha doing over here this time of night?

Looking for deals in the market?" Krea stood in front of her father's smithy with a broom in her hand. Her papa didn't like when ashes from his forge collected in the street.

"Hi, Clarion!" called Carleton, one of Krea's little brothers. He leaned over the small wall partially blocking the view of their papa's forge. There was a large streak of soot over his nose.

"Hi." Clarion crossed one foot behind the other and gave the boy a diminutive curtsy.

"Carleton!" Blacksmith Burne called out between thundering strikes of his hammer on the anvil. "Never leave before a job is done!"

Carleton grinned and trotted back to his father. Rolling her eyes, Krea looked on. "He's only six, yeah? Give him a break, you big lug."

"Go inside and help your mother!" Burne didn't even look up from his work on what Clarion supposed was a barrel hoop. The metal glowed redder than the sun. She wondered how any of them could stand staring at it.

Krea leaned the broom against the front of the house. "Ma's the one who sent me out here," she muttered to Clarion. Her face brightened. "Hey, why don't you come inside, though, anyway? I'll show you what I'm wearing tomorrow."

In the heat of all that had happened that evening, Clarion had almost forgotten about the springtime ball— and how she'd once had no reason to dread it. Now it would mark the last moment she truly owned her family's final legacy.

The blacksmith's cottage was a little larger than Clarion's despite being so much closer to its neighbors. However, the crowd inside made it feel much smaller.

"Clarion's come over, yeah?" said Krea as they entered.

"Ricker, no! You don't put that in your mouth. Drop it!" Dena, Krea's ma, bounced her baby boy in one arm as she rapped her knuckles atop the head of one of her twins like he was no more than a dog. "I said, drop it, didn't you hear? Spit it out!"

When the boy finally did as bidden, a small ball of iron came tumbling out from between his lips and rolled across the floor. The family's orange and black calico cat jumped out from beneath the parents' bed and batted it under the kitchen table.

"Krea, snatch Eald, will you? Let her out." Dena bounced her baby again and went over to the fire, where she stirred whatever was cooking with a cast-iron ladle.

Dena must have known what would happen. The twins were shrieking as they began chasing the cat, who was after the ball. The cat yowled and gave up her chase to jump sideways with her back arched at a ridiculous degree in order to scare off her tormentors.

"Oi! Stop that, you little dunderheads!" Leaning down to reach toward her cat with one hand, Krea pushed at one of the twins with the other. "Here, here, kitty! Kitty want to go outside?"

"Ma, it's cold!" said the other twin, grinding to a halt. "You're not going to make Eald spend the night outside?"

The baby started wailing then, just as the cat's hisses got louder. Dena seemed nonplussed. "Are you going to leave 'er alone then, eh? Or am I going to spend all night chasing you so you stop chasing her?"

"You're not the one doing the chasing." Krea and her brother were making a game of her blocking him from moving forward. She used both hands to stop River and he was pressing forward, swinging his arms back and forth, with a grin on his face.

"We'll stop!" Ricker gestured at his brother. "Won't we, River?"

River stopped pushing against Krea, causing her to tumble forward. Luckily, she was already on her knees. This caused him to burst into laughter. The cat lowered her back slowly to the ground and slinked under the bed.

"All right, all right, think you're so funny, don't you?" Krea stood up and slapped her thighs to send some of the dust flying. She turned to Clarion. "*Anyway.* Let me show you the dress."

Dena jumped, dropping the ladle handle and clutching her chest. "Goodness me! Clarion! I didn't even notice you." She bounced her baby all the way to its tiny cradle and then elbowed Krea, who was rifling through the trunk at the foot of the bed. "You should have said something."

"I *did* say something." Pulling out a pale yellow dress, Krea held it out above her. "Honestly, woman."

Dena wiped her hands on her apron. "Now you're sounding like your father."

"Whose fault is that?" Krea's puckered lips sweetened into a smile as she twirled in a circle with the gown aloft, as if the dress were her partner. "In't it lovely?" She spoke as if to the dress. "Ma mended an old one of hers."

"Ay, and it was no small feat binding all those holes the moths ate in it so no one would notice them." Dena stared after her only daughter, but her stern face broke into a grin. "She'll be one of the belles of the ball now, won't she?"

Clarion dropped the flint into her pocket and wiped her hands on her apron before fingering the dress as Krea held it out for her. This close to it, she saw the little ribbons tied throughout the material that must have been used to cover the holes, but they really weren't that noticeable. "It's beautiful," said Clarion. "Will you wear that bonnet with it?"

Krea smoothed the loose curls that tumbled out from her dirt- and ash-stained bonnet. "Oh, no. I'm wearing my hair loose."

"You'll do no such thing," cried Dena. "Do you want the village to think you're a harlot?"

"Ma, what a thing to say!" Krea took the dress back and folded it nicely. "I know Elena's going without a bonnet."

"Well, everyone knows the mayor's daughter is a maiden through and through," said Dena. "It's *your* reputation I'm worried about."

"I'm a maiden, whatever you think! Ain't no boy worth thinking to be otherwise who'd ever asked me out... Until today." The last part Krea said under her breath, but Clarion heard it. Krea's mother, fortunately, didn't seem to. Krea's face reddened as she tucked the dress back into the chest and slammed the lid shut. "I'll wear a bonnet if it'll stop you talking about that, but I ain't wearing this rag." She tapped the bonnet at her forehead and took a giant step over one of the twins, who was crawling on the ground. "What're you wearing, Clair? You know?"

Clarion had thought about it. Elena had offered to let her wear one of her new dresses, but Clarion had noticed she hadn't extended the same invitation to Krea, and she didn't want to be the cause for another skirmish between the two of them. "Probably the same dress I wear for every special occasion." She jumped back as another twin appeared from behind her and scooted straight through her legs. "If Mother hasn't sold it."

Krea's eyes narrowed and she took her friend's arm in hers, guiding her over to the relative peace of the open window at the back of the house. "Your ma's been selling your things again?"

"Yeah. She sold my favorite two pigs." Clarion couldn't look her friend in the eyes, so she looked out at the alleyway behind Krea's house that ran between two main roads. It was dusk now and she could hear the lamplighter making his way down the street. Though there'd be no lamps lit down here, where the blacksmiths and their neighbors tossed some of their garbage.

"Royse and Randel?"

Clarion nodded. A flicker of lamplight danced across the alleyway. She figured it must be the lamplighter walking past. "Gone, after I came home from Jacosa's."

"But how are you going to keep up the farm? They was the last of your sounder, eh?"

Clarion let out a deep breath. The light grew closer now, more jostled, and she swore she heard the clop of horse hooves. "She wants us both to clean houses."

"Hmph."

"But that wasn't all. She—"

"Oy!" Krea turned around to sneer at one of the twins, who'd rammed right into her. "Give us some space, yeah?" She turned back to her friend leaning on the windowsill. "Sorry to hear that. I know you'd rather be with the pigs, muck 'n all." She cocked her head and squeezed onto the sill beside Clarion, leaning over to stick her head outside. "What's that? A carriage, through here?"

Clarion leaned out to get a better look, but Krea was taller than her, and she had to settle for peering around her shoulder. It was a carriage, moving slowly, almost as if the driver were keen to hide the sound of the procession coming through. But there was no masking the sound several horses and a carriage made.

There was a lamp attached to a stick beside the driver, and that was responsible for the light that flickered and danced all over the filthy cobblestones and mildew-covered walls. The driver, an older man with flecks of gray all over this dark hair, lowered his hat as he approached. "Good evening, ladies. If you'd be so kind as to keep this to yourselves for the night. There's nothing to see here."

Krea and Clarion pulled their heads back inside and stared at each other, not sure what to make of it. Before they could respond, the driver had vanished from view.

But there was a window on the ornate wooden carriage, and Clarion saw a face in profile that stole her breath away. It was a young man with dark fringe that poked out from beneath the brim of a black hat. She only saw him for a moment, and she shouldn't have felt anything, really. She didn't have time to study him, to do more than notice the slight strong hook of his nose, the robust ruddy hue of his skin. But her thoughts were focused on him even as two other horsemen followed the carriage and then the carriage disappeared down another alleyway, the echoing clops of the animals at last dying out to nothingness as if the procession were never there at all.

Clarion didn't stop thinking about him until Krea's voice snapped her out of it. "That boy was handsome, yeah?" At least she wasn't alone in thinking so.

But she'd never before felt that explosion in her chest, that loss of focus on the world around her. Never because of a *boy* anyway.

Maybe never about anyone.

She immediately felt guilty for thinking that. She'd have to tell Elena. But no. Of course she didn't have to say anything. It was nothing, just a moment of weakness. Although... She and Elena had to have a talk regardless.

"Is that who I think it is?" Krea leaned back out the windowsill, and Clarion followed suit. They both saw Jacosa, clear as day in the flicker of the nearest streetlamp, even with the shawl over her hair that she clutched tightly at the base of her throat.

"Oy, Jac—" Krea began, but Clarion covered her mouth and held a finger to her lips.

Krea nodded and Clarion dropped her hand. The two stared after her, watching her disappear down the alleyway across the street, trailing after the carriage.

CHAPTER 4

t was a good thing neither Krea nor Clarion had to keep their secret for long—Krea couldn't keep it for more than a second, she told her ma the instant she peeled away from the window—as it was all made clear by the next day.

Well, it was made mostly clear by the next day.

Clarion couldn't stop thinking about the carriage, and how it had stolen through the alleyways at night, and that face. She didn't even notice how the mystery eased the pain that had drawn her to Krea's to begin with. She sat in the back of Jackin's cart, her hand atop the sheet that covered her harp. (It was still *her* harp, if just for a little while.) Her mother was on the other side of the harp, hitching a ride along with it to the mayor's mansion, having offered both her and Clarion's services to help prepare for the ball.

Clarion didn't even bother changing into her better dress since she was going to be scrubbing and cleaning for hours before the ball began. She thought of going back and changing later, but she didn't want to leave the harp behind until she had to. And besides, she knew Elena wouldn't dream of letting her wear her old dress. She was going to have to wear one of Elena's dresses, no matter how it might hurt Krea.

She wondered if she might convince Elena to send an invite to Krea early to ask her to join them. But she wondered too if Krea would take that as an insult, as a sign that Elena thought she could only show up in rags and needed to be "fixed up" to be presentable.

Clarion was tired of trying to outthink every potential quarrel between the two of them. Tired of trying to prevent what seemed unpreventable, what always worked itself out anyway.

"Yes, of course Clair will show you where best to put it."

Clarion hadn't heard half of the conversation between her mother and Jackin, hadn't done more than smile halfheartedly and nod at anyone who bade them good morning as they passed through the town. A brief thought of disappointing her father for dwelling more on her own thoughts than those of others flashed through her clouded mind, but it was just one of many thoughts that popped up and floundered, one of many that kept leading back to that carriage and its passenger stealing through the early night.

"Clair? *Clair?*" Eustace took Jackin's hand to climb down the parked carriage, amazed that her daughter was still staring off into space.

"Yes? What? Oh." Clarion took in her surroundings and realized they'd pulled up to the front of the mayor's house and she'd been none the wiser. She scrambled off the cart, not noticing Jackin's proffered hand. She pulled the sheet off the harp and started tugging on it.

Jackin rested a hand on her shoulder. "We got it." He nodded as two of the townspeople who helped out around the mayor's house on such occasions came out to assist with the harp. Clarion stepped back, staring at her harp as the men handled it, cringing with every jostle as they tugged it down the cart.

Eustace grabbed Clarion's hand and pulled her away.

"Come on. Let them handle it. You can direct them in the foyer."

Clarion stumbled but let herself be dragged forward and up the steps. The doors were already propped wide open. Men and women bustled around the entryway, in and out of the large ballroom.

Eustace dropped Clarion's hand as she stepped inside, spotting Gytha, the mayor's housekeeper, at the back of the ballroom.

Clarion stared at the grand, open ceiling, so faded when exposed to the sunlight. It looked so much warmer when the chandelier was lit in the evening and the entire room glowed with fire edged in by darkness. She was still staring at it, her thoughts drifting, when Jackin and the other two men passed by.

They put down the harp with a thunk, causing Clarion to jump, and Jackin wiped his brow on his sleeve. "Phew. You think the back of the room, Clarion?"

Clarion covered her mouth with her cuff, trying not to let Jackin see how much the thump of the harp had frightened her. It wasn't hers to be worried about anymore, not really, but she couldn't very well stop caring about it just because it belonged to someone else.

"There." She let out a deep breath and pointed to an alcove halfway down the length of the ballroom between two pillars. The alcove was surrounded by three large windows. "The sound might carry better to both sides of the ballroom from there."

Jackin stared at her a moment too long, and Clarion directed her attention to the large table being set up for the buffet to make him think she hadn't noticed. She heard rather than watched him and the two men resume their trek across the ballroom as she focused on the two women who had to make way for them as they headed in her direction. Instead of walking toward her mother, as Eustace no doubt intended she do, she retreated backwards, back to the foyer, back to where it was darker, where she could think and hide

27

and not be noticed.

"A ball doesn't look so tantalizing in the daylight, does it?"

Clarion couldn't move any farther. A hand gripped one of hers and held it aloft beside her shoulder. She hadn't even noticed she'd been reaching behind her, looking for the wall to hide against.

She turned slightly and looked up, catching a glimpse of dark hair against a reddish cheek, the edge of a nose with a slight downward hook.

She let out a small, almost inaudible cry and pulled away. Her hand left his easily; he'd caught her gently as if she were a butterfly to admire and then to let go. He removed his hat and bowed. Instinctively, Clarion took her skirt in both hands and curtsied.

"Magnus, son of Destrian, lord of Rosewood." He placed his hat back atop his head and readjusted the brim. "But I prefer Mack."

"Lord?" asked Clarion, before she even thought to say her own name. She wasn't thinking straight. Here was the young man she'd seen in profile in the mysterious carriage, the one who'd made a fool of her thoughts all evening and morning since.

Mack smiled, and Clarion imagined an artist painting those lips as the final stroke in a magnum opus. "Yes, your mayor jokes with my father that lords are no longer relevant here, nor have they been for fifty-odd years."

"You wouldn't know it from how he keeps up this house," Clarion muttered. Catching her mistake, she quickly put her hands to her mouth. When she dared to peek at Mack again, she found his smile had grown wider.

"The thought had crossed my mind as well." Mack leaned his forearm against the wall for which Clarion's hands had been unconsciously searching. "So tell me. Are you a rather bold maid or... ?"

"I'm no maid." Clarion clenched her fingers together. "Well, I'm not a maid of this household. They asked my mother and me for additional help setting up for the night's ball."

Mack frowned. "I wondered. Forgive me." He closed the small distance between them and took her hand in his again, only this time she could look into the pale brown of his eyes atop the high cheekbones that marked his face. He couldn't have been any older than Clarion herself, but there was such confidence, such poise in his expression, Clarion was sure he had what her papa might have called "an old soul." "These didn't seem the hands of a housekeeper."

Clarion laughed. She knew there were several calluses from the harp and dirt caked beneath her nails. She hadn't had time to clean them yet, had thought it pointless before she was due to spend the day cleaning anyway. "These are now. But they once were the hands of a pig farmer and harpist." She didn't know why, but she didn't want to pull her hand away.

The smooth, bold forehead that poked out from beneath his tresses wrinkled as he arched his eyebrows. "A pig farmer harpist? You are full of surprises, aren't you?"

"Master Magnus," said a man in a black suit who descended the stairs.

At the same time, Clarion heard her name called from behind her in her mother's most concerned voice, and again from the stairs as Elena appeared a few steps behind the man.

Without so much as a moment's hesitation, Mack and Clarion's hands retreated to their own sides, their moment alone over almost as soon as it'd begun.

"I take it that's your name?" asked Mack quietly as the small crowd approached them from either side. "Clarion?"

Clarion bowed her head slightly. "There goes all my mystery." She could hardly believe the bravado that had taken over her in his presence.

It was short-lived as her mother took her by the arm. "Where did you get off to? We're to help in the kitchen."

"Master Magnus, your father would like to speak with you," said the man, who bowed toward Mack. He glanced at Clarion and smirked. She recognized him as the driver of the carriage who'd spoken to her the night before.

"Clarion!" Elena looked from Clarion to Mack to Eustace and back. She was in one of her plainer frocks, her hair still in plaits. Krea was right, though, that she wouldn't be wearing a bonnet, as she daringly walked around without one even now, despite the men around. That it was her home surely couldn't justify the boldness, with so many servants and guests around.

She tucked one ankle behind the other and curtsied at Mack. "Milord." She turned away before he had time to finish removing his hat. "Mistress Eustace, if it's all right, may I ask Clarion to help me get ready?"

Eustace let go of Clarion's hand and scratched her elbow. "I'd like to give her time to get ready for tonight, but your father engaged us both to help set up the party."

Elena took up Clarion's arm almost as soon as Clarion's mother had dropped it. "This *would* be her helping *me* get ready for the party." She started tugging Clarion toward the stairs. "I'll talk to my father," she called over her shoulder. "I assure you, she'll still get paid."

Clarion didn't take note of her mother's expression because she spent the half a minute tumbling up the stairs watching Mack. His eyes never left her.

"No need to thank me," said Elena quietly as they walked through the second floor hallway. "I know how you feel about scrubbing pots and sweeping floors."

As they were about to reach Elena's room, a door several rooms away opened and Elena paused, putting her back to her door. Confused, Clarion watched her and followed suit. A tall, thin man almost drowning in dark furs exited the other room, trailed by two other men in less resplendent attire and Elena's father, Mayor Judd.

Elena took her skirt in both hands and curtsied as they neared, and Clarion copied her. None of the group so much as slowed their pace, although they nodded their heads in the girls' direction. When Clarion dared to look up, she saw some of Mack in the first man's countenance, felt his dark eyes linger a beat too long before he turned and took the stairs.

Elena grabbed Clarion's hand the moment the men were out of sight and pulled her inside her room. A maid was unfolding gowns and spreading them out on top of Elena's bed.

"Thank you, Mariah, that will be all for now," said Elena, clasping her hands together. "Clarion will help me. You're needed in the kitchen."

Mariah hardly looked up from the floor as she passed, but Clarion swore she spared her one scathing look, as if she knew she was responsible for the swap in jobs—or worse, she knew exactly why Elena had dismissed her.

Once the door shut tight behind Mariah, Elena threw her arms around Clarion's shoulders and kissed her.

Elena marched over to her bed and began making a mess of the careful array of clothes. Clarion fingered her lips and watched her. "Elena," she began, not sure how to even start this conversation.

It wasn't like she didn't love Elena. When Elena had first asked if she could kiss her, Clarion had said she could. Elena was beautiful, and although she'd known her since almost as long as she could remember, although she loved her as a friend first, as someone like a sister... Something had changed between them at some point, and Clarion was just as curious as Elena as to what that might be. But that was months ago—almost a year ago now—and Elena no longer asked. There'd grown an understanding between them, and Clarion wasn't even sure she really understood.

"Did you decide against that silly notion of wearing your one nice frock?" Elena held up a pretty blue dress made of smooth material that deepened her already deep blue eyes. Her arms fell and her face soured. "Unless you seriously intended to run home and change after a day of cleaning." She tossed the dress down and picked up another one, this one in golden yellow. "I can't imagine why your mother thought it suitable for you to help clean for the ball!"

Clarion bristled at Elena's tone. "Everyone celebrates at the springtime ball. Even those who helped set it up." It was true. There weren't enough rich people for the mayor's family to hobnob with them exclusively. Although that may have been why this neighboring lord and his son were invited.

Her face distressed, Elena lowered the yellow dress. "I didn't mean that." She folded the dress over her arm and started scattering the other ones. "That you wouldn't have come if you helped clean." She smiled timidly. "It's just... You're *my* friend. You shouldn't have to clean to earn your respite."

Her friend? There was some of the confusion beneath the "understanding" the two of them shared. Clarion regarded Elena's profile as she tossed some of the dresses atop a chest at the foot of her bed. She had an elegant, sloping profile that sometimes made Clarion's heart beat faster, but it'd been a while since she'd felt that.

Her heart quickened only a little now.

Elena sat on the bed on a small area she'd cleared of dresses. Her usually-proud features softened as she held her hand out, beckoning Clarion to sit beside her. Clarion hesitated a moment, but she did as wordlessly bidden, sliding her hand into Elena's.

"Father is trying to arrange a marriage between me and that *Magnus*." From the way she emphasized Mack's name, Clarion knew the young man did not have the same effect on Elena as he did on her.

But Clarion's mind jolted as she pondered it. The two of them together would be the loss of both people—the only two people—who had ever stirred something inside her, something strong, something special.

She felt immediately guilty for thinking that of *two*

people. She removed her hand from Elena's and folded her hands in her lap instead.

Elena mistook the meaning behind the gesture and grabbed Clarion by the shoulders. "I don't *want* to!" She threw her hands up. "I was *thankful* Father didn't think any of the boys in town were good enough for his daughter." She twirled a coil of her silky hair around her finger. "I should have known he would just import me a husband from somewhere else."

She stopped playing with her hair and spoke hesitatingly. "What if... I don't know. What if you married Jackin?"

"What?" Clarion choked on her astonishment.

"I *know*, and I know that Father probably wants to import him a proper lady wife, too, but..." Elena spoke so quickly, her hands fluttering about her face, that she stumbled on her own words and had to pause to swallow. "But everyone knows how Jackin feels about you, and I could see him fighting Father so he can marry you, and maybe just me being married to Magnus would be a good enough family connection—"

"How Jackin feels about me?" Clarion thought back to when Jackin wound up asking Krea to the dance. Krea, at least, had no idea how Jackin felt about Clarion. Frankly, Clarion had hoped she'd just imagined it. Even Elena had never brought it up, never encouraged it.

Although she had reason before not to encourage it.

Slipping her arm through Clarion's, Elena rolled her eyes. "You know he wanted to ask you to the ball, right? When I found out he somehow got stuck with Krea, I figured you played dumb and she was just oblivious." She chewed on her bottom lip. "Jackin always did care too much about not hurting other people's feelings. Even at the expense of getting his own feelings hurt."

Elena so rarely talked about her brother when with Clarion. Clarion felt like this was the first time she'd seen any proof that Elena even cared about him—at least in the past few years, as they drifted apart. But she still didn't understand the matter at hand. "If you were to marry Magnus," said Clarion, the taste of the words unexpectedly sour on her tongue, "you would leave and go with him, right? You wouldn't be here in the same household. What good would it do for me to marry your brother?"

Elena took both of Clarion's hands in hers. There were tears edging out from the corners of her eyes. "I know. Don't you think I know that? But surely we'll visit each other, as sisters-in-law, and... We can't be together." Elena hid her face behind her palms.

Clarion hesitated before gently caressing the soft velvet of Elena's house dress. "Maybe that's... for the best."

Elena took in a sharp breath and peeked through her long, delicate fingers. "What do you mean?"

Clarion turned her attention to her own coarse skirt, feeling the roughness of the wool even through her calloused palms. "I'm not sure. I had fun... with you. But ever since my papa died, I haven't felt... I haven't wanted to be with you, in that way."

"Since your father died?" Elena wiped her sleeve against her nose in a most unbecoming way, which she would never have done in front of anyone but Clarion. "Clair, I'm so sorry about your father. Really, I am. I know that you especially couldn't handle the loss of a parent. I've tried to be supportive—"

Clarion bristled at the "you especially," but since Elena had lost her mother at such a young age, she supposed she had a right to compare their losses. Clarion felt so much weaker when she compared them, even selfish, because she'd had five more years with her father than Elena had had with her mother. "You have been."

"Then what are you saying?" Elena swallowed, choking on her own words. "What has your father's passing to do with us?"

"Nothing. I don't know." Clarion found it hard to keep the tears forming from falling. But now didn't seem the right time to dwell again on the loss of her father. "I just... Didn't want to play around anymore."

Elena stood and flung her hands out to her sides. "We weren't *playing*! *I* wasn't playing. Were you?"

Clarion shrugged, unable to meet her eyes. "Not at first, maybe. I don't know. I don't know, all right?"

"You said you weren't attracted to any of the boys in town, either! That this... Whatever this is, that I'm not..." Elena's voice cracked as it grew quieter. "That I'm not crazy, to be in love with you."

Clarion stiffened and met her friend's gaze. It was the first time she'd said those words, at least the first time she'd said them quite like *that*. Elena looked so earnestly down at her, her eyes splotched with red and swollen from crying.

Clarion swallowed. "I've felt attraction to boys. To a boy. To a man."

"So you lied to me?"

"No. I mean... At the time, I hadn't."

Elena began to pace back and forth. "Your father died, you fell apart, and like under a spell, you transformed into a girl like Krea?"

Fell apart. What did Elena think of her? She felt broken, but she didn't need Elena to tell her that. "No. I don't find *every* boy attractive..."

Elena crossed her arms. "So just one." She tossed her head. "May I ask which?"

"No, it's nothing. It's meaningless."

"It wouldn't happen to be the *only new young man our age* to appear in the town in oh, the past few hours?" Elena banged a fist against the post at the corner of her bed. "Clarion, you just *met him* downstairs! How could you throw away everything we have in only a minute?"

"I saw him last night. Briefly." Clarion wrung her hands together. She felt stupider and stupider every minute this conversation kept going.

"Oh, that's a relief. So you've known him *two*

minutes then." Elena thudded across the room to her dresser and flung open one of the drawers.

Clarion stood on shaking feet and followed her. "I'm not in love with him."

"Good." Elena flung several pairs of stockings out of the drawer onto the floor and rummaged around in the remaining contents. "So you're not entirely insane." She stopped and pulled out a coil of green ribbon, frayed and worn at the ends. "You're just a liar." She shoved the ribbon at Clarion's chest.

Clarion took hold of it instinctively and recognized it as her own ribbon she'd once tied through Elena's hair when her plait came loose. "I'm not a liar." She stared at the ribbon and thought of the feelings that had gone through her mind as she'd tied it through that hair, how Elena had turned her head when she'd finished and asked if she could kiss her, how Clarion had numbly nodded, and how, before she could even think about what had Elena had just asked, she'd felt the comfort of Elena's lips against her own. It was her first kiss. *Their* first kiss.

"You said you were like me."

"I am. I was."

"Then you wouldn't feel that way about men at all!" Elena spoke so loudly, she gasped at herself and stared at the door, waiting for someone to barge in and catch her in her admission. No one did.

"Maybe... I can be attracted to both?" Clarion wasn't sure what she meant. She wasn't sure what it meant that she'd only wanted to hold hands with two people, that she'd only imagined her fingers dancing across the cheeks of one young woman and one young man.

"Then you're not like me." Elena grabbed Clarion by the elbow and dragged her to the door. She opened it and shoved her outside before Clarion could say another word.

Elena was about to shut the door behind her, but she peeked her head out. "And now I hope I *do* marry Magnus so I can dangle something you can never have over your head and see how *you* like it." She slammed the door so loudly, a gust of stale air blew Clarion's hair back.

Clarion waited at the door for half a minute before walking toward the stairway, the ribbon clutched to her chest, her eyes on the floor, her thoughts lost once more.

"I never wished to be the cause of a quarrel between friends."

Clarion's foot stopped moving halfway to the ground. She looked up and her eyes widened to find Mack and his manservant two paces before her.

Mack moved to remove his hat for another bow, but Clarion dipped her head quickly in recognition and scrambled around him to get down the stairs before he even had the chance to say more.

Chapter 5

larion did not wear one of Elena's fine gowns for the ball, nor did she run home to change into her own finest. Her mother had fretted and tried to fix her hair—"If you'd told me you'd planned to wear this when you were playing the harp, I wouldn't have had you scrubbing the hearth!"—while splashing a little water on her face to do away with the dirt and soot, but Clarion did not care if she was dressed in her worst dress for the ball. It was only the last chance to play the harp as her own—perhaps the last chance to play the harp ever again, if Elena didn't want her to come to the mayor's house anymore—that kept her there at all.

"Where's Elena? I haven't seen her with you all evening." Krea's face was flushed from her fourth time around the dance floor with Jackin (not to speak of the three other dances she'd given to Tenney and Layne after all). "Every time I think I spot her, she's dancing with someone else, but I figure it's all just a trick of the light." She nudged Clarion, who stayed seated beside her. "Elena dancing with half the town boys? Imagine."

Clarion had watched as Elena was passed from Layne to Tenney and back to Mack. Her small, delicate hand looked like it could be crushed in each of the men's eager grips. "That's her." There were few other girls in town around the same age, so there was no girl Krea could confuse Elena for. Clarion knew Krea had known, that she really wanted an explanation, but Clarion busied herself by plucking a string and pretending it still needed to be tuned.

Taking hold of her bright yellow dress, Krea swished her skirt back and forth to the jovial tune. Clarion had not yet been asked to perform her harp—the rest of the band would ask her to when they were in need of a break, and the crowd was far too excited to quiet down with one of Clarion's more somber pieces.

"Where's Jackin?" Clarion asked instead. She'd seen him earlier, when Krea had been dancing with the other boys, but she'd excused herself to the kitchen each time she thought she saw him headed her way.

Krea nodded toward the buffet table at the back of the hall. "Said he needed refreshments." Studying her friend, Krea put both hands on her hips. "Say, what you wearing that for? Didn't Elena spare you a dress?"

"We... quarreled."

Krea tapped the side of her nose. "Thought as much, what with Elena hanging all over them instead of you." She tugged on Clarion's elbow. "But that's no reason for you to sit out on all the fun. I coulda lent you something if you needed it."

Clarion would not be moved. "No. I could have dressed better. I just... lost interest."

Krea stopped tugging but held her friend's arm still. "Do you think you should ask Jacosa? For a charm to bring a fight to an end?"

"I don't think she has one of those," said Clarion, pulling her arm free. "And even if she did, she shares little but her medicines and saves the rest for parlor tricks."

"Speaking of..." Krea peered over the crowd. "Where is she tonight? She didn't do that thing with the flowers that turn into doves to start off the festivities."

"I don't know..." Clarion gnawed at her lip. She'd been so preoccupied, she hadn't once thought of Jacosa, not even after her strange behavior the previous evening. Her gaze swept the room, and Krea was right, the town witch—gardener, what have you—was conspicuously absent. But no sooner had the thought entered her head than her stare rested on Elena and Mack, hand in hand, dancing toward each other and away, their eyes never breaking contact. Elena looked radiant—she was smiling wider than Clarion had seen her smile in far too long. Mack... Mack in profile took Clarion's breath away.

The song came to an end and the crowd burst into applause and beleaguered breaths. Clarion was certain Elena and Mack held each other's hands a moment longer than the other dancing couples did, but they too joined in eventually. But they clapped for only half a minute before Mack grabbed Elena and guided her away from the floor.

Feeling a tap on her shoulder, Clarion jumped and looked up. It was Krea, inclining her head toward Barlow, the leader of the band.

He bowed, removing his hat to reveal his shiny scalp beneath it. "I was only asking if you were ready for a song? The boys and I thought we'd take a break."

"Oh!" Clarion swiveled her legs so she could get into position. "Of course. I'm sorry I didn't see you earlier."

Returning his hat to his head, Barlow smiled and joined his fellow musicians in a beeline toward the refreshment table.

The ballroom was humming with dozens of separate conversations, everyone's attention focused on their partners, their neighbors, or the food. Clarion looked to see if anyone at all was watching—she'd prefer if they weren't—but even her mother was lost in conversation with the mayor and his housekeeper many feet away. She caught Jackin's eyes on hers from the wall across the way, two cups in his hands, and Krea waved. "Good luck," she said, winking before she made her way through the crowd.

Clarion lay the fingers of one hand against the strings and held the other aloft. She waited for that feeling that overtook her, that confidence that burst through her from somewhere deep inside—*"It's here, little one, right here in the pit of your stomach"*—and she began.

"They told me you had left for the land above. I told them you would never leave me, my love. But when I looked for you, you had gone. I couldn't give up; I searched all over 'til dawn."

With each word, another conversation in the ballroom seemed to die, like a snuff over each flame on the chandelier above the crowd. Clarion couldn't focus on the growing silence, or she'd lose her own flame, the one that soared through her and warmed her from her fingers to her toes as she played her father's last legacy to her.

"Were you stolen away by the kings of old? Or did I know ye not, so I've been told? I'd like to have faith that I knew ye well. That you love me still, and in the land above you dwell."

Clarion's gaze drifted from her fingers to the crowd—she wasn't sure why. Her fingers kept moving, the strings kept pushing into her skin, but she pushed back, her whole body trembling with the effort.

"The years have passed, and I still don't know. Were you ever truly mine or was it all for show?"

Clarion saw him—Mack, alone, without Elena in sight. He held his hat in his hands against his abdomen, and he seemed to move forward with every pluck of the harp. He'd somehow come so close, she could almost touch him if she let her fingers stop playing. But she couldn't, not now, not when the fire burnt so brightly inside her.

"Are you warm at night in another's arms? Should I mourn or curse you, have you come to harm?"

Mack's eyes burned into hers, and she felt more alive than she had in months, than she had ever. She returned the gaze, felt the fire flow from her and to him and back.

"I'd like to have faith that I knew ye well. That you

love me still, and in the land above you dwell."

As soon as she plucked the last note, Clarion pulled her hand back like she was snatching a fly out of the air. The room was still, as if she'd plucked out all the air with her song.

The mayor cried out and was the first to bring his hands together, although Clarion didn't know that for certain. The room echoed their leader's applause, and there were even a few whistles from the band over at the table. But Clarion didn't notice much of that, for her gaze never left Mack, and he was as still as if he'd seen the clouds part and the sky reveal all its secrets.

Following her third song, Clarion worked her way through the crowd to head outside. She could barely remember the other two she played, not after the way she'd locked eyes with Mack for so long. But the man she'd assumed to be his father appeared at Mack's side soon after she started her second song, and he went off with him, leaving the ballroom. She couldn't even find Elena among the people enraptured with her music, although she did notice Krea and Jackin and her mother and the mayor make their way forward.

She had to make the excuse that she was in need of fresh air, that she wasn't ill, just overheated, to convince them all to let her go without an escort. Besides, she knew there was a quiet area that let out into the back alley through the kitchen back door, and she needed to be alone with her thoughts.

Only she didn't find herself alone at all. Voices carried through the open door from the alleyway behind the kitchen. She checked over her shoulder to see the few people left who'd volunteered to run the food and dishes back and forth from the kitchen weren't paying her much attention. She hesitated only a moment before the kitchen emptied out entirely. Then she waited around the side of the ajar door, where she couldn't see the people in the alleyway but could still hear them, knowing full well she was eavesdropping and she wasn't even sure why.

"...she was a skilled dancer, that's for sure. Lovely to look at." Clarion didn't recognize the voice, but she guessed it belonged to Mack's father because of the voice she heard next.

"Yes." Mack's tone didn't express the same confidence and poise it had earlier.

"Yes...?" His father made it seem a question.

"Yes, but I don't love her. I... I don't think I can."

Clarion wondered if it was possible to love someone so quickly—surely no one expected him to be in love with Elena after one day. But it seemed like Mack was sure it was possible—to be in love, to know.

"You can't if you tell yourself you can't." The man sighed. His breath sounded deep and resounding. "Besides, did I ask you to fall in love with her? I only asked you to marry her."

He made it sound so perfectly reasonable.

"Why is it so important that I get married?" Mack swallowed so hard, Clarion could hear it. "Why do I have to leave home to search for a bride?"

"Are you in love with someone back home?" asked his father. "A village girl?"

"No."

Clarion was surprised to notice she'd been holding in a breath.

"Maybe."

Clarion's heart practically stopped. She dared to move closer to the door to peek through the crack and get a better look at them. Mack's father put his hands on his son's shoulders. "I know what it's like to be restless at your age. Believe me, son. That's why I want you settled. A good wife will knock all sense of adventure right out of you."

Clarion wasn't sure that was a good thing, but what did she know? She'd never been tempted by a sense of adventure. Her friends and mother wouldn't have heard of it.

Mack's gaze traveled to the ground. "A good wife or a wife I love?"

"A *good* wife you can learn to love." Mack's father straightened the cravat at his collar. "I'm a lord here, Magnus. I almost threw that away once... I won't have you do the same kind of foolish thing I did."

Clarion inhaled sharply. She wondered if Mack's mother was a commoner.

"Foolish? If that woman is telling the truth, I'd have to call what you did a little more than foolish, Father—"

"You believe *her*?"

"Clarion?"

Clarion whipped her head around. Jackin appeared from the hallway clutching a large glass bowl containing only the smallest bit of punch.

Clarion curtsied slightly and tucked a loose strand of her hair beneath her cap. "I was just about to step out for some air."

Their conversation, though brief, didn't go unnoticed. Mack's father stepped inside the kitchen, although Mack was not with him. He looked first at Jackin, then at Clarion. "Ah!" he said, clapping his hands together. "The lovely harpist. I didn't recognize you at first under the trappings of this kitchen." He studied her still-dirty clothing, as if to say it wasn't that she looked out of place here, more that it was hard to picture her as the songstress.

"Thank you, sir." *I think*, she added in her thoughts.

The man removed his hat and bowed slightly. "Lord Destrian of Rosewood, at your service." As Clarion curtsied back, he had already turned to Jackin, his hat back on his head. "Your father has you helping with refreshments now, does he?"

Jackin shrugged as he put down the bowl. His gaze flicked toward Clarion. "I offered to help."

"That was mighty kind of you." Destrian put an arm around Jackin's shoulders and guided him toward the hallway. Jackin's eyes widened and he threw one last look over the man's shoulders, but Destrian didn't seem to notice. "Does a man good not to forget his lesser, to help shoulder their burden. I was wondering if you might tell me more about your fair sister, and whether or not she's of the same frame of mind..."

Clarion lost track of their conversation as they stepped out of sight.

"Was that thing about stepping out for air the truth or just an excuse? Either way, care to join me? It *is* lovely outside."

Clarion almost forgot about the young man still left outside in the alleyway. Her pulse quickened as she stepped around the door sheepishly, peeking out at Mack.

He leaned against the wall opposite the mansion, a stone wall that surrounded the living quarters for the staff, although only Gytha the housekeeper and Mariah the maid were full-time servants of the family at the moment. As Clarion approached, Mack was looking up, but he spared her a glance and a charming half-smile.

"Were you spying on me?" he asked, although he didn't seem to have lost his humor.

"No." Clarion wrung her hands together. "That is, not on purpose."

Mack nodded and lifted a leg to park his foot against the wall behind him. "The accidental spy. How disappointing." He tucked his arms behind his back and pushed harder against the wall. "Usually I can charm a woman into obsessing over me on purpose."

Clarion could feel herself blush. *If you only knew.*

Mack jutted his chin toward the sky. "You have to

see this. The moon is so bright tonight."

Clarion had lived countless nights when the moon was bright and she'd never really cared one way or the other. Evenings were for gathering around the fire, for one of her papa's stories, for her mama working her needles. But she didn't care what Mack was looking at, so long as it gave her an excuse to sidle up next to him, her back against the wall.

She stared at his face a moment too long, and he noticed. He grinned sheepishly at her and pointed up. "No, look."

Clarion did, embarrassed that she'd been caught in the act of staring at him. She saw the moon and found it quite nice, how it peeked out through the clouds almost as full and bright as the sun. But then her eyes caught something else, something strange. What she first thought to be a gap in the clouds revealing the night sky behind it appeared now to be a shadow on the clouds themselves, the silhouette of a castle.

She laughed.

"What?" asked Mack. His arm brushed against Clarion's as he shifted slightly.

She copied his stance, right down to the sole of her foot against the wall. "Nothing. I just... I thought I saw something on a cloud."

"What makes you so sure you didn't?"

Clarion smirked, her thoughts long since directed away from the moon.

"Where did you learn to sing and play like that?" asked Mack.

"My papa." Clarion could feel the heat rush over her face. It was all she could do not to topple over. "My... father."

Mack chuckled. His laugh was higher in pitch than Clarion's papa's had been, but there was something about it that reminded her of the laughter they shared together. Maybe it was just the infectious nature of it.

"You're more and more of a mystery the more I think I get to know you," said Mack. "Is this the pig farmer papa?"

"Yes, but... He's gone. He died a few months ago."

Mack's smile fell. "I'm sorry. I shouldn't have laughed."

"No, it's all right. You didn't know, and I like laughing when I think of him."

"Well, he taught you well. Unbelievably well." Mack ran a few fingers over his cheeks and chin, almost as if tracing a beard that wasn't there. Although now that Clarion was drawn to the area, she thought she saw the slightest shade of one. "That first song of yours... really spoke to me."

"It's an old ballad." Clarion bounced the back of her head self-consciously against the wall. "Father said it was his great-grandfather who wrote it."

Mack's lip turned up in a half-grin. "So you're from a family of musical pig farmer harpists with the ability to mesmerize everyone with only a song?"

"I don't know about that," said Clarion. "Father's ancestors were the lords here until my grandfather was unseated by the mayor's father."

"I knew I sensed nobility in you." Standing away from the wall, Mack put his foot down, giving Clarion his full attention. She could feel his gaze travel up and down her body, and she shifted uncomfortably, swapping one foot leaning against the wall for the other.

"Hardly. We've been pig farmers since before I was born."

"But it's in your blood. And it's hard to destroy what's in the blood, no matter how those around you may try." Mack sighed and leaned back against the wall beside Clarion. He was lost in his thoughts a moment, gazing above him, before he pointed again to the sky, to the clouds passing over the moon. "It's probably your noble blood that causes you to see things there."

"What am I supposed to see?"

Mack leaned closer, ever so slightly. Clarion could practically feel the warmth of his breath. "What do you want to see?" His voice was quiet, almost a whisper.

Clarion examined the clouds again, in fear that if she kept gazing into the moon reflected in Mack's eyes, she might lose herself entirely.

Although it was nice to be lost in his eyes. Nice to think of something not painful, even though the bitterness of her last conversation with Elena hung at the edges of her thoughts. She took the green ribbon from her pocket, running her thumb and forefinger up and down it as she stared above.

The clouds had shifted since she'd last looked. The moon was even more covered.

She squinted at the silhouette. Her mind was playing tricks. It really seemed like there was a house there... No, several houses. A village.

She fanned herself. "I think I need more air," she began. "It looks like there's—"

A thunderous boom shook the earth, and she stumbled, the foot she'd leaned against the wall tumbling to the ground. Mack grabbed both of her upper arms and pulled her to him, wrapping his own arm around her neck and laying a hand gently on the back of her head.

Buried in his chest, her legs unsteady as the ground shook beneath her, Clarion foolishly thought of how he smelled of lemongrass.

When the shaking finally stopped, Mack loosened his grip, but his hands remained on her head and back. She pulled backwards to look at him, but he was looking left and right.

Mack cleared his throat and dropped his hands entirely, taking a step back. "The ground shakes here?"

Clarion frowned. "On occasion." She'd dropped the ribbon, but she didn't feel like bending over to pick it up.

She peered around Mack's shoulder to look inside

the kitchen to see if anyone had come to check on them. The bowl Jackin had brought lay shattered on the floor, the red punch leaking all over the stones.

"I think it came from this way. That is, I heard something right before the quake..." Mack straightened his hat and walked to the end of the alleyway behind the mayor's mansion. Surprised that Mack had a particular idea of where the shaking had started, Clarion followed, stopping only to grab her ribbon and stuff it back into her pocket, dirt and frayed edges and all.

Mack had stopped in place, his lips slightly parted. Clarion followed his line of sight and gasped.

The clouds had practically descended over the town, and Clarion felt the moist nip of the air. But despite the fog, there was something that stood out, although it had to be half a mile away.

A gigantic plant that reached from the ground to the sky.

"That's near Jacosa's," Clarion said, rubbing her eyes to make sure she wasn't dreaming the vision.

"Jacosa?"

"The town witch." She cocked her head. "That is, she tends a garden and it's full of healing plants—"

Mack took Clarion's hand in his. "We have to go," he said, as if there would be no argument.

Clarion spared a brief glance over her shoulder. Although she could hear the distant murmur of the crowd at the ball, she saw no movement.

"All right," she said. Mack smiled at her before tugging her away.

Chapter 6

he stone fence that enclosed Jacosa's garden was broken toward the back. The tree beneath which Clarion, Elena, and Krea had sung together just the day before had toppled over entirely, and Clarion had to step around one of the stone bricks from the upended fence that were scattered about the dirt road as she and Mack approached.

Mack still clutched Clarion's hand, squeezing it as if the touch brought him strength to confront the scene. Mack and Clarion craned their necks upward, but there was no end to it. No end to the giant, vividly green tree that had taken the other tree's place.

"Have you ever seen a tree so large?" asked Mack.

"No…" Clarion squinted and saw the leaflets that grew haphazardly this way and that. "It's a stalk!"

Mack drew closer, pausing only to climb laboriously over some of the stones, and turning to look over his shoulder to make sure Clarion could safely navigate the rubble. He reached out with his free hand to tug on her arm gently so she could gain steady footing at the top of the hill with him. When she stood beside him, he smiled, and he touched the giant, green plant.

"You're right," he said, squeezing her hand harder. "It's springy."

Clarion couldn't believe how occupied her thoughts had been, how overwhelmed her senses had become at the sight of the large stalk, because now she was intensely aware of the heat that generated between their palms. "Jacosa?" she called out, eager for another distraction and wondering if the witch woman was nearby. Her house, at least, appeared to have escaped the chaos that had ripped through one corner of her garden and half the dirt road beside it.

Mack let go of her hand and grabbed hold of one of the sprouts while Clarion climbed back down the rubble toward the house. The door was wide open and a fire was dwindling in the fireplace, so Clarion called out again. "Jacosa?"

There was no one in the house. The witch's sole hen erupted into a loud squawk and flapped its wings as it appeared from beneath Jacosa's bed. Clarion screamed and clutched her chest as the animal passed by her feet.

"Are you all right, Clarion?" Mack called.

Clarion laughed in spite of everything. "Yes. The hen just startled me." She clutched her skirts and climbed back toward the base of the stalk. Mack stood with one hand on a sprout a foot or so above his head, his boot on another. "What are you doing?" asked Clarion.

Grabbing for an even higher sprout, Mack grunted. "Breathing."

"What?"

Mack laughed and brought his foot even higher. "I'm climbing!"

"I can see that, but... why?" Clarion reached the bottom of the stalk and pushed a hesitant palm against it. It *was* springy. Despite being thicker than the thickest tree trunk she'd ever seen, she was worried it wouldn't support him.

Mack stopped and looked down at her, laughing

between deep breaths. "Don't you want to know where it goes?"

Clarion was taken aback. She gestured upward. "It *goes* nowhere. It goes up."

Mack let go of one of the sprouts to wag a finger at her. "That's where you're both wrong and right." He grunted again as he climbed higher.

"Are you mad?" Clarion could barely hear her words over the wild thumping of her heart. "You're going to fall!"

"Thank you... for your... confidence." Punctuated by deep breaths, Mack's voice got farther and farther away as he climbed.

Something came tumbling down and Clarion screamed, not sure whether to try to catch it or back away. She covered her face.

She heard laughter from above her and she peeked through her fingers. Mack's hat lay at her feet.

"Keep that for me, will you?"

Clarion scooped the hat up. "Mack! Lord Magnus! Come back here, please!"

She could only see his boots now. The rest of him was lost in the mist and the darkness of the night. She stepped back as far as she could without tumbling and craned her neck to get a better view. She couldn't see where the stalk ended. It just seemed to go on and on and blur into the fog.

Mack's voice was distant now, like an echo. "You know what you saw!" His boots vanished into the fog.

Clarion clutched the hat so hard, she was afraid she'd tear it into pieces. "Mack?" There was a scratch in her throat. "Mack! Magnus!" Her voice was growing hoarse.

But there was no reply.

Trembling, Clarion approached the unbelievably tall stalk and poked it again. Every inch of her mind cautioned her against what she was about to do, but she didn't know what else *to* do, how to convince Mack to climb back down and stop this madness. She placed his hat on a large upturned stone nearby and shook her limbs loose in front of the stalk. She'd never been any good at tree climbing, but Krea wasn't half bad, and she'd seen her do it. She'd also seen her spit on her palms first and rub them together. It was a bit revolting, but Clarion wasn't in a position to be tidy.

She grabbed the highest sprout she could reach from the ground and stuck her foot on the lowest. "All right," she said quietly to herself. "I can do this."

It was probably only a few minutes, but it felt like half an hour later, and she was still only three more sprouts higher. Her arms ached, and every time she reached for another sprout, it was like she was close to tearing her muscles. Her foot kept slipping. The soles of her shoes were worn down and she could find little purchase on the leaves.

"Mack?" she tried to call upward, but her voice cracked and her teeth chattered. It was colder up here in the mist.

She swung her arm out, gritting her teeth through the pain it caused her, and grabbed hold of a new sprout. Just as she lifted her foot to climb higher, though, she realized she was holding the leaf too close to the end. At about twelve feet off the ground, she slipped and started falling, only just barely managing to slow her fall by grabbing hold of another sprout.

The sprout snapped off the stalk, and she was still clutching it tightly as she landed in the dirt on her rump, just narrowly missing one of the stones from the broken fence. She looked up again, but there was no sign of Mack.

She screamed in frustration and threw the sprout aside.

Scrambling to her feet again, she cried out his name one more time. "Mack!"

But there was no answer. She wasn't sure what to do. Jacosa was nowhere to be found—was she hurt when this giant stalk appeared out of nowhere?—and she didn't fancy getting Mack in trouble if she went to get a search

53

party and his father got wind of it. What if he didn't forgive her? The thought of losing his affection as suddenly as she'd seemed to have gained it overwhelmed her more practical side. It drowned out her worries that he could get himself hurt—or worse.

She realized it had been a long time. Too long a time.

Finally, she heard something. Hearing anything—any difference from the silence that had grown in Mack's absence—quickened Clarion's pulse and brought hope to her heart.

"Mack?" she said again. She peered up. A dark figure appeared through the mist and then grew closer and closer, the swishing sound louder and louder. The sprouts from the stalk began raining down on Clarion and she backed up, aware the figure was sliding down the stalk quickly.

There was a loud thump as the figure landed on the ground.

She spit some of the leaves out of her mouth and wiped hair out of her eyes.

"Mack?" said Clarion. It wasn't him. The figure was slapping her knees and shaking dirt from the hem of her skirt. "Jacosa?"

"Oh!" Jacosa stopped slapping herself to clutch at her chest. "Goodness gracious, you scared me, child."

Clarion was in no mood to feel remorse. "You climbed that thing?"

Jacosa looked at the trunk of the stalk and at the layer of mist far above them. "So I did."

Clarion's breath hitched as she realized all of the visible sprouts, the things Mack had used as hand- and footholds, were littered on the ground around her. "Did you see Mack?"

"Mack?" Jacosa looked at Clarion as if she were delusional, as if *she* were the one who'd just slid down a giant stalk that seemed to grow for infinity.

"Lord Magnus! He's a young gentleman from

Rosewood, visiting the mayor with his father—"

"And I'm supposed to have met him... up there?" Jacosa hitched a thumb toward the stalk.

"Yes! He climbed up there shortly before you came sliding down. Surely you passed him along the way?"

"Can't say I did." Jacosa flicked some more dirt off her shoulder.

"But then? What? Where?" Clarion could barely get the words out of her mouth. She grabbed hold of the stalk's trunk and carefully edged around it, her feet slipping every few seconds. "Mack?" she called again, clutching to the stalk, afraid of tumbling down, and she was barely more than a few feet up a hill. She couldn't imagine having climbed like Mack had, having fallen... What if he'd fallen on the other side?

It took her far longer than she would have liked to travel around the gigantic stalk, to call out his name, to peer into the misty air. Jacosa lived at the outskirts of town, but still, she was surprised more people hadn't noticed the giant stalk after the earthquake, hadn't come to see what it could possibly be. Ball or no ball, fog or no fog, they couldn't *all* have missed it.

She heard the thwacking before she was all the way around again.

"What's that?" she called, screaming a little as her foot slipped again. She didn't want to land on the pile of rubble. "What's going on? Jacosa?"

The sound didn't let up. When she finally came back to where she'd started, she found Jacosa at the trunk, whacking it with an ax.

"What are you doing?" demanded Clarion, tripping over an upturned root from the fallen tree in order to get closer to the older woman.

Jacosa held a hand out. "Stand back." She didn't wait for Clarion to move before she whacked it again.

"Stop!" Clarion moved to get between the stalk and the ax, but she took no more than a step forward before she jumped back and screamed. Jacosa would not stop whacking the stalk.

"Are you mad?" asked Clarion, and she felt like she'd been asking that question of people all day. "I told you, a young man climbed up there!"

"Didn't see him." Jacosa wiped her brow and whacked again. She was making remarkable progress despite her weak appearance.

"I don't care if you didn't see him." Clarion went the long way round, climbing over several roots to approach Jacosa from behind. She put a hand on her shoulder in between whacks. "I'm telling you, he went up there, and you can't knock this down until he gets back down."

"Can't wait." Jacosa chopped again. The stalk bent to the ax's will more readily than a typical tree trunk would, its insides spewing juices like blood.

"Why not?" Clarion placed a palm on her forehead. "What are you trying to do? What's *up there*? And what do you think will happen if you knock that whole thing down? It's just going to... collapse in the fields. Maybe it'll hit the town!"

Putting the ax head down into the dirt, Jacosa sighed. She leaned against it like a walking stick and breathed heavily. "Thanks for all the theories. Those are always helpful. Why don't you be useful and grab me a few of those beans you'll find in my cupboard on the top shelf?"

"Beans."

"Yes, beans." Jacosa waved a hand at her and raised her ax again. "And hurry."

Clarion didn't know how the beans would help anything, but she'd seen Jacosa's plants come to life. She was looking at one, she assumed, that grew impossibly tall. She ran toward Jacosa's cottage, crawling down the upturned roots and stones, nicking one of her wrists and cursing, not even caring when she accidentally kicked Jacosa's hen out of her way. She grabbed hold of the cabinet doors and pulled them open to rummage around for signs of beans. There were seeds and sprouts in small pots of all shapes and colors, but she ignored them, grabbing a handful of dried red beans from the top shelf instead.

By the time she made her way back to Jacosa, the witch was a quarter through the stalk's trunk.

"Good. Give them here." Jacosa tossed the ax to the ground and held her hands out for the beans. "Hate to waste them, but 'haste makes waste' and waste is exactly what we want from this beanstalk."

"Beanstalk?" Clarion emptied her palms into Jacosa's and stared at the stalk in wonder, unsure if the unimaginable thing had come from one of those beans. Was she going to grow another one? Would they ride it to the top as it grew and search for the lost young lord?

Jacosa put a bean between her teeth and tore the bean in two. She spit half of the bean onto the ground and wedged the other half into the oozing, green open wound she'd made with the ax. She stepped back then, grabbing Clarion by the arm and taking her with her.

"What's going to happen now?" asked Clarion, but her words were drowned out as a sound like a sheet of hail broke out from the stalk. Countless red dots spread up and down along the stalk from the place where half of the bean had been placed. The sound was like termites tearing through wood, only the horde of these red creatures wanted to devour the stalk entirely.

"What's going on?" shouted Clarion, her voice rising over the swarm. The sound was growing louder, like each dot was birthing several more with every scream. She saw the red spreading on the hilltop, pouring from where Jacosa had spit the other half of the bean. "They're eating the stalk!" She swirled on the old woman. "Jacosa, they're going to destroy the stalk, and Mack will fall—"

When she thought of the moment afterward, Clarion wasn't certain whether Jacosa tugged on her arm or stumbled and pulled Clarion along with her, but whatever the cause, Clarion slipped down the rubble on the hill and hit her head on a stone. She just managed to recognize the place where she'd been planting for Jacosa the day before and took notice of the sprout that had already formed so soon. It grew beside Mack's hat, which had apparently tumbled down the hill after her. Her recognition was overwhelmed by the screeches of the red creatures, and the little sprout and hat alike vanished in a wave of red.

Chapter 7

Although Lord Destrian and Jackin both remembered that Clarion was the last person they'd seen near Mack, neither was inclined to believe her tale that he'd climbed a giant beanstalk into the sky.

"Dreaming, or delusional, the poor girl, you can't blame her," Mayor Judd said the moment Clarion had told her tale. She'd hesitated toward the end, feeling the room full of people judging her.

"No, I..." Clarion tried to sit up in bed, but she moved too quickly, and the room around her spun. Eustace stood from her chair at Clarion's bedside and coaxed her to lean back. "Ask Jacosa," Clarion said, allowing her mother to fuss. "Jacosa," she repeated.

Eustace reached behind her and fluffed her pillow. "Yes, Jacosa was the one who found you. Passed out in her garden. She was worried you'd gotten into some of her herbs meant to help with insomnia, and she noticed you'd hit your head on the way down."

Clarion gazed beyond her fretting mother to the lit fireplace. There was hardly enough room to house the three of them—when there had been three of them—in their small pig farmer's cottage. Now, with everyone concerned over Mack's disappearance, there was a crowd threatening to burst the house at its seams. The mayor spoke with Lord Destrian and two of his servants in hushed tones beside the mantel, and Jackin and Elena sat at the small table. Both looked at Clarion with a mixture of anxiety and suspicion.

"My son *would* do such a thing, I am sorry to say." Lord Destrian paced back and forth in the small space before the fire. "I know it may ruin his chances with your daughter to admit that, but the fact is, I've had such a hard time corralling him, ever since... Ever since his mother entrusted me with his care."

Clarion got a better look at Elena as Eustace sat back down. Elena focused instead on her nails, not looking the least bit worried that her potential betrothed was nowhere to be found. Clarion reached into her pocket beneath the blanket, but she realized she had been changed into a different outfit and that the green ribbon wasn't there.

Mayor Judd waved a hand. "Boys will be boys, and all will be forgiven, I'm sure." He stopped to look at his daughter and waited for her to respond with an unconvincing smile before he turned back to his guest. "I'm sure he'll turn up."

"But your lordship," said one of the servants, the one with whom Clarion had spoken on more than one occasion, "he took none of the horses. The mayor reports none of his missing—"

Lord Destrian stopped pacing and cut him off. "So he took another horse. So he walked right out of the town, hoping to convince a passing carriage to take him away. Anything to avoid commitment or something that might threaten to make him settle down."

Grimacing at his words, Clarion shuddered when she caught Elena gloating at her. So Mack had other girls in other places, had caused this feeling in others? She should have known she was being a fool. But even so, that didn't mean she wished him harm.

"Mother," she croaked, her voice wavering, "where's

Jacosa? Have any of you been to her garden? Have you seen the damage?"

"Hush now," said Eustace, patting her daughter's leg. "Jacosa is busy mixing herbs to help with your wounds."

Pulling her arm out from under the blanket, Clarion stared at the wrist she'd cut during the chaos. It was bandaged and there was a red splotch on the white cloth. But it hardly mattered. She tried to get her mother's attention again. "But the damage in her garden! If the beanstalk was eaten, surely someone at least saw that."

Elena laughed, a hollow imitation of the laughter that used to sprout warmth throughout Clarion's body. "There was a giant beanstalk that reached into the sky? And it was *eaten*—that's why no one saw it?"

There was a knock at the door and Eustace patted Clarion's leg before getting up to answer it. "Let her be," she said in hushed tones to Elena as she passed. "She's hurt her head and she can't be blamed for her rantings."

"She can be blamed for plenty else," mumbled Elena, but the comment went unnoticed as Eustace opened the door.

"Clarion!" Krea peeked over Eustace's shoulder. "I wanted to see how you were doing."

"I'm afraid it's rather cramped, but come inside, dear." Eustace took a basket from Krea. It was just like Krea's mother to send a loaf of bread and other goodies whenever someone fell ill, even if they barely had enough for their own family. Krea was no longer wearing her fanciful dress, Clarion noticed. They all had changed, and she felt stupid for not noticing it earlier. Despite her conviction she was right, her head really did ache. She wondered if it'd only been a day since the ball, or if she'd slept for longer.

Krea took a noticeably long time to squeeze between the mayor and his son, putting her hands on the back of Jackin's chair and mumbling her apologies with a knowing smile. She took Eustace's chair beside Clarion and clasped

Clarion's hands in hers, her eyes widening like she'd found Clarion at her death bed. Clarion wondered how bad she looked.

"What happened?" Krea demanded. "Ma told me not only were you hurt, but you were there when the visiting young lord went missing?" When Clarion, dazed, hesitated to answer for a matter of seconds, Krea dismissed her as too ill to explain herself and turned back to Jackin. "You found her in Jacosa's garden?"

"Jacosa found her. Turns out the old woman wasn't feeling well and she missed the ball because she'd stayed home to nap."

"You'd think a witch of all people would be back on her feet in no time with all her herbs and concoctions." Krea squeezed Clarion's hand, but her gaze fell on everyone in the room but her.

The mayor excused himself from the gathering of men at the fireplace and stepped over to Eustace, who was placing Krea's bread on the table. He put a hand on her shoulder and gestured toward the door. Clarion just barely heard him as they left the home together. "Eustace, seeing the state of things while here... Might I have a moment?" Clarion worried they'd be discussing her care and health, like she'd be an invalid for the rest of her days.

"I forgot you'd gone home by then," said Jackin, and Clarion didn't fail to notice the brief flash of hurt that crossed Krea's face. "It was some hours later, when the ball was just about over. Jacosa appeared, disheveled but calm as could be, and asked for help carrying Clarion to a bed. Said she was too heavy to lift on her own, and she'd left her where she'd found her, asleep on that hill."

"I didn't know that," mumbled Elena. "I was... I'd gone to bed early. Doesn't she have a seed that makes heavy things lighter?" Perhaps she was starting to question Jacosa's story instead of Clarion's, as everyone seemed wont to do.

Few heard or noticed, though, as Clarion shot up at

Jackin's admission, ignoring the pounding in her skull. "So you did see Jacosa's garden!"

Krea patted Clarion's hand. "You saw the garden, too. We've all seen the garden."

Pulling her hand out from Krea's, Clarion shook her head. "Not like this! It was damaged. The stone fence had broken. The tree at the top of the hill had uprooted."

"Which Jacosa explained must have happened during the latest quake," added Jackin. He stood, peering down at her over Krea's shoulder. "She was worried you were caught there during the quake, but I told her I saw you not moments before at my home." He frowned. "I suppose if you and the lord's son set off as soon as we left you..."

"We didn't," said Clarion firmly. "We were still behind the kitchen when the quake shook. But the stalk..."

Jackin rolled his eyes. "I can assure you there was no beanstalk, giant or otherwise." He looked over his shoulder at the lord's servants, and they nodded. Clarion supposed they'd been with Jackin to help transport her home.

Lord Destrian, who'd been rubbing his chin, squeezed past Jackin and Krea to stand at Clarion's bedside. "What *were* the two of you doing there?"

"Father suggested she went to see why Jacosa hadn't shown up for the ball," said Jackin. Clarion wondered why Jackin was so quick to jump in with an excuse for her.

But the reason for his interference became clearer when Lord Destrian refused to break eye contact with Clarion. "Is this true?"

Clarion shook her head and looked at her lap, tired of feeling all of the eyes on her. Mistrusting, doubting, coddling eyes, every one of them. "We spotted the giant stalk after the quake."

"And you thought to investigate?" said Lord Destrian brusquely. "Not step back inside to tell any one of us— anyone at all—but head off to the edge of town, just the two of you? Unchaperoned?"

Clarion felt her face darken at his unspoken

suggestion. "We didn't think, really. Mack..." She winced. "That is, Lord Magnus was enraptured by it, and we set off before we thought better of it."

"I should think so," said Lord Destrian, glancing at Elena at the table behind him. "You were aware I had in mind for him the mayor's daughter?"

Clarion cleared her throat. The pounding in her chest would not stop. "Yes, but—"

"And yet you set off in the dark with him anyway, fell victim to his fanciful excuses to get you alone, to abscond with him to the countryside for who knows what kind of tomfoolery?"

Clarion couldn't believe Mack's own father would accuse him of being such a rake, and all the while still seem like he was angrier at her, at a girl he hardly knew, than his own son. She pinched the blanket over her thighs. "I saw it, too!"

Lord Destrian scoffed and returned to his men at the fireplace. He spoke in harsh whispers to them, leaving Clarion, Krea, Jackin, and Elena to exchange glances and wait in silence, hanging their collective heads as if they were all guilty of something.

The visiting lord strode back to the bedside, his countenance twisted. Jackin had to jump back to get out of his way, grabbing hold of Krea's shoulders, and making her blush, despite everything else going on around her. "I just want to know if he was with you until you fell unconscious!" said Destrian. "Did he leave you before then? Where did he go?"

Clarion quivered and focused on the blanket in her hands. "Up. He went up."

Lord Destrian grunted and snatched his hat from the coat rack near the door before storming outside. His two servants looked at the group of young people and inclined their heads slightly. One paused beside Elena. "Should she say anything of use..." he whispered, leaving the rest unsaid.

Elena nodded, and the men followed their master outside, leaving the friends alone. The door was still open, and the mayor and her mother looked on as the lord started walking down the road. The mayor nodded at Eustace and scurried after the lord and his servants. Eustace stepped inside and stood beside the open door, clutching her palms together. "Perhaps it's time the three of you got home as well," she said. "I'll send word if there's any change."

Clarion didn't like feeling as if she were merely a witness instead of an active participant in what was going on around her, especially when she was at the center of it all. She was tired of feeling that way and realized now as she was sitting in her bed, letting first Krea and then Jackin wish her a speedy recovery, that Mack was the first person who'd made her feel like she needn't be coddled. That she was capable of adventure. And she'd let him climb up that stalk alone, too afraid, too weak to follow.

She clutched the blanket so hard, the rough-spin wool made indents in her palms.

"Tell your mother thank you, dear," cried Eustace after Krea. She clutched both Elena's hands in hers and leaned close to her ear. Clarion couldn't make out everything she said to her, but she did hear her say they would see her soon.

Once her friends had left, Clarion finally noticed the tears forming at the corners of her eyes, the slight blurriness of her vision from either the moisture or the pounding in her head. She wiped her nose with the back of her hand.

"Clair," said Eustace as she picked up a shirt that needed mending, which she must have gotten from someone in the town. She sat beside her daughter. "Perhaps all this tragedy... shall prove our fortune."

Clarion wiped her eyes and stared at her, but her mother was humming and passing her needle through the cloth. "What?" asked Clarion, not sure she'd heard right.

"Well, it brought the mayor here, and he told me he was appalled that the two of us were living in such conditions."

Clarion glanced around the room. It was a small cottage to be sure, but it was cozy and not so terribly dilapidated considering her papa's recent passing. It probably needed another sweeping, and some of the fence around the pig pen needed replacing, but they'd both been busy, and besides, Eustace had sold the last of their pigs.

"With the lord and his men staying on for longer than they considered initially," Eustace continued, "the mayor can't manage with one housekeeper and one maid alone. And with you needing looking after for a little while, I'm going to have to turn down a lot of work for the next few days."

"What are you saying?" Clarion asked, dreading that she already knew the answer.

Eustace put her work down on her lap and beamed at Clarion. "He invited us both to move into his servant house as soon as you're better, to be his full-time servants!" She threaded the needle through the hole again and pulled the thread tight. "We won't have to worry about money anymore."

Clarion's head pounded, and she let herself sink back into her bed, her head dropping against the pillow. She closed her eyes and saw flashes of red dots multiplying, of Mack's retreating figure, of Elena's angry face. Before she fell asleep, she dreamed of her papa.

"Little one, this house is your home. It may not be much, but it's yours, and sometimes just knowing what's yours is enough to make it worth more than all the fancy jewels in the world."

Eustace sold their home two days later, and she and Clarion moved into the mayor's servant house before the sun had even set that evening.

Chapter 8

larion would never believe she'd imagined it all. And considering what they did know Jacosa's garden capable of, she'd never understand why no one—not one person—seemed to think it even *possible* she wasn't making things up. Except maybe Elena. But she hadn't visited her again, despite being one building away.

There was another earthquake one night when Clarion was recovering, but still no one reported a beanstalk as far as the eye could see. Then again, she'd been in the garden during one earthquake, and there hadn't been a beanstalk then. Still, when Clarion had asked her mother if it was foggy the night of the latest quake, she did say it was, and for her not to worry about it. The quake was so slight, Clarion never even rolled out of bed. It was soon forgotten, and Clarion began her new job almost the moment she was on the mend.

Mayor Judd poked his head into the kitchen that first morning. "Mariah, I was wondering if you might ask Lord Destrian and his men if they're all right with ham tomorrow instead of tonight? Gytha informs me she'll have to send for more pigs from the neighboring town, as we ate the last one from the butcher's last night."

Clarion stopped mid-scrub of the cast iron pot she was working on cleaning. *Royce. Randel.* She hadn't been able to stomach the leftovers from that dinner because she couldn't stop thinking of them. But her mother had eaten her share.

"Yes, master," said Mariah as she put plates away. The woman—probably a decade and a half older than Clarion—hadn't said more than two words to her since Clarion and her mother had moved into the servant's building. Clarion did catch her looking down her nose at her on occasion, as if to say she knew what Clarion had gotten up to with her mistress every time she was asked to leave the room, and she didn't approve.

But she hadn't said anything to the mayor, as far as Clarion could tell. And Elena wasn't any better. She hadn't even *seen* her. Clarion would have thought the sudden disappearance of the man who'd sort of come between them would have softened Elena somewhat. But even with him out of the way, Elena wasn't keen to forgive. She'd also never understand that it was never about Mack, really. And that Clarion's attraction to Mack didn't negate the feelings she'd once had for Elena.

"Oh, my daughter was asking for you," said Mayor Judd.

Clarion dropped her sponge inside the pot.

"Yes, master," said Mariah. She closed the cupboard door, curtsied, and made her exit. Of course, it was *Mariah* Elena had wanted to see. Clarion recognized the twinge of jealousy that pinched at her throat, even though she knew she had no reason to worry that Elena had moved on to her own maid. It was just that Mariah still got any of Elena's attention, even if it was all one-sided.

"Clarion," said Mayor Judd, clapping his hands together and strolling to the sink. "How are you feeling as of late?"

"Fine, thank you, sir." Clarion fished inside the pot for the sponge and started scrubbing again.

"Are you adjusting to the work well?" Mayor Judd's voice sounded shaky, a little awkward. Clarion supposed he'd never really talked to her alone for long. He smiled sheepishly as he stood beside her. "Better than mucking with pigs, no doubt?"

Clarion didn't want to lie, but she could hardly blame him for ruining her life. She couldn't even blame him for ruining her whole family's, since it was his grandfather who had done that—and ages ago. She cleared her throat. "Yes. Thank you."

She knew she should have said more, should have thanked him for ripping her and her mother from poverty. But there was a happiness in that place that'd been ripped from her along with her mother's stress and the worry about having enough food on the table.

"I was wondering if you'd be up to focusing on your other duties." Mayor Judd examined the stack of dishes Clarion had yet to get to and plucked a half-eaten tomato from a plate, popping it into his mouth. Clarion suppressed a shudder. "That is, before I proposed to your mother that the two of you move into the servant's quarters, she'd asked about my hiring you to play the harp on occasion." He gestured to either side, chewing the tomato with too much zest. "At first I wasn't sure it'd be appropriate—and there was the issue of your injury—but I'm thinking now, now that the poor soul has been missing more than a week, you might play for us at dinner tonight. Lighten the heavy hearts of my guests and grieving daughter."

Yes. "Grieving daughter." Clarion wondered if Elena's father truly had no idea where Elena's inclinations lay or if he simply wanted to be stubbornly ignorant.

Clarion performed a small curtsy without taking her fingers out of the pot. "Certainly," she said. At the very least, it might bring herself some comfort.

"Excellent." Mayor Judd clapped his hands together once more and then stood there a tense moment. He closed one eye and pointed at her, cupping his chin with his other hand. "I wonder if Elena might spare you a better dress. I know it's just an informal dinner, but it might make the evening feel more significant."

Clarion froze up again. She forced herself to finish the scrubbing. "If Elena will allow it."

Mayor Judd waved a hand in her direction as he headed for the hallway. "Oh, I'll make sure she'll allow it. She has enough dresses. She won't miss one for one evening. I'll speak with her now."

"Mayor," said Clarion, her heart racing, "you needn't—"

"I *will*." He fingered a ring on his thumb, and Clarion wondered if it'd once rested on the fingers of her forefathers. "I've found it rather strange that since you've become a member of the household, Elena has treated you as such. Yes, you're a servant, but you're a good friend to her, too."

So he has no idea why *things have changed between Elena and me*, thought Clarion. She tucked a stray strand of hair beneath her bonnet with her pruned hands. "I appreciate it," she lied, "but I was wondering if before that, I might go help Jacosa."

"What for?" Mayor Judd's brow wrinkled. "I pay the woman good money for her herbs. I never did understand why Elena volunteered to help garden."

Clarion really wanted to examine the garden for herself. To grab the woman by the shoulders and make her reveal the truth to everyone. At the very least, to ask her why she'd lied, when a young man's life was at stake. "It's just... I said I'd be coming this week. Before all this. And after that last earthquake, she probably needs more help than ever fixing up her garden."

Turning, Mayor Judd shook his head. "Don't you worry about it. Leave that to others. I'll pay for any herbs you and your mother need from now on." Just about to exit, he stopped. "Oh, I asked Jackin to invite your other friend— the blacksmith's daughter." He straightened his cravat. "I thought she made a fine addition to my son's arm at the ball, and since I don't know of any gentleman's daughters near enough to make a match for Jack... Well, in any case." He tilted his hat at her and left.

Putting her hands on her hips, Clarion examined the stack of dishes left to wash. Her eyes traveled from the stack to the doorway through which she'd exited to stand beside Mack that unforgettable night. She could sneak out the back, be gone before anyone noticed. If they asked her why she'd never finished the dishes, she'd feign a headache. She was just recovered, after all, and—

"Aren't you finished with those dishes yet?" Stomping into the kitchen, Gytha grabbed the poker beside the fireplace, stoking the dying embers. "I need you to go help your mother with the gardening outside."

She could *still* feign the illness...

"The master told me all about cleaning you up for tonight's dinner," said Gytha, dropping the poker and rubbing her hands on her apron. "But you'll have plenty of time to finish your chores first."

Clarion sighed and picked up the plate from which the mayor had stolen an extra bite. She almost cried as she scraped a half-eaten slice of bacon into the bucket for the compost.

◈◈◈◈◈◈

Clarion was already into her fourth song of the evening before her stomach rumbled. Loudly. She had to go a little off-melody to drown it out with a tune.

Only Elena seemed to notice. She peered across the dining table at Clarion over the top of her wine glass.

"I wish I could be of more help." Mayor Judd took his knife to his chicken, and the scraping of the utensil on the plate grated in Clarion's ears. "But as you can see, mayors don't have quite the purses of a lord and we have only the women here to serve us."

He paused to let Eustace refill his goblet. "Thank you, dear," he said, although he wasn't that much older than her.

Clarion tried to play louder. She'd held off on singing with her music, considering the fact that a portion of the table could hardly keep quiet.

"I understand," said Lord Destrian. He picked at the feast on his plate, hardly making any headway into it. "Besides, I made use of the townspeople those first few days, the ones who volunteered. I'm confident nothing bad happened to him, that he just went his way to another town. I've sent out letters to every town I can think of, asking if the lords and mayors have had any sight of him." He sighed and put his fork down. "I'm thinking of posting a reward, a sizable sum to get anyone he might have charmed into not revealing his whereabouts to come forward." He stared at Clarion. "Still, I'm sure he'll waltz right back through those doors when he's had time to think over everything he left behind." He gazed at Elena, whom Clarion thought looked lovelier than ever in a red satin gown. "And *everyone*."

The table fell into an uncomfortable silence, the only sound the plucking of Clarion's fingers across the strings of the harp and the occasional clink of utensil on plate.

"Say, that's a nice dress, Clair," said Krea, often competing with the mayor to be the first to fill the dead moments of near-silence. Krea chewed on her meat as she spoke, and Clarion was sure she didn't imagine the mayor shuddering. "Borrow it from Elena, did you?"

Both Elena's and Clarion's eyes averted at the mention of the exchange. Krea frowned.

"I hear she got it from my closet," said Elena, spooning a dainty scoop of beans onto her plate. "I don't

72

know. I let Mariah choose it for her. It's an old dress anyway."

Clarion finished the melody and demurely accepted a glass of water from her smiling mother. That half hour spent with Mariah fixing her up like she often did Elena had to be among the most awkward moments of Clarion's life. At least Mariah said no more than ten words the entire time. Although it was the most she'd ever spoken to her.

Clarion handed the glass back to her mother and wiped her moist palms on her skirt, not feeling the least bit bad about it.

"I think you look marvelous," said Eustace quietly to her daughter as she took the glass back to the kitchen.

Elena tensed at the compliment, but no one but Clarion seemed to notice.

Krea was too busy almost choking on her food. She'd been about to say something, and she was still chewing. She collapsed toward the table, slamming her palms atop some forks and spoons and sending them flying. Jackin and Lord Destrian's servants sent their chairs flying backward to get to her side. Clarion tried to get between them, but there was no room. Mayor Judd stared, horrified, and Elena's eyes widened in shock. Lord Destrian took a sip of his wine.

"Fine!" choked Krea, slamming the table over and over with her palm. She swallowed loudly. "I'm fine. Just... choked a bit." She panted. "Fine."

Jackin grabbed her cup of wine and brought it to Krea's lips. She recoiled at the strong odor and started gagging.

"Gytha!" called Mayor Judd, pushing his chair back and crossing the room to the hallway. "Gytha! Eustace! Mariah!"

Eustace and Gytha appeared from the hallway leading to the kitchen, their fast gait slowing down as they looked at the spectacle.

Mayor Judd pointed to Krea and wrinkled his nose as if she were a rat discovered beneath their table. "Please take her... Take Miss... Just take her to the kitchen so she can calm down."

Eustace and Gytha swooped in, Eustace crying, "Stand back! Let her breathe!" to get the men to move aside, and they walked arm-in-arm with Krea to the hallway.

"I'm fine." Krea coughed. "I just choked a little..."

Clarion could hear her mother comforting her friend as they retreated out of sight. Mayor Judd cleared his throat and straightened his coat. He gestured toward Clarion. "Please. Continue."

Clarion watched him, her brow cocked, and waited until all of the diners were once again seated before she lifted her hands and positioned them on the harp. As she was about to begin, she noticed Lord Destrian staring at her, the goblet still in his hand. She couldn't decide what kinds of thoughts lay behind those eyes. She just knew they weren't good ones, not as far as she was concerned.

She started playing again.

"Well," said Mayor Judd, dabbing at his lips with a napkin, "it's nice to pretend, if only for a minute, that we can enjoy the finer things in life in comfort." As he unfolded his napkin onto his lap, he nodded toward Lord Destrian. "No disrespect, your lordship. I'd be beside myself if I lost any more of my family..." He stared at both Jackin and Elena in turn.

"Did your late wife enjoy music at dinner?" asked Lord Destrian. He swished the contents of his glass around.

"Yes," said the mayor. "She couldn't play, but she could sing. She liked to sing with the children—"

Elena stood up from the table. "May I be excused? I have a headache."

"Of course, dear." Mayor Judd leaned over to take Elena's hand in his. "Rest up. Be well."

Clarion searched for Elena's gaze as her first love retreated from the room, but Elena walked with her nose held high, never once glancing in her direction.

Lord Destrian put his goblet down and wove his

fingers together. "Have you ever thought of remarrying?"

"No," said Mayor Judd. "I mean. I have Gytha to run the household anyway." Mayor Judd's eyes lingered on Clarion for an uncomfortable moment. "Although I do admit to being overly concerned with who my children will marry." He scratched the back of his neck. "Perhaps my son needs a young woman from the town who exhibits more grace?"

More grace than... Krea? wondered Clarion, sure she noticed Mayor Judd's opinion of the girl lessen considerably over the dinner. Her fingers stumbled in the tune as she realized he probably now meant her.

Sure enough, Jackin's face beamed as he turned around to gaze at Clarion. She felt herself trip up again as she shirked under his attention.

"What of you, your lordship?" asked Mayor Judd. "How long have you been a widower? Any thoughts of remarriage?"

"Oh, I'm not a widower." Lord Destrian picked up his goblet again and stared pointedly at Clarion over the top of his glass as he took a sip. "But I have often wished I were."

"Oh, I'm sorry," said Mayor Judd, choking, "I thought..."

But Clarion couldn't hear the rest of his apology. She plucked the strings louder, louder than need be, drowning out the creeping feelings that gripped her lungs like a vice, louder and louder until she felt the skin on her index finger crack.

"Ah!" she called out, stopping the melody mid-tune.

"Are you hurt?" Jackin was at her side before she even realized what had happened.

"It's just a small cut." She stood and curtsied toward the table. "If I might be excused."

"Yes, yes, of course, my dear," said Mayor Judd. "Gytha should have something for you."

"Let me escort you," said Jackin.

"No," said Clarion, cupping her injured finger tightly. "I'd rather you not."

Sparing a glance at Lord Destrian, whose eyes bore into her, dipping down and up, Clarion left through the hallway to the kitchen, with no intention of finding Gytha.

Chapter 9

s she strode through town, Clarion wrapped a piece of cloth she'd grabbed from the kitchen around her finger. At least it wasn't a bad cut; it would probably stop bleeding in a matter of minutes. Every time she stopped to look up at the pale moon, she noticed the sky was obnoxiously clear, the few clouds disappointedly devoid of shadows. She was grateful, though, that so few people roamed the streets at this time of night, and that the few who spilled out from the taverns and houses paid her little heed. She'd been grateful to see the fire on in the servants' house and figured Gytha and her mother had taken Krea there—probably for some of Jacosa's herbs to calm and soothe the poor young woman.

Clarion wondered if Krea knew how close she had come to having Mayor Judd's support in marrying his son, and how she no longer seemed to be in the running. It was little surprise the mayor might consider Clarion a better match for his son after that display at the dinner, but what of Lord Destrian? Surely he wasn't hinting that Clarion might be a match for him. A man old enough to be her father. She had to have been imagining that look. But after years of recognizing that way Jackin looked at her, Clarion wasn't so certain it was all in her head.

The thought horrified her. But if he found her worthy of his own gaze, might that then mean he'd consider her a worthy bride for his son?

Clarion felt herself blushing at the ridiculous thought, which reminded her of why she'd finally left the mayor's mansion behind, permission or no. Jacosa was the only person with answers, the only one who knew she hadn't been entirely dreaming.

She was the only one who could get Mack back.

Once she exited the heart of the town, she stopped at the crossroads that would lead to her home—to her former home. Part of her wanted to walk by, to see what the new owners had done to the place. Did they even need the pig pens? Would they tear them up and turn them into gardens, like her mother had wanted to do?

Did any of that matter?

She turned toward Jacosa's, wishing she'd thought to bring a lantern. The moon was bright, but she'd never been this way alone in the dark. Even with the wide-open spaces, which should have quelled her fears, she couldn't shake the feeling that something could pop out at her at any moment. She increased her gait, walking as fast as she could without running—a silly voice in her head told her whatever was "out there" might be more likely to try to catch her if she was running—until Jacosa's garden finally came into view.

The tree on the top of the hill was notably absent, but even if everyone else were to be believed instead of her, she expected it to be gone, toppled in the quake alone. As she drew closer, she noticed some of the stones seemed askew or out of place, although someone—probably more labor from the town—had tried to rearrange the stone wall meant to keep critters out of Jacosa's garden. She placed a hand atop the wall and peered over it. A quarter of the seedlings were shorter than the rest, clearly replanted after the others. Although Clarion still wondered why Jacosa's magic plants grew so much faster than any of the normal crops anyone in the town tried growing themselves. But that was probably because she *was* a witch, whether she liked the title or not.

Jacosa's hen burst out from between the taller seedlings and Clarion jumped.

"What are you doing here?"

The voice came not from Jacosa's cottage, as Clarion might have expected, but from behind her. She'd been a fool not to believe her instinct, not to figure out who was following her earlier.

But the voice was recognizable, and although it caused her some discomfort, it actually made her far less frightened than the idea of being out here on her own.

"Why did you follow me?" Clarion asked as Elena walked up beside her, placing a basket atop the stone wall.

"Jackin told me you cut yourself," she said, reaching for Clarion's hand.

Instinctively, Clarion pulled her arm out of reach. "What do you care?"

Elena opened the wooden cover of the basket and brought out a small jar. "I didn't want you to bleed all over *my* family's harp."

Clarion tucked her hand tighter against her chest and walked around Elena toward the gate, giving her friend a wide berth.

"All right," said Elena. "I'm sorry. Okay? Is that what you want to hear?"

Clarion paused, touching the gate. "You had a right to be angry with me."

"Maybe so," said Elena, grabbing the basket with one hand and carrying the jar with her other, "but I shouldn't have let my anger go on for so long. I'm sorry. About the harp comment. And ignoring you and—"

Clarion wrapped Elena in her arms, not bothering to hide the tears that slid down her face. "I thought you'd never speak to me again," she whispered.

Elena shifted awkwardly to put the basket down

atop the wall again and patted Clarion's back. "To tell you the truth, I thought about it." She pulled back, and Clarion couldn't help but notice the single streak of shine that ran from one eye to her chin. "Now let's see that finger."

"It's just one of my calluses that cracked," said Clarion as Elena put the jar down beside the basket and then unwound the wrapping. Sure enough, the bleeding had stopped. Elena's nose wrinkled as she held the wrapping with the tips of two fingers and tossed it atop the stone wall.

She popped open the jar, still keeping hold of Clarion's hand in hers. Feeling Elena's soft skin on her somewhat rough palms, Clarion felt ashamed and awkward and grateful all at once.

"Even so," Elena said, "a little poultice will work better than a dirty cloth." Smiling and locking eyes with Clarion, she massaged the mixture into the small wound.

Clarion couldn't stand gazing into her lovely pale eyes for more than half a minute. She noticed the open basket and strained her neck to peer closer. "It looks like you've packed for a full picnic."

Elena let Clarion's hand go and grabbed the cover for her poultice jar, closing it up and dropping the jar back into the basket. Her hand lingered on the basket cover, halfway between shutting it and keeping it open. "I wasn't sure what you intended to do. I saw you leave from the window in my room. I figured you weren't leaving to have a little cut looked after." She twirled one of her plaits of hair around a finger. "But I also knew you wouldn't properly treat it."

Clarion laughed and peered into the basket. "Food?" She took the cover from Elena and rummaged through the contents, pulling out one thing after another. "A blanket? A jug of water? How were you carrying all that?"

"It wasn't easy." Picking up the things Clarion had removed from the basket, Elena arranged them back inside the wicker. "But I thought you might be going... Wherever Lord Magnus went."

Clarion leaned both elbows on the stone wall and stared at the place where the impossibly-large beanstalk had been. "I would if I could."

"That's what I thought." Elena shut the basket gently. "You know, I... Lord Destrian mentioned offering reward money."

Elena fidgeted, all traces of the anger Clarion had seen in her gone. What had changed her? "Do you think he was serious?" Clarion shifted toward her. "And that he'd offer it to you... To Mack's fiancée?"

Elena cringed. "You know, you only knew the guy a day. Or two." She crossed her arms tightly over her chest. "Why do you love him so much?"

"I don't." Clarion brushed some hair out of her face. "I do feel something, but it's not what you think. I wasn't about to run off with him to a quiet part of the countryside to do..." She shook her head. "No, I felt something for him. But it wasn't love."

"Not yet," said Elena. Clarion didn't respond. "Why 'Mack,' though?"

"It's what he told me he preferred to be called."

Elena leaned against the garden gate. "He never told me that."

Clarion shrugged. "Maybe he thought you too elegant to refer to him that way."

"And you weren't elegant enough?" Elena raised an eyebrow. "I saw the way he looked at you, after he saw you playing."

"I wasn't exactly the picture of elegance that night," said Clarion, remembering the dress and the dirt.

"Which was my fault, I know." Elena chewed her lip. "You just... You didn't seem to care how much you hurt me."

"I did care! I do." Clarion grabbed both Elena's hands in hers.

"Clarion, I... I want to find Lord Mag—*Mack*."

Clarion cocked her head. "You? Why?"

"First of all, just because I don't really want to marry

him doesn't mean I wish him harm." Elena squeezed Clarion's hand. "And secondly, I thought with some reward money—money Lord Destrian gives directly to me, to *us*, money I don't have to pry away from my father... We could go somewhere else."

"Elena..."

"Stop. Don't." Elena pulled her hands away and cradled one arm with her palm. "I knew it was stupid. Lord Destrian expects me to be his daughter-in-law. He's not going to hand me some money and let me go on my merry way. I just thought... Maybe he'd be grateful enough that he might. It might be my only chance."

Clarion threaded her fingers together. "And if I didn't go with you?"

Elena rubbed the side of her nose. "I figured that was likely. I just thought... Well, your papa is gone, and you don't get on so well with your mother. And it's not like we'd never be back to see our parents, Jackin, Krea... Just, well, we'd be someplace else. Someplace that's ours and ours alone."

"But... Elena, I *love* you, I do..."

Elena's voice cracked. "Don't say that. Please. Not if you don't mean it."

"I *do*! I just... I'm not sure I want you to be my one and only love my entire life."

Elena turned her face away, but Clarion could see she was rubbing her eye. "Well, maybe I can love someone else, too," she said, her tone projecting a shaky strength. She faced Clarion again. "Only not a man. If I marry, I won't love him at all. Not like I loved you."

Clarion took Elena in her arms, feeling strange to be the one to embrace her so boldly when she stood there trembling, so used to being the one swept up in a hug. Elena cried a little into her shoulder, but she didn't let her tears fall for long. She pulled back after only a minute and grabbed Clarion by both her elbows.

"What if we find this boy and split the money?

Maybe I could go off on my own, and you could use it as a dowry to marry him."

"I'm not going to *marry* him." Clarion laughed softly. "I hardly know him."

"Then use it to buy back your harp or your home or... Whatever! Clarion, you're the best chance any of us has of finding him. Where did he go?"

Clarion pointed to the newly barren top of the hill and let her finger linger there. And then she traced where the beanstalk had once been, higher and higher into the sky.

"Up," she said, and she walked around Elena to let herself into the garden.

Chapter 10

ou're still sticking to your story?" asked Elena, dropping her heavy basket at the bottom of the hill with a clunk.

"It wasn't a story." Clarion clutched her skirts higher and kicked at a few stray small rocks left at the top of the hill, looking for evidence. She crouched closer to the ground, picking at the dirt to find a trace of anything—the sprouts, the leaves, the red dot-like creatures.

"Jacosa?" called Elena, tiptoeing around the plants in the garden to knock on Jacosa's cottage door. "Are you home?"

Clarion scurried to find something, *anything*, sure the witch would just deny the beanstalk even though she'd climbed down it herself.

The door gave way to Elena's pounding and she went inside, calling the woman's name.

Clarion dug faster and faster in the dirt. Finally, she unearthed something, but she wasn't sure what it was. It was green, no bigger than her hand. She held it up to get a closer look in the moonlight. It looked like half a lima bean, with a large sprout coming out of it.

Jacosa's hen bawked and floated over Clarion's

shoulder. She tumbled backward into the dirt as the hen bobbed its head and climbed down the hill, curiously examining Elena's basket. It poked at the wooden top, lifting it up an inch or so and pulling back, fascinated to see the cover rise and fall.

"Clarion, Jacosa isn't home." Elena strode quickly out of the cottage, her hand clutching a small, dark pouch. "But this was on the table with a note that just said your name." She wasn't so careful as she walked through the plants this time to climb to the top of the hill.

Clarion stood and brushed off her skirt best she could before taking the bag from Elena. She opened it. Inside were three lima beans.

"The note just said my name?" she asked. "Nothing else at all?"

"No. I looked at both sides. There was nothing else." Elena clenched her fist. "Were you expecting an order? What do these do?"

"No. And I don't know." She held the bean up to the moonlight and turned it this way and that. A thought struck her and she bent over, searching the ground for the partial bean she'd dropped.

"What are you looking for?" asked Elena.

"This." Clarion held the piece of bean with a sprout in her palm beside the complete bean. Elena leaned over her shoulder. "They look like the same type of bean."

Clarion bit down on the inside of her cheek. *It might seem crazy, but...* "Stand back," she said, backing up a few paces and holding an arm out to keep Elena from following her.

Elena stumbled and grabbed hold of Clarion's shoulder. "Watch out. I almost tumbled."

"Sorry," said Clarion. She pointed down to where the basket lay, Jacosa's hen nowhere in sight. "Stand down there."

"Why?"

"Just... stand down there. Okay?"

Elena frowned but picked up her skirts and climbed down the hill to stand beside her basket. "What am I supposed to do now?" she asked, waving both arms outward.

"Wait and watch." Clarion took another step back and then tossed the bean and the sprout in her hands at the top of the hill, running down the hill as fast she could, tripping a few times until Elena ran forward to catch her and stop her momentum.

Their faces so close, they gazed into each other's eyes until Elena's eyelashes fluttered and she turned away to look back at the hill. "What was supposed to happen?"

Clarion straightened herself and looked up at the hill. "I don't know, I guess. I thought maybe... a giant beanstalk would grow."

"By throwing a bean at the ground?"

Clarion shrugged. "Maybe Jacosa went back there. And she wanted me to follow her."

"Back... up?" asked Elena.

"Jacosa came down from the beanstalk. *She* tried chopping it down, before she threw one of her beans at it and these little creatures came out and ate it. Maybe this time she had the little creatures eat it from the top down, so it would disappear even before she got back, and no one but me would be any wiser." Clarion felt ridiculous the moment she spoke those words.

Elena raised an eyebrow. "And what if those beans in that bag were the creatures?"

Clarion tapped her fingers to her temple. "They would have activated as soon as I threw it... Oh!" She scrambled back up the hill, not caring when she stubbed her toe on an errant rock.

"Clarion! Wait!" Elena climbed after her and stood beside her as Clarion searched the ground. "Now what?"

"She bit it before she threw it." Clarion's lips soured. "Maybe it has to be broken first."

Elena sighed and roamed around the hilltop,

scouring for Clarion's tossed bean. "Well, it's lost now," she said, kicking at the dirt.

Clarion held her little pouch above her head. "I still have two more."

"And you want to waste one, just because we can't find it? Maybe if we wait until morning..."

Clarion was already removing a bean from the bag and she held it before her lips, her legs swaying slightly. "Go back down and wait?" she said, inclining her head toward the basket.

Crossing her arms, Elena made her way back down. "Okay," she said once she reached the bottom. "I'm here." She sounded exasperated. Like she hoped Clarion might give up her schemes once she'd tossed all the beans.

Clarion chomped down on the bean and quickly spit both halves back into her hand. The pieces shook, bouncing as if brought to life. Clarion almost jumped right down the hill, even though this was exactly the outcome she'd intended. She quickly ran forward a few steps, dropped both pieces to the ground, and then ran down the hill, holding on tightly to her bonnet as she felt a rush of wind from behind her.

The earth shook and she fell to the ground before she reached the bottom of the hill. Elena ran over on unsteady feet, nearly falling herself, sliding to the ground to grab Clarion by the shoulders. "ARE YOU ALL RIGHT?" she shouted, but it was hard to hear her over the rumbling.

Clarion nodded and crawled away from the hill, as close to the stone wall as she could get, Elena at her side. They slammed their backs against the wall and stared upward, their mouths agape.

As the stalk grew, mist descended from the air above. When the rumbling ceased and the giant beanstalk stopped shaking, Elena broke the silence. "You were right. They went up."

"Argh! It's no use." Elena kicked the trunk of the giant beanstalk, muttering something about the spongy feel of the giant plant on her toes.

Clarion laughed between ragged breaths. This was the Elena she saw that few others did, the Elena she had loved even when she couldn't be reasoned with. Clarion wiped her sweaty palms over her apron, patting the bag with the last bean tucked away in her apron pocket. She stared at her fingers; her wound had cracked open just a bit again, and another callus threatened to tear.

Elena, her face shiny with sweat, her bonnet on the ground and her hair frizzy, wagged a finger at Clarion. "Neither you nor I have the strength to climb that thing more than a few feet, let alone..." She stepped back and pointed upward. "How far does it go up anyway? And do you think we'll really find some cave or cottage or... They can't *still* be up there, can they?"

"He never fell back down." Clarion shrugged. "He would have fallen if he wasn't off the stalk by the time it collapsed."

Elena paced back and forth, ignoring her. She nearly kicked the basket she'd brought to the top of the hill, thinking they might need to bring food and drink along. Until she realized there was no way she could climb *and* carry the basket. "And why hasn't anyone from town come out here to see? Fog or not, it's a *giant beanstalk*. I know Jacosa lives a bit out here, but you said you saw the other one from my house, right?"

"Yeah, but Mack and I... We were already kind of looking that way. Who else knows to look over here when there's an earthquake? And it's not like there's a stalk every time there's a quake. Plus..." Clarion pointed upward.

Although the skies had been clear when they'd set

out, a wave of fog had enveloped the top of the beanstalk once it'd stopped shaking.

Elena crossed her arms tight. "They should still know. Papa should have checked on me after the quake, and he'd find me missing—"

"—and his thoughts would immediately turn to a giant beanstalk in Jacosa's garden?" Clarion frowned. "If you want to get back, he *is* probably looking for you."

"Your mother, too." Elena walked up to the beanstalk and kicked it again. "No. I'm not telling them about this and losing out on the chance to claim the reward money."

"Elena—"

"*No.*" She gripped a sprout for what seemed like the thousandth time in the past hour. "Besides, if we both leave, I could see this 'magically vanishing' by the time we bring them all back to see. Or if just I leave, I could see you gone along with it."

"I wouldn't go without you," said Clarion.

Elena dug her foot unsteadily into a space between two lower sprouts. "But that's exactly what you had planned to do before I showed up, wasn't it?" She jumped back down and grunted.

"Yes, but now you're my partner in this." Clarion stepped forward to take her turn, spitting on her palms and rubbing them together.

Elena let out a disgusted noise. "Seriously? *That'll* make all the difference? A little bit of spittle?"

Clarion grunted as she moved her legs and stood on the second-lowest sprout. Her muscles ached from the many tries already. "It can't... hurt." She flinched as her palm wrapped around another sprout and she tore her callus open again.

Elena paced at the bottom of the beanstalk, both her hands on her head. "This isn't working, Clair. It just won't work." She sighed. "I don't know how in the world Magnus and Jacosa could possibly..."

"What?" asked Clarion after a moment of silence. She let out a deep breath as she balanced on the third-lowest sprout. She looked down, and her friend was nowhere to be found. "Elena? Elena?" Panicked, she started climbing back down. When she reached the bottom, she heard sounds of rummaging from Jacosa's cottage.

"Don't just walk off on me like that," said Clarion, entering the cottage. "After what I've seen here..." She stopped. Elena had made a mess of the place in just a matter of minutes.

"I thought of something," said Elena, unloading a drawer's contents onto Jacosa's empty bed.

Clarion cringed as Elena sorted through seeds and dried beans and other herbs on the older woman's duvet. "What?"

"You remember how everyone told you Jacosa found you passed out in her garden after the earthquake?"

"Yeah." Clarion rubbed her forearm. "Which was a partial truth, but it was the aftermath of the beanstalk vanishing that made me pass out. And Jacosa *knew* that."

Elena crossed in front of Clarion and ripped another drawer out of the witch's cupboard. "I thought it strange even then." She shook the second drawer onto the bed.

"Well, thanks for standing up for me when no one else would," Clarion retorted dryly. She reached forward and then pulled her hand back. "Do you really think you should be messing with Jacosa's stuff? Aren't you afraid she'll curse you?"

"With a floating rock that hits me on the back of the head? No. Ah!" She stopped her manic plundering and held up a dark red bean in her hand.

Clarion approached her. "What's that one?"

"Kidney bean." She shoved it into Clarion's hand and frowned, scouring the pile again. "But there's only one."

Clarion pinched it between two fingers and held it up to the beam of moonlight that penetrated the cottage through Jacosa's open window. "I don't remember what this

90

one does."

"It makes things lighter." Elena snatched the bean back from Clarion's hand. "I wondered why she didn't use it on you to make you easier for her to carry, if you were in such grave danger." She gestured around her. "Or why she didn't let you just rest here, for that matter."

"So you did find something off about her story." Clarion grimaced. "I thought *no one* believed me."

"Well, I wasn't sure about *all* of your story." Elena chewed her lip a moment. "I thought you'd concocted a story about a giant plant to hide something."

"Hide what?"

"That you helped Magnus—Mack—leave town."

Clarion crossed her arms. "If you thought I was so in love with him, why would I help him *leave*?"

Elena shrugged and sat on the only small free space left on Jacosa's bed. The moonlight glowed on her, like a ragged princess surrounded by autumn foliage, except the herbs and seeds and beans were all dried and of different colors. "I don't know. Maybe he promised he'd come back for you. Maybe he charmed you into thinking it was a good idea."

Clarion went to sit beside her but thought better of disturbing the mess and leaned against the wall beside the bed's pillows instead. "If he wanted to escape his father, I have no idea why he'd need my help."

"I just assumed... Maybe he used you for a little distraction on the way out."

"You and everyone else in town apparently."

Elena rolled the bean between her fingers. "Well, his father implied it. I don't know what my father thinks."

Clarion let out a breath. "He seemed to imply I'd make a good wife for Jackin."

Elena's fingers froze. "I take back my suggestion you marry him." She shuddered. "I don't want you marrying anyone you don't want to."

Clarion nodded, but Elena didn't let her say

anything more. She slapped her hand on her knee. "In any case. I wondered if Jacosa just wanted to make a show of there being no giant beanstalk here, so when you came to and told them the visiting lord had climbed up one and vanished, they could also say they'd seen no such thing."

Clarion jutted her chin toward the mess on the bed. "Doesn't she have anything there that would just make me forget?"

Elena's fingers traced the pile. "Not that I know of, but who can say? But even so, she obviously *didn't* want you to forget, or she wouldn't have been able to leave you the beans to grow another stalk."

Clarion turned to look out the window at the trunk of the beanstalk visible from the cottage. "But why does she want me to know about them? Why did she bother destroying that last beanstalk at all?"

"I expect we can find out." Elena held up the bean. "Once we use this."

Chapter 11

"Do you know what you're doing?" shouted Clarion as she scrambled after Elena, who neared the top of the hill and was sliding her basket over her arm.

Elena shrugged. "Does it matter at this point?" She snatched her bonnet off the ground and shook it out to let the dirt go flying.

"Have you seen Jacosa use that before?" asked Clarion as Elena put her bonnet back on and tried tying the closure beneath her chin one-handed. "Come here," grunted Clarion, tying the ribbon for her.

Elena studied Clarion as she did, and Clarion felt the weight of her former sweetheart's gaze on her. She tried to keep herself from blushing, but she had no idea if she was successful.

"Where's the green ribbon?" asked Elena. "The one I..."

"In my drawer," admitted Clarion, relieved she'd found it and didn't have to lie. "A memento of the past."

Clearing her throat, Elena swallowed and took a step back from her once she was done, saying nothing more about the ribbon. "Jacosa crushed the bean and sprinkled it on one of the rocks she wanted moved in her garden, remember?"

Clarion thought a moment. "I guess so... You noticed which bean she used to do that?"

Elena tapped the side of her head. "I'm observant."

"I know."

"But that wasn't the first time I'd seen her use it." Gazing up, Elena took a few steps back. "She used it on one of Tenney's father's cows once when it wouldn't move out of the road. She fed it to the animal then."

Clarion stepped beside her, a sickening sensation settling in the depths of her stomach. "Why not sprinkle it on the cow?"

Elena tilted her head. "Either because it was heavier than the stone or because it was a living thing are my best guesses." She readjusted the basket on her elbow, as it seemed to be swinging from the weight. "Or maybe eating it made the cow go even higher. It had to get over a fence, so I remember it floated higher than the stone. Jacosa and the men helping her had to hold tight to all four of its legs and Jacosa was quick to shove something else into its mouth when they got it where they wanted it. One of the men was almost pulled off the ground right over the fence with it."

"So... You mean for us to eat it?" Clarion hoped they could come up with another idea, although she felt they were almost too far gone into this plan to turn back now. "But there's only one bean and two of us. I'm not sure half a bean each will work as well as we need it to."

"One of us eats it." Elena grabbed Clarion's arms and wrapped them around her own waist, then slid her free arm around Clarion's back, pulling Clarion closer. Clarion felt a rush of heat invade her cheeks and she wondered, not for the first time, exactly why she'd been so certain she wanted to stop being sweethearts with someone who could still make her feel like that. "The other floats like the farmer right along with her."

"But we don't know what Jacosa fed the cow to make

it fall back down to the ground—"

"And we don't have any intention of falling back to the ground. In fact, I'd think that'd prove a very bad idea."

"But—" Before Clarion could protest any further—or offer to be the one who ate the bean, as she intended—Elena lifted her palm to her mouth, her basket dangling against her chest as she did, and crunched down on the bean.

"*Elena!*" said Clarion, but she tightened her grip as her friend started slipping out of her hands.

"It's working!" said Elena, gleefully. She sashayed her legs a little as if trying to walk forward. "Let's try to stick close to the stalk!"

Clarion looked down and saw they were already farther above the hilltop than they'd ever gotten when climbing the stalk directly. She squeezed Elena, holding on for dear life. The beauty felt so much lighter than she once did in her arms, almost as if she were barely there at all.

Elena laughed and finally reached the stalk, letting her fingertips graze its surface. "Why did Jacosa even *bother* climbing?"

Afraid to mention how hard her heart was thumping, Clarion wrapped her feet around Elena's ankles, thinking she would be safer climbing the beanstalk after all, if only her muscles had had the strength to make the journey that way. "Maybe she didn't. She could have floated, too... Or took something to get stronger!" Clarion shouted over the rush of the wind.

The pair hit the layer of fog, and it was like a mist of rain pelted over them both. Elena closed her eyes a moment and opened her mouth, drinking it in and laughing.

"Elena!" called Clarion. "Watch out!"

Elena's eyes popped open just as her head was about to slam into a large, protruding sprout. She grabbed hold of it with the hand not clutching Clarion and cackled, even as the basket slid down her arm and hit against her chest with a thud, pushing the sprout below her and using it as leverage to spur the pair of them higher even faster.

"Ah!" screamed Clarion, clenching her eyes tightly shut. It was hard to see anything in the fog more than a moment before they approached it, but even so, she knew closing her eyes was a bad idea. She couldn't help it.

"Clarion, we're *flying!*" Elena reached for another large sprout and used it to fling themselves higher. "Jacosa should grow these by the dozens! Can you imagine? An entire town full of people who can fly from one end to the other?"

"We're not exactly flying from one place to another," choked out Clarion as she forced herself to open her eyes. "We just keep going up. And up."

"I don't care!" cried Elena, laughing again. Clarion wondered if the bean had made her friend go mad. "I love it!" She kicked her foot off another sprout.

"Slow *down!*" said Clarion, who made the mistake of looking down. She couldn't see much but mist and fog below her, but she felt dizzy anyway, knowing they were far, far above where they could safely fall back to the earth again.

"No time! I don't know how long this lasts," said Elena, using another sprout to launch them even higher. She sighed and shifted the basket between Clarion's chest and her waist. "This keeps getting in the way."

Clarion trembled at the small distance the basket put between her and the young woman to whom she clung desperately. "We should have left it below."

"And have nothing to eat or drink? I think not." Elena grabbed another sprout. "If this is a rescue mission, Magnus could be stuck in a giant tree or mountain cavern somewhere, having gone a week without food."

"How could there be a tree or mountain?" asked Clarion, her voice straining against the wetness in the air. "We'd see the base of it below."

"Don't know," said Elena, cackling again as she kicked off from another sprout. "But I have no idea what else we could find up here."

As she spoke, her head burst through the last of the mist into a startlingly clear sky glowing in the embers of a soon-to-be-breaking dawn. She gasped.

"What?" asked Clarion, timidly, but then her own head poked through the last of the fog, and she forced her eyes to widen. They'd reached the top of the stalk—there was a *top* to the giant beanstalk—and they didn't find a tree or a cavern at all.

They found a town. A town on a bed of clouds.

"What in the world...?" asked Elena. Her jaw stayed open even after her sentence died out.

"It's a... How?" posed Clarion. She grimaced, as she noticed they weren't stopping. "Elena, we're still rising! We have to check this place out."

"I *know* that." Elena twisted around and started kicking forward. "I just don't know... how to stop." Her face was awash in panic and she kicked. Clarion tried to cling tighter, almost as if she were trying to bring her down with her, but it was no use. She could barely feel her friend's weight in her hands.

"Try kicking back to the top of the stalk!" shouted Clarion. The basket fell from between the two girls as they struggled, but neither tried to grab it.

"I *am* trying!" said Elena, kicking harder and harder with her hands out, as if she were swimming. "Clarion," she said, looking down. "The basket landed on the cloud! We can walk on the *clouds!*"

Clarion spared a quick glance below. Sure enough, the basket was there beside the hole in the clouds surrounding the beanstalk, and if it weren't for the panic washing over her, she would have thought to marvel more at the fact that Jacosa's chicken of all things burst out of the top of the basket and hopped toward the village.

"That's... good." Clarion grunted. "I figured those buildings had to be built on *something*."

Elena struggled and struggled and finally her fingers

reached the top of the stalk. She gripped it tightly and pulled them both toward it, letting out a huge sigh as Clarion gently released her hold and found her own cluster of sprouts to stand on.

"Are you still flying?" Clarion asked, panting.

"Yes," said Elena, embracing the top of the stalk tightly. "But this is keeping me here."

Clarion frowned. How were they going to get her down and keep her from flying even higher into the skies?

"Clarion, look!" Elena let go of the stalk with one hand without thinking and pointed to where the chicken was walking, toward the edge of town some distance away. As her legs started to ascend again behind her, she quickly clutched the stalk again.

The chicken walked past the cottage at the very outskirts of the village and barely came up to a tenth of the height of a single stone that made up the outer wall.

"What?" asked Clarion, not believing what she was seeing.

"They're *giant!*" said Elena. "The buildings are made to house *giants!*"

CHAPTER 12

larion didn't have time to argue with Elena about giant people and giant buildings. Besides, she'd be the last one to deny someone's seemingly fanciful story, considering everything she'd seen. Considering the size of the buildings she was looking at right now.

But more importantly, she was looking for Jacosa. Mack as well, of course, but Jacosa was the only one who could help Elena, who could do nothing but cling to the top of the beanstalk and hope she didn't float away. Clarion prayed the effect would wear off in time, but she couldn't take that chance. If only she knew where to go.

Despite seeing the chicken and even the buildings stay put on the cloud, despite being in a hurry to help Elena, Clarion still only tentatively lowered her foot once she had finished climbing down the stalk and reached the cloud. It felt like she was standing on a pillow. Clarion put her other foot down and wobbled, letting go of the last sprout. "I'm going to find Jacosa!" She cupped her lips and strained to look up. "I'm going to get help!"

"Okay!" said Elena, her voice distant. "And, um... Hurry?"

Clarion hurried as best she could, but it felt not only

like she was touching pillows with her feet, but like she was walking on them, which made it difficult to steady herself. But she didn't have time to get used to the strange gait the cloud ground forced on her, so she pushed and she struggled and she made herself go forward. As Clarion approached the village, she kept expecting the buildings to get smaller, but they actually did get larger. It was no trick of the eye; these buildings were meant to house people at least a hundred times taller than the people in her town. And just walking to the edge of the town was taking far too long; the longer it took, the more anxiety she felt about leaving Elena behind, but she didn't dare stop to look back, to waste a single second. When she finally rested her hand against the corner of a building—just a tiny portion of one stone of the building—she turned around to see if she could still make out the top of the beanstalk clearly.

Instead, she saw someone running toward her on the cloudy ground. She was bouncing every few steps and leaping in unbelievable bounds, waving her arm over her head.

"Elena!" cried Clarion, and she made her way back toward her.

When they at last met, Clarion grabbed hold of her by both hands. Elena felt weightier than she had before, but there was still something off about her, like she wasn't actually there in her grasp.

"I started sinking," said Elena, lacing her fingers through Clarion's. She burped and then smiled. "Although I don't think it's entirely worn off."

Clarion tugged her closer, holding her in her arms. "You could have floated off, letting go of that beanstalk!"

Elena blushed and then burped again. "I couldn't exactly stay clutching the beanstalk when I was losing my float. Good thing the bean lasted as long as it did." She pulled away and frowned. "We left the basket."

Clarion pulled her toward the town. "That's the least of our problems."

Several feet away, one of the doors of a giant house opened. A foot practically the size of the mayor's house appeared, followed by a leg that almost went on as high as the beanstalk had. A woman stepped out, as slow as can be—at least, it seemed slow to Clarion and Elena. She looked every bit like any other woman would in their own village, as far as Clarion could tell, but she was so much—*so much*—taller.

Perhaps thanks to the softness of the clouds, they didn't notice the movement at first, but when the woman turned around to shut the door behind her, the air shook with a thunderous noise, the same kind of earth-shattering groaning they heard during earthquakes. The woman's slow, giant steps were quiet on the clouds, but her breathing sounded like a wind storm.

Elena ran, dragging Clarion behind her, both of them bouncing along the clouds. "We have to get out of sight!" she shouted.

Luckily the cloud ground was so soft, neither felt any strain or injury when they landed following one of Elena's leaps. She reached for the wall of the cottage, grabbing on to a small protrusion hanging off one of the giant stones to slow down their pace.

They both plastered themselves against the wall, breathing hard.

Clarion heard a strange noise somewhere nearby... Like a cluck.

"What are we supposed to do?" asked Clarion. "How are we going to find two tiny people if this entire town is full of people like *that*?"

"How are we so sure they haven't been squashed at this point?" asked Elena. She winced. "Sorry." Moaning, she doubled over and Clarion scrambled to stop her fall.

"What's wrong?"

"I don't feel so good," said Elena. She reached back to grab Clarion's arm. "We need to find Jacosa."

Clarion, panicked, looked around her and found

what might have been a mouse hole nearby in the building if mice were as big as people. It's where the clucking sound seemed to be coming from. She started dragging Elena toward it, wincing as the rumbling grew louder and louder the closer they came.

Elena's face twisted as she climbed into the hole. "It's like I swallowed a whole house full of air." She inhaled sharply. "Is that... Jacosa's hen?" A tuft of white feathers disappeared into the darkness.

"Maybe," said Clarion, raising her voice to be heard over the rumbling. "It was in your basket." She guided Elena to the wall of the hole. "Rest here."

Elena leaned back against the stone, her hand still clutched to her stomach. "And what if... a giant mouse... walks through?"

Clarion's lips pinched into a thin line as she stood back to observe her friend. "Then you let it know you have no giant wheel of cheese."

Elena laughed and then belched some more and seemed about to vomit. Once she recovered, she smiled weakly. "Find Jacosa. Please."

Clarion leaned over to brush some of Elena's hair out of her face. "I will." She paused. "Thank you..."

Elena nodded and burped again, resting her fingertips at the base of her throat. "Just find her."

Not knowing what else to do, Clarion crawled farther into the hole toward the warm glow at the end of it. She tentatively placed a hand at the edge as she peered inside. It looked like a normal home, albeit many times larger. A blast of air hit Clarion's face as something—a leg, she figured out—passed by in front of her. A giant-sized man was walking around a table.

As the giant man turned around, Clarion noticed his lips move. The rumbling—that bone-shaking rumbling— was him *speaking*. Clarion felt proud for figuring that out, but she had a hard time understanding everything he was saying.

"...be pleased," said the giant man. (Or so Clarion thought. It strained her ears to even hear that much.)

"...take me to him," said another voice, a far quieter voice, a more *familiar* voice.

Hope surging through her body, Clarion climbed out of the hole and ran as fast as she could to get under the table. It took her a while to cross the length of the table, but the giant legs had moved to the other edge, and she wanted to make sure she was actually seeing what she was seeing. Despite everything, part of her still felt like this was a dream.

There was more rumbling above her and then the giant legs walked slowly toward the cottage door, each step a thunderous pounding that practically sent Clarion soaring a few inches off the ground. She peered around a table leg that was far bigger than any tree back home and saw the giant man holding his hand out in front of him.

A tiny woman stood on his palm with a chicken on her arm.

"JACOSA!" screamed Clarion, unable to believe her luck. Of all the houses Jacosa could be in, for her to be in the first one they'd tried... Elena would be saved.

The giant man opened the door in a slow motion.

No, thought Clarion. *They're leaving!*

"JACOSA!" she screamed again, picking up her skirts and running after them. Clarion thought she saw Jacosa turn toward her, perhaps even smile, but she wasn't sure, so focused was she on getting to that door before it shut in front of her.

"JACOSA!" she tried again, waving her hands above her. She hesitated when she reached the open door, unsure if she should dart through and risk being squashed, but she was running out of time to decide as the man began to pull the door closed behind him.

She saw the cuff of his pants was folded, making a small pouch area for someone of her small stature to ride along in.

She grit her teeth and ran forward. The practice of climbing the beanstalk helped her find the strength to climb up his shoe and settle in between the starched folds of fabric.

❧❀❧❀❧❀❧

Clarion was sure she'd never felt so sick in her life, but she clung on to the giant man's pants as he took slow step after unnervingly slow step through the cloud-formed streets farther into the village. She couldn't get off. She had to stick with Jacosa.

But she was hardly able to take in anything around her. The movement was too much, the sounds of talking coming from far, far above her pounded in her ears. She was certain they passed other pairs of giant legs, but eventually, she had to close her eyes and climb deeper into the pants cuff, closing out the world.

It was the first time in a while her papa invaded her mind.

"Little one," he'd said, tapping the stool they kept next to the harp. "Time for a lesson."

"Oh, Papa," said Clarion, kicking her legs wildly under the dinner table as she spooned another scoop of porridge into her mouth. "Do I have to?"

"If I say no, and I ask again tomorrow, and you still don't want to, then when will you ever learn?" He smiled and winked. "Come on, now, just a few minutes."

Clarion pushed her chair back from the table and shuffled her feet to the stool. "I don't like playing, Papa." Clarion flexed her digits. "It makes my fingers hurt."

He took her hand in his. "All the best things in this life will cause you some pain," he said. "But they're worth it, I promise. So long as you never give up because the pain seems *frightening."*

Clarion rolled over and clutched the pants cuff tighter around herself, like a giant blanket. A part of her wanted to give up, and she knew that was why her mother, Elena, Krea, and even Jackin, whom she was barely close to, could sometimes treat her like a delicate flower. She didn't want to be thought of as brittle glass, even if part of her felt that way. Elena was relying on *her*. Mack was relying on her—although now that she knew that this was the place he'd disappeared to, she hoped against hope he was safe up here somewhere. But she couldn't leave without finding out. She had to do something.

When the giant man finally stopped moving, Clarion removed the hand she didn't realize she'd placed up against her ear and loosened her grip on the blanket-like cuff. She let the cuff fall and blinked her eyes. They were no longer outside. The giant had taken Jacosa to another home—a far grander one.

Clarion bit her lip, wondering if she should get out or not. The man seemed to be standing near a table, which would provide her cover. Taking a deep breath, she took the chance, scrambling down and landing with a thud on the floor. She winced instinctively before realizing there was no way the giant could have heard her. She was a mouse to him. She scurried to the nearest chair leg.

And then couldn't believe her luck.

They were near a fireplace—a roaring fire, large enough to consume her entire town, she thought. And the mantel was strangely decorated in ascending bumps carved into marble. Though merely decorative for someone of the proper size, they'd also serve as stairs for someone of her size.

She peered around the table leg, wondering if she should risk it. There were a half a dozen pairs of legs here, and the rumbling of their speech was too much for her to bear. But she had to be sure Jacosa was still there, that she could signal her somehow.

Would a giant spot her? Did she spot every mouse that scurried around her own home?

Clarion gripped her skirts and decided to do it. She ran for the mantel, which she found frustratingly far away. When a giant slowly picked up its feet and walked near her, she felt that terrible lurching in her stomach again as she was lifted off the ground against her will. Still, she kept going, determined to get to the mantel before any of the giants spotted her.

She threw her hands out to the third step, daring to stop and calm her breathing, let her heart rate slow.

The feet seemed to be coming closer.

She pressed against the wall and retreated into the darkness, realizing how close she could have come to being squashed. Only when the giant legs passed did she start climbing the mantel while pressed into the shadows against the wall, the stairs seemingly endless above her. One hand settled on the wall, the other against her ear as she climbed. She couldn't tell how long it took to reach the top, but her legs ached and her breathing quickened. She had to collect herself before she could properly take in the scene around her.

There were at least four men and several women giants. One of the men and one of the women who stood hand-in-hand were dressed in finer clothes than the others, like they were the lord and lady of the town—or if like Clarion's town, the mayor and his wife. Most of the others were coming and going, bringing out a pitcher to fill a goblet the fancily-dressed man held or taking away empty giant plates. The man on whom Clarion had hitched a ride stood beside a table, his hat in his hands. On the table stood tiny Jacosa and her even tinier chicken, who ran around her, bobbing its head.

The giant lord and his wife laughed and the woman pressed her fingertips together over and over in an excited clap, her face positively alit with awe.

The lord said something, and Jacosa curtsied, saying

something back. Clarion could make out a word or two, but it was mostly thundering rumbling. She had no idea how Jacosa was speaking as loudly as they were, nor how she could hear them clearly.

The lady approached the table and held her hand out to the chicken, who ran onto her palm. She smiled as she brought it to her face for a closer look. The lord's face beamed with something akin to pride as he gazed at her.

Clarion thought she was imagining it at first, but Jacosa turned from the giant lord and lady toward the fireplace. She waved her hand quickly and pointed right at Clarion.

That settles that. She knows I'm here, thought Clarion. But that made sense, since Jacosa had left the beans with her name on them.

Jacosa tilted her head and widened her eyes, shaking her pointer finger even harder until suddenly dropping it to clutch the sides of her skirt and smile back at the lord and lady.

Clarion realized she wasn't pointing at Clarion for any of the giants' benefit. She was pointing *near* Clarion for her own. She frowned and searched the shadows of the marble mantel. The heat from the roaring fire warmed her chilled toes even through the soles of her boots. Luckily, the fire wasn't hot enough to make it impossible for her to walk on the surface.

The giants grumbled something again. Clarion covered her ears with her hands as she gazed at the knickknacks all around her, each almost as tall as her house had been. There was a giant, unlit candle, and a snuffer that was three times her height. There was a large basket with matches in it that easily reached Clarion's head. But it was the basket that was proportioned to Clarion's height beside it that caught her eye.

Like someone had expected her to climb that staircase. Like someone had expected her to find it.

She stepped closer to find a note atop a small pile of

green, dried herbs. "Eat me," it read.

No explanation, no hint of what to expect.

Clarion bit her lip and glanced back at Jacosa. She was rifling for something in one of her many pockets, pulling out beans and herbs as the three giants now milling about looked on.

She thought of Elena in pain back in the mouse hole, and Mack somewhere in this place, with no hint of where to find him. Jacosa was her only way to help either of them, and she clearly wanted Clarion to eat these herbs.

She grabbed a small handful and stuck it in her mouth. It tasted sharp and tangy, and it seemed to clear her sinuses as she chewed and swallowed, eager to get the taste out of her mouth. She closed her eyes as the unpleasant taste faded. She felt tingling in her fingers and toes and wondered if she was about to start flying or do something else strange and unusual.

"It's surely the cutest thing I've ever seen."

"You wouldn't get much of a meal out of it, if you tasted it. It'd get wedged between your teeth before you swallowed it." A man laughed deeply and heartily.

"I would never *eat* it!" A woman seemed appalled, but she laughed, too. "I'd make it my most adorable pet."

Clarion opened her eyes and scrambled to the edge of the mantel, too shocked by what she'd heard to bother being careful not to be seen.

She could *hear* the giants. And it sounded like normal speech in her ears, not that loud, thunderous rumble she could barely make heads or tails of.

"Ah! Found it." Jacosa held up one hand and shoved a handful of herbs back into her pocket. "I didn't grow many of these—they're harder to grow than you might think. They have to appear amongst the green peas like a diamond in the rough." There was something between her finger and thumb, but Clarion couldn't see it, even when she thought to lie on her stomach and put her head as close to the edge of the mantel as she could without falling over.

"What's that?" asked the giant woman, gently petting the little chicken with her index finger.

"A dried yellow pea. A special dried yellow pea." Jacosa gestured for the woman to give her the hen. "If Your Grace loves the hen so much, I should love to give it to you. With something special added."

Your Grace? thought Clarion. It was a title she didn't hear for lords and ladies.

The giant woman put the chicken back on the table beside Jacosa. Jacosa cooed to it and slipped the pea into its mouth.

"What's... special about it?" asked the giant lady, cocking her head.

"Watch," said Jacosa. She clapped her hands together and the chicken squawked, laying an egg before scurrying away from its former master.

The giant man reached for the egg and held it on his palm to examine it. "It's gold!" he exclaimed. "The hen lays golden eggs!"

"It does now," said Jacosa. She curtsied. "And it will for many lifetimes, many more times the life of an average bird, if you treat it well. Keep the animal, and may you enjoy many years of its golden blessings."

The giant lord's laugh bellowed, and even though Clarion's ears had adjusted to the level of the noise, she still found herself covering her ears at the volume. She let out a little cry without even realizing it and was surprised to find the giant man's laughter suddenly cut out.

"What's this?" asked the giant lord, approaching the mantel. Clarion stood cautiously, not sure if he could see her or if she still had hope of stealth. She realized that after ingesting the herb, the giant's movements no longer seemed labored and slow.

"Another tiny woman?" said the giant lady.

"Another gift," said Jacosa.

Clarion stepped backward until her back plastered flat against the massive unlit candle behind her. The giant lord's hand reached toward her, a smile like that of a mischievous boy who'd found forbidden treasure warping his giant, cracked lips.

Chapter 13

"She's a pretty little thing, isn't she?" The giant lord scooped Clarion into his palm and nudged her to stand toward the middle of his hand with a finger. Clarion jumped and glowered at the giant fingertip that poked her backside.

"And she's talented," said Jacosa.

"Talented?" The giant lady's nose wrinkled. "Can she lay golden eggs as well?"

Jacosa laughed and stepped back as the giant man put his hand on the table beside the garden witch; Clarion didn't hesitate to scramble off and clutch at the older woman's arm.

"What's going on?" hissed Clarion. "What do you mean, I'm a gift?"

Jacosa turned her head slightly and said as quiet as could be, "They can hear you clearly when you've taken the aloe. It's how they spotted you. Be quiet." Her face still had a fake smile plastered on it and her eyes flickered toward Clarion.

Clarion wanted to plead her case for Jacosa to help Elena, but she wasn't sure it was the best idea. *If the giants knew about another "tiny woman," they might make a spectacle out of Elena, too,* she thought. She tapped her foot, deciding it best to wait until the giants were distracted.

Stepping away from Clarion, Jacosa curtsied again. "Clarion is a musician. She can play the harp and sing like a dream."

The giant on whom Clarion had hitched a ride, the one who'd brought Jacosa to this grander home, flinched beside them. Clarion hadn't even thought to focus on him before, but she realized he was younger than the others. Perhaps about her own age. If giants aged like people did. It was hard for her to make out his features from where she stood, although she could see that he, like the other giants in the room, had dark hair.

"A little songstress?" The giant lord laughed. "I'd have her play the harp, but we have none in her size." He cupped his chin. "Unless..."

"No," said Jacosa, too quickly, shaking her head. "There's so little left. I need to grow a new crop, and it's not always a precise magic when given to our kind."

The giant lord shrugged. "She's more fun as she is anyway." His wife glared at him, but he didn't seem to notice. "Can she sing without the harp?"

"*Anyone* can sing without a harp," said the giant lady, huffing. She reached out to shuffle the little hen into her hand, and Clarion practically tripped over herself to step back as the big hand got closer.

Jacosa smoothed her skirt. "She could, but it wouldn't be the same."

"I can make a little harp," said the young giant, and it was the first time he'd spoken since Clarion could hear the large creatures clearly. "But I'll need to take her home with me to size it right against her small hands."

The giant lord adjusted his belt over his rather rotund stomach. "You think you can, Wilkin? All right then."

Wilkin put a hand, palm up, on the table. Clarion stared up at him, and he nodded at her. She looked at

Jacosa, who slipped her arm through Clarion's, although she kept her eyes on the lord and lady. "I'll make sure she has everything she needs before I go back home to grow more herbs."

"Jacosa," started Clarion, doing her best to keep her voice down, "what—"

Jacosa squeezed her arm tightly and directed her toward the waiting palm. "Thank you again, Your Graces." She tilted her head. "Enjoy the golden eggs."

She stopped as they reached the middle of Wilkin's hand, a smile plastered on her lips. If the young giant man was going to take them back to that first cottage, Clarion was headed exactly where she needed to go to save Elena, Jacosa in hand.

She just had to make it through another ride on a giant without losing all of her stomach's contents.

⁂

The ride back to Wilkin's cottage was better than the ride from it. Jacosa explained the aloe Clarion had ingested helped adjust all of Clarion's body to life in this realm. It was why she could hear clearly what the giant people said, why she could speak to them and be understood. It was why she no longer felt like a quake was invading her eardrums every time any of these giant people moved.

But Jacosa didn't explain *what* this realm was, and how it possibly existed.

Even so, Clarion had other pressing matters to deal with first. "Elena's here," she said, tugging on Jacosa's arm when they were some distance from the mansion. "And she needs your help. She ate a bean that made her float. That's how we managed to climb the stalk."

Jacosa raised her eyebrows. "She *ingested* the bean

113

that makes heavier things lighter?"

"We couldn't climb the stalk otherwise." Clarion frowned.

"Why did you bring her with you to begin with?"

"She followed me." Clarion dared to spare a glance upward and behind her, but she still couldn't make out the giant Wilkin's face, not with the newly-risen sun shining behind him. "I left her in a mouse hole back in that first cottage. She's not... She's not feeling well."

"I imagine not." Jacosa rolled her eyes. "I'll have to take her back down the beanstalk and give her a special mixture of herbs to counteract the side effects. The floatation spell is not for living creatures."

"She said she saw you use it on a cow once."

Jacosa shrugged. "And I fed it the proper mixture of herbs right after, before it had time to negatively affect her." She coughed. "Plus, it was a *cow*."

Something bristled in Clarion at that comment. Clarion thought briefly of her papa's pigs, and how even though she knew what most of them—what all of them now—had been destined for, there seemed a difference between treating them cruelly in life, and giving them peace and comfort for what time they had. But that no longer mattered. That was so far removed from where she was now in so many ways. "Can you help Elena in time?"

As the giant man approached his door and opened it, Jacosa nodded. "She'll live. Can't guarantee she'll be comfortable for the next few days, though."

"The next few *days*?"

"She'll be recovering. Once I give her the poppy stalk, she'll be out for a while." Jacosa paused as the man moved them toward his table, resting his nails against the wooden surface. She lifted the hem of her skirt and walked down between a giant wooden cup and a bowl overflowing with two humongous bread rolls. Clarion followed, watching the giant man warily as he approached the corner of his cottage where there was a workbench.

Clarion felt something poke her arm and whipped around to accept the human-sized basket Jacosa shoved at her abdomen. "That's full of enough aloe to last you several weeks if need be."

"Several weeks?" When Clarion had pictured rescuing Mack, she'd thought she'd find him stuck in a cave far, far out of sight. Maybe injured. Perhaps simply being a fool. She thought they'd climb down together, that she'd be home before anyone even noticed she'd left.

She was the one who'd been a fool.

Jacosa fished out a shawl from the top of the basket and wrapped it around her shoulders. "Take a handful every morning so you can communicate with the people here and so they don't cause you so much disorientation."

Rifling through the basket, Clarion found nothing but piles of the dried herb. She tucked the foliage into a pocket in her apron. "What do you expect me to do here?"

Jacosa tucked her hands beneath her arms. "What did you come here to do?"

Clarion glanced at the giant man, who'd pulled a stool up to a workbench in the corner. He grabbed several tools and sat down to work by the glow of a candle. "Find Mack," she whispered, in case her newly booming voice carried across the room. Finding a land full of giants at the top of the beanstalk didn't change that fact. She couldn't let it, not even if her heart hammered and her head pounded and she felt as unsteady on her legs as she'd ever felt in her life.

Except, perhaps, when she'd lost her papa. And if she could get through that, she could get through this.

Jacosa nodded. "I figured you wouldn't let well enough alone. So stay here because here is where you'll find him." She walked toward the edge of the table in Wilkin's direction.

Clarion let the basket fall to her feet and lost her footing as she accidentally stepped onto a bread crumb the size of her head. "But where are we? How does such a place exist?"

Jacosa ignored her, cupping her hands around her mouth. "Wilkin! A ride, if you please!"

Wilkin looked up from his workbench and stared at the two small women for a moment before pushing his stool back from the table.

Clarion grabbed Jacosa's arm tightly. "Answer me!"

Jacosa didn't tear her eyes from the giant man approaching. "It's a place the observant in our town have always known existed. Just think of that song you like to sing."

Clarion frowned. The tale of a man whose lover disappeared—a lover everyone thought had deserted him, but whom he insisted was snatched away to a kingdom in the sky. She thought it poetic. And it certainly never mentioned the *giants* who lived there.

"What am I supposed to do?" she said quietly, her grip loosening.

"Well, if you hadn't brought a friend in need of treatment, I could have stayed and helped you." Jacosa smiled, but something cast a shadow over her face. Wilkin stopped before the table and held his palm out to Jacosa. She climbed on. "The mouse hole, please," she said, as if speaking to a carriage driver. She lifted her nose in the air. "Ask Wilkin for anything you need. Just be careful of his mother."

"His mother?" asked Clarion as Wilkin laughed. It wasn't a pleasant laugh. Clarion walked the length of the table, following them, so she could see Jacosa leave. Wilkin crouched to the ground and held his hand out to the mouse hole. Lacing her fingers together, Clarion prayed Elena was still in there and still well enough to get help.

Wilkin cracked his neck as he straightened up. "Are you hungry?" he asked. So he wasn't going to explain whatever the comment about his mother meant.

Clarion thought of the bread crumb as big as her head. "I suppose," she said. Maybe food would help her figure out what she was supposed to do.

Wilkin walked to the cupboard and opened it, pulling out a wedge of cheese that was half the height of Clarion. "Just a crumb for you," he said, breaking off a corner as he approached her again. He held it out to her, and Clarion had to use both hands to take it from him, her sore arms actually flinching at the weight of the biggest slice of cheese she'd ever had to herself.

"Thank you," said Clarion, quietly, putting the cheese on the corner of a giant wooden plate and breaking off a mouthful.

Wilkin stared at Clarion as he chewed on his own portion, and although his face was somewhat hidden in the darkness, Clarion thought she saw something like admiration in his light-colored eyes.

Clarion opened her mouth, about to ask about her purpose there, or who else might be keeping little people as "gifts" and "playthings," when the door behind her opened.

Wilkin moved quickly to approach the older woman who entered. "Mother. Good morning."

Wilkin's mother sneered and raised a hand, tossing a bucket to the ground with the other. "Yes, yes, *good morning*. A morning like any other, full of hours of scrubbing." She shoved at his chest, and he stepped aside. "I don't want to see a single face right now. I just want some cheese and bread, and then to take a nap..." She stopped suddenly, clutching her chest. "What's this? What happened to that old woman mouse?"

Wilkin cleared his throat. "Jacosa went home. She left this other one behind... For Their Graces."

"Then what's she doing *here*?" growled Wilkin's mother. She shook her head. "Oh, I won't have it. Bad enough you or I have to ferry that little witch creature every time she shows up, but she's leaving one of her kind behind? No, Wilkin. No."

Clarion stepped back, her heart thumping, as the woman's mangled giant hand reached out to snatch her.

CHAPTER 14

larion didn't see the point in her scrubbing a plate big enough for a giant. But Wilkin had only been able to calm his mother by explaining he was "sizing" her for a little harp for the king and queen—yes, that's what he called them; Clarion had never met real royalty before, but she laughed at the thought because truly, the more important issue was she'd never met *giants* before—and that Clarion would help with the housework while that was being done.

The giant woman hadn't seen anything wrong with that.

"All right, then," she'd said, grabbing a plate off the table and dropping it and Clarion down a few feet into her basin. "Clean up." She tore a corner off a sponge on the counter nearby, dipped it in a bucket of sudsy water, and threw it at her. Clarion had to run to dodge it.

It took her at least an hour to run the sponge piece over the entirety of the plate, and her back ached because she'd had to bend and push the sponge with both arms. She'd collapsed at the bottom of the basin at the end of it, breathing hard, not caring that her skirt got wet from the layer of moisture coating the sink.

She was hungry and wished she'd eaten more of the cheese piece before she'd dropped it back on the table. She had to use the privy, but she knew she wouldn't find any in her size, and she was frightened to find out what would happen if either giant spotted her squatting beside the plate she'd spent so long cleaning.

Still, there was no stopping nature, so she did it anyway. She tried to get as far from the plate as possible.

Her hair was coated with sweat beneath her bonnet, so she removed the hat and wrung out the moisture, leaning on the sopping sponge like it was a pillow.

"Finally done, are you?" boomed the older giant woman. "Here's the rest." She grabbed the clean plate and put down another, stacking two wooden cups, two wooden spoons and even a giant knife atop it all. Clarion looked up, her eyes wide, and the giant woman shook her head. "I'll soap this up for you," she said, grabbing the piece of sponge out from under Clarion, and causing the girl to fall over, hitting her cheek against the hard, wet surface of the basin.

Clarion choked back tears as she pushed herself up, holding up her now-soaked bonnet. She didn't feel bad about the urine at all anymore.

"Oh, enough with the blubbering," said the giant woman as she approached, soapy sponge piece in hand. "It's just a little water. It'll dry out when you're done with the dishes." This time, at least, she placed the piece gently beside Clarion.

Clarion hiccupped and put both hands on the sponge again, running it over the edge of the new plate, her tears mixing with the soapy water on the wooden surface. With a grunt, the giant woman walked away.

By the time Clarion finished the second plate, she'd about run out of tears. She collapsed next to the plate, staring at the cups and wondering how she could possibly climb up to clean them. The giant woman hadn't even thought to tip them over so she could climb inside. But she could tackle the utensils next anyway. The gleaming blade of the knife frightened her, though, and she wondered if she could possibly run the sponge over it without cutting her feet, but there'd be no avoiding it, as the edge was the part covered with what was possibly butter.

She couldn't believe she missed scrubbing the mayor's floors. She missed rolling in the mud with the pigs, but that was less of a surprise.

She was so thirsty. She'd risked relieving herself in the corner of the basin earlier, but she was too afraid to drink up the sudsy water.

As she dragged the sponge to the nearest spoon, her shoulders aching, she felt the basin beneath her shake.

She froze. It took her another minute to realize it wasn't an earthquake but snoring.

The giant man appeared at the side of the basin, a finger to his lips. He held his palm out to Clarion, who hesitated a moment before walking onto it. She realized then, as uncomfortable as it was, she much preferred having a palm held out to her than just being grabbed like a doll.

"Mother's sleeping," Wilkin whispered as he carried Clarion to his workbench. "I'll finish the dishes for you. But first..."

He placed his hand down on his workbench and Clarion walked onto it. A piece of wood almost three-quarters her height and a pile of strings of metal stood beside her.

"Should I have looked for gut?" asked Wilkin, referring to the strings.

Clarion crouched beside the strings and ran her fingers over them. "No," she said quietly, shaking her head. "I played on metal at home."

Wilkin pulled his stool closer, as quiet as could be, and sat down. "You must have been a lady where you came from," he said, picking up the wood. He held it up beside her, and she took the hint to stand beside it.

"No." She reached out to touch the wood, imagining her own harp there as he put his thumb on the wood at

120

about the right height for a harp her size and grabbed a sharp little knife. "The harp wasn't mine... Not anymore."

Wilkin carved a mark into the wood where he'd held his finger. "But it used to belong to your family?" He spoke casually, more like he was trying to make conversation than he had any real desire to know.

"Everything good in my town used to belong to my family." Clarion's knees shook from all the work she'd done and she plopped onto the table, causing a bit of the wood shavings to fly upward around her like dandelion seeds. "But that was before I was born."

Wilkin traced his knife over the wood in the shape of a harp. Clarion wondered if he intended to carve it all out of one piece, if he could possibly be skilled enough for that. Her eyes started closing, so she hugged her knees to her chest and tried to squeeze herself into staying awake.

Wilkin's knife stopped. "Oh," he said, putting the wood and knife down on his table some distance away from Clarion. "You must be exhausted. You can rest." He pointed to a dark corner at the edge of his bench against the wall. At some point during the day, Wilkin had put together a Clarion-sized bed made of several folded giant cloths—or perhaps he'd let Jacosa sleep there before; considering she wasn't certain what Jacosa did there, Clarion had no idea how long she'd usually stay. There was even a pillow made out of a fluff of cotton. Clarion really wanted to stay up, to learn more about the world she was in, to ask where Mack might be, but the labor of the day had exhausted her on top of attempting to climb the beanstalk and worrying about Elena.

Mack would have to wait. She was physically incapable of helping him. Maybe her loved ones were right. Maybe she was too weak to do anything on her own. But surely there was no way another tiny person would be overlooked in this town. She could find him tomorrow. Clarion shuffled across the workbench, dragging her feet to the inviting makeshift bed. She removed the top cloth and was about to climb in, not even caring that she was still wet.

She felt a tug at the back of her dress. Wilkin had pinched it with two fingers.

"Sorry," he said, and Clarion could have sworn she saw his cheeks darken. He pointed to another cloth Clarion hadn't noticed, one that hung at the corner of the room where the two walls met. "There's more cloth back there; I tore it into several pieces. I thought you could dry yourself and then wrap yourself in the cloth. I'll hang your clothes near the fire so they dry overnight."

Clarion gazed at Wilkin warily, but she was too tired to argue. She stepped behind the sheet and shook off all her clothes, snatching the pieces of cloth to use as instructed. She was sure to grab the dried herbs out of her pocket and tuck them safely beneath a stack of sheets. She didn't want to lose them and have no way of communicating with the giants around her.

"I should have made you new clothes," said Wilkin. Clarion could see him pick up the block of wood and the carving knife again through the silhouette of the hanging cloth. "But Mother would have asked what I was doing."

Clarion couldn't help herself. Perhaps it was the exhaustion or the fact that she was in a world she never imagined existed. She laughed and covered her mouth hard to stop it as soon as she remembered she was supposed to keep quiet.

She peeked out from behind the cloth and stepped out with one of the towels wrapped around her torso. She was definitely imagining the blush on Wilkin's cheeks as he leaned closer and plucked her discarded clothes up. She figured he *must* realize she was the size of a doll to him, after all.

She tried to see if she found his face handsome, if she could imagine these giant creatures as anything other than anomalies. With the dying light of the fireplace, it was hard to get a good picture of his face as he draped the clothes atop some of the warm stones nearest the fire. He seemed pleasing enough. But again—she was the size of a doll in his hands.

But maybe she could use his discomfort to her advantage. Perhaps he just wasn't used to speaking to women at all, thanks to a domineering mother. After just a day in his mother's presence, she was starting to think of her own as far less egregious.

"Wilkin," she said, her voice soft and quiet. "Am I the only... That is, is Jacosa the only other person my size who's been here?"

Wilkin's shoulders stiffened as he finished patting the small clothing flat on the stones. "Why?"

Wilkin's slight reaction didn't go unnoticed. Clarion walked to the edge of the table, adjusting her towel so she could hang her legs over the side. "It's just... No one in my town knows about this place. Except Jacosa, apparently. Do you all know about our town?"

Wilkin returned to his stool and picked up the wood and tool again. His hands quivered slightly. "We know. We've always known."

"And no one comes to visit us?"

Wilkin's tool stopped carving suddenly. "Jacosa assures us we couldn't fit."

Clarion laughed, not even meaning to. She swung her feet and stretched her toes. "I hadn't thought of that. Still, I find it strange. You all live in the skies above us and yet... How does that work anyway?"

Wilkin resumed his carving in slow, steady strokes. "How does what work?"

"There aren't always clouds in the sky." Clarion raised her hands above her, wincing as she felt her towel start to fall, careful to quickly tug the material back over her chest. "Does your town travel with the clouds?"

"Jacosa doesn't seem to think so."

"How did she...?" Clarion took a deep breath. "How did she find this place?"

"The little witch from your town has always found

her way here," said Wilkin. "She sometimes brings others with her."

"Others?" Clarion straightened her back. "Has Jacosa brought others... before me?"

Wilkin opened his mouth but snapped it shut as his mother let out a snore that practically shook the workbench Clarion was sitting on. He looked at his mother for a moment until he was satisfied she was only stirring in her sleep. "I didn't mean Jacosa particularly," he said, burying his nose back in his work. "The witches before her used to bring more little people here."

That would explain the songs, I guess, thought Clarion. *Although Jacosa never mentioned witches before her. Is it a family trait?* She crossed her legs and stared at her bare feet, surprised she wasn't shivering, but even a dying giant fire radiated enough heat to keep her small body warm. *Should I just ask him about Mack? That seems like something he would have mentioned. If he wasn't purposely keeping Mack a secret.*

"Was there a small man who came here—"

Wilkin whipped his head around and turned back, a finger to his lips. He listened intently as his mother's snores grew louder for a moment before he finally let out a deep breath.

"You'd best get to sleep," he whispered, nodding toward the bed. "I'll put your clothes behind the sheet I draped for you when they're dry."

Frowning, Clarion stood. She chanced it once more. "You've never seen a man my size here?"

"If there was ever a living, breathing man your size here," said Wilkin, "he wouldn't have stayed that way long."

As she pulled the towel acting as a blanket up to her chin, Clarion felt she had to be satisfied with Wilkin's answer, although she was certain his words were covering up something he left unsaid.

Chapter 15

larion's second day in the land in the clouds was much like her first. Wilkin expected little of her, although he didn't talk much as he worked to build her harp. When his mother returned, she expected far more, but Wilkin stepped in to finish her tasks once his mother had fallen asleep. Clarion's mind kept active with thoughts of how she should slip out the mouse hole to search for Mack, but a part of her felt it hopeless, that her best chance was to wait for Jacosa's return and rely on the wily woman's assistance.

It was on the third morning that she thought to ask Wilkin, "How often does Jacosa visit?"

"Whenever she feels like it." Wilkin didn't so much as shrug as he affixed a second string into the soundboard he'd finished making the night before. It was crude, but it was starting to look like a harp. Clarion didn't think to ask how Wilkin was sure he could make one, how he knew to make each string sound different.

Not that she cared if it actually worked. It would never be her family's harp, and this place would never be home.

Still. What was his family's profession? His mother

cleaned houses, and there seemed to be no sign of his father. He could hardly be an instrument maker without more instrument parts strewn about the cottage.

Clarion mulled this over as she swept her little makeshift broom across the kitchen table, trying to move a crumb half the size of her head to the edge of the table. "Have you ever made a harp before?"

"No," said Wilkin, "not exactly."

Not exactly? Clarion paused to wipe her brow. "Have you made a different instrument?"

Wilkin grunted and Clarion shook her head. With each passing day, she was unsure waiting for Jacosa was her best option. But the thought of scurrying around in a village of giants made her even less enthused. She could convince Wilkin to take her around, maybe, especially when his mother was gone...

Clarion heaved the crumb over the side with one last burst of strength and sat at the edge of the table, purposely exhaling loudly.

Wilkin paused and looked up from his work. "Would you like some water?"

"Yes, please." Clarion waited for Wilkin to pour some water from his own mug into the thimble he'd been using as her cup. It splashed over the side and dripped down to his toes. He grabbed the thimble with his other hand and shook out the wet one.

Even though Wilkin held the thimble with just two fingers, Clarion had to use both hands to take it from him. She dipped her chin in like a dog in order to take a sip. "So what have you made?" she asked, gently putting the too-large "cup" on the table beside her and wiping her mouth.

Wilkin hesitated, almost certainly about to walk back to his workbench, then sat in the chair nearest her. "I make... whatever needs making. Little odds and ends."

"Was your father a tradesman?" asked Clarion, genuinely curious. "Did you learn from him?"

Wilkin laughed, and even though his voice was

softened to her magicked ears, something in the bitter sound shook Clarion from her head to her toes.

"My father isn't a tradesman. He hardly taught me anything."

"He's alive?" Clarion knew it wasn't her business, but she was curious nonetheless. Estrangement was so rare in her village because everyone in town would look upon the couple poorly. Were there jobs that took working men away for long periods?

Wilkin's mouth soured, but he said nothing, just stared into his drink.

Clarion decided to let well enough alone. It had no bearing on what she was doing there regardless. "But the king let *you* make the harp. Doesn't your town have a blacksmith here? A carpenter?"

"We do." Wilkin grunted and squeezed his mug tighter in both hands. "We did."

"*Did?*" Clarion didn't like the sound of that.

Wilkin took a quick sip of his water, almost choking on it. But Clarion could hear what he mumbled into his mug nonetheless. "The king grew displeased with them."

Clarion traced her fingers over the rim of the thimble beside her. For some reason, she thought maybe the water smelled of lemongrass. So the king was tyrannical? There was so much she didn't know about the village. Were there other villages of giants, and how did one travel from one to the other? How did the village stay put while the clouds moved on? (She supposed it must if Jacosa had been there more than once.) Where did they get their resources? Could crops grow on cloud ground, and did water flow for that matter? But her curiosity was secondary to her need to find Mack and go back to check on Elena. She had no intention of staying in this world after her goal was accomplished, even if it meant her curiosity would never be satisfied.

"What... happens when the king is displeased with someone?" asked Clarion, certain she should at least know that if the man expected her to be a tiny songstress for him.

Wilkin lowered his mug. "They're... no longer allowed here."

He wasn't saying everything, Clarion was sure of it. Clarion wondered if she could use Wilkin's unhappiness with this place, with his king, to her advantage, although she wasn't sure she could promise to take him with her. A giant in a village full of people her own size was even more impossible than a tiny person in a village of giants.

He would have to go unsaved. She had her hands full trying to be someone who could save both Mack and Elena. "What's going to happen to me? Does the king expect to have need of me forever?"

"I don't know." Wilkin frowned and put his mug down on the table some distance behind Clarion. Clarion bounced a little at the movement, even though her daily dose of aloe kept it from being dizzying. "Jacosa seemed to make him think you were a gift, a toy to play music at his whim, but your people don't give away their neighbors anymore than we can give away our neighbors."

Clarion shook her head. "No, they don't. You're right about that." She took a deep breath and decided honesty was the best tactic. "I only played along because... I'm looking for someone."

Wilkin didn't look surprised. "There are no others your size here," he said, as if guessing her next question. "And if you ever want to get home again, it's best you go as soon as possible. The next time the beanstalk grows back."

Clarion froze. "The beanstalk is gone?" *Of course,* she thought. *Jacosa destroyed it every other time.* But would the mayor and Lord Destrian believe Elena this time?

Wilkin grunted. "It is. I thought about suggesting you hide until then, but Mother would notice your absence as soon as she got home, and she'd report it to the queen. She does cleaning for her, and she's rather eager to stay in her good graces."

"It doesn't matter," said Clarion, whose fingers

brushed the pocket in her skirt, leading her to realize she still had one bean there. Would it work to just throw it down the hole in the clouds where the stalk had once been? "I'm not going back without Mack. Magnus."

Wilkin stared at her a good long while, and Clarion noticed for the first time since she'd arrived that in the silence of a morning, you couldn't hear the birds chirping from up here. She marveled at the thought of giant creatures to go along with giant people.

When Wilkin spoke at last, Clarion wondered at the edge in his voice. "Do you like this... Mack?"

"I hardly know him," admitted Clarion. She considered how truthful she should be—if Wilkin was honestly sweet on her despite her size, jealousy might prevent him from helping any further—but that, at least, wasn't a lie.

"Then why do you care?"

Tucking her hands beneath her thighs, Clarion swung her feet slowly. "I don't know. I want to say I'd do the same for anyone I witnessed climb that stalk and never return." Wilkin let out a breath and pushed his chair back, standing. Clarion thought about what she'd said, and how hard it was for her and Elena to climb it. Could she have done as much for someone else? Would she have even bothered? Elena had. But Elena claimed to be helping for the reward money. Still, Clarion wondered if it was mostly for Clarion's sake. "That's not entirely true," she said before she even thought it through. "I knew him only a few hours really. But there was something palatable between us. I didn't even know I could feel that way about a man before."

Wilkin clutched the back of his chair and gazed at his little companion. Clarion couldn't look back at him for fear she'd undone what good will the giant young man had for her by admitting her feelings for one of her own kind.

"There's a ball this weekend," said Wilkin, utterly surprising Clarion with the segue. "I know the king is hoping you could perform for him. It's... The king and queen often like to bring out their playthings for these events."

"Their playthings?" asked Clarion. "You mean like... the hen. And me."

Wilkin nodded and pushed the chair back under the table, careful not to get it anywhere near Clarion's fragile body.

Clarion shot up. "And if they've been keeping Mack a secret, perhaps they'll bring him out, too!"

Wilkin's eyes widened. "So you mean to go? You think you'll find a little man there?"

"I think I'll find *my* little man there!" Clarion bit her lip, considering the other alternatives. If Jacosa had never found Mack, he would never have known to eat the aloe, and he'd have been lost and terrified in this confusing world. But Jacosa hinted that she had met him—and maybe he'd figured out how to climb that mantel and found the basket of aloe Jacosa had left behind. But what if he'd been squashed? The thought was too terrifying to think of. No, Jacosa had met him and either presented him as a gift to the king and queen or told him to stick close to the shadows and far out of view. Why she didn't just bring him back with her, Clarion had no idea—but it was far from the only thing the witch had to answer for. No, either Mack was in a box somewhere in the mansion waiting to be brought out and put on display, or he'd be observing the giants, and what would be more likely to draw his attention than a ball?

She clasped her hands together as if in prayer. "Please tell me you'll have the harp done in time."

Rubbing his hand across his long nose, Wilkin sniffed. "All right. I will."

Clarion grinned and was about to thank him when an unimaginably shrill roar echoed throughout the air and the table began shaking beneath her. Clarion stumbled, the thimble spilling and splashing across her feet. Her hand reached out for the edge of a bowl a few feet from her, but her steps were unable to carry her steadily toward the towering wood above her, the bowl's edge sliding out of her grasp.

She wasn't sure how long it lasted, wasn't sure if her aloe was failing her prematurely, because she had never before felt so nauseous and dizzy, and she swore she heard gibberish echoing throughout the scream.

"FEE, FI, FO, FUM!"

Wilkin's hand shot out to the table and Clarion fell into it, gripping on to his finger as her cheek pressed against his skin. She realized he was shaking, too, that he gripped the edge of the table hard with his free hand.

Finally, after what felt like minutes, the sound stopped. Clarion pulled her head away from Wilkin's hand, her arms still trembling and her grip still tight on his finger. "What was that?"

Wilkin stood straighter and wiped some sweat off his brow. "The king," he said as he gulped. "He must have grown displeased with someone. That was the sound of him razing a house to the ground. It happens every few days as of late."

Clarion's spine stiffened as she wondered if the quakes she had known back home were the result of the giant man's rampages. She'd never imagined how much more frightening the sound and vibration would be from here.

"If the king finds out you ever plan to leave him... Maybe you should hide now after all..."

Clarion couldn't hear much else of what Wilkin said. Her thoughts were drifting, her ache for the comfort of her home, the pigs, and her papa's arms around her stronger than ever.

Chapter 16

"This is going to be impossible." Wilkin's mother held the cut of silk she'd received from the queen earlier in the day. "I don't know why, if she was to be a gift, Jacosa didn't outfit her in something nicer."

And this is actually one of Elena's outfits. Considering the worn condition of her fine dress, Clarion lowered her arms as Wilkin's mother sat down on the stool. The woman had grabbed her like a doll and set her on Wilkin's workbench, going on and on about how the king had asked her to make Clarion a nice dress for the ball that evening after work. Which left her only a matter of hours in which to make it.

Wilkin leaned in to pick up the finished harp so his mother didn't ruin his entire week's worth of work. He raised his eyebrows at Clarion, who shrugged and sat down as his mother took a sharp tool to the fabric.

"It'll be crude," said his mother, tracing the outline of a dress. "It might be best if you wear it over that sole piece of fabric you thought to bring with you."

Clarion nodded but didn't say anything. Despite all her bravado as of late, she could never bring herself to talk

132

around Wilkin's mother. She felt so inconsequential around her. So inhuman. Like how her own mother viewed the pigs.

"I'd make you make it," she grunted before settling into silence for some time, "but we haven't needle and thread small enough."

Clarion was thankful for that, as she had no idea how to make a dress. Behind his mother, Wilkin gestured toward Clarion's little bed and changing corner of the table and Clarion made her way there. Wilkin placed a thimble of sudsy water and a small piece of sponge behind her towel curtain. "You should wash up for the ball."

Wilkin's mother paused in her work, a needle held high above her head, to glare at her son. "What are you so concerned about her washing up for?"

"I just thought—"

"You *thought* like your father would." She sniffed and went back to her sewing. "Maybe if I'd agreed you should be married off, your thoughts would stray further from the gutter more often. Nothing like marriage to cure one of all those kinds of ideas, let me tell you."

Clarion cocked her head a moment but figured it was none of her business. She stepped behind the curtain and wrung the excess water from the sponge.

Wilkin's mother stopped in her work again. "Give the plaything its privacy, boy. Go deliver that harp. The king's been asking to see it."

"I thought I'd bring it with Clarion tonight—"

"*Clarion?*" The tone of the giant woman's voice made Clarion flinch. "What have I told you about getting ideas and talking to these little people?" Clarion's heart thumped at 'little people.' Had they seen more than just her and Jacosa then? "You'll call her whatever the king decides to call her, and you won't even see her after today, except when the king feels fit to bring her out for his amusement." She sniffed and tugged a little too hard on her thread. "Now get moving."

Clarion peered around the corner of the towel

barrier just enough to see Wilkin nod in apology. She remembered his final plea from that morning that she hide before the ball that evening, that she flee the first chance she was able. That no man was worth becoming the king's plaything, that no one was worth staying here in this strange land among people so much taller than herself.

A small part of her, the terrified part, the part that wanted to do nothing but think about the past and all she'd lost, wished she'd done it.

But what was done was done, and Wilkin left, shutting the door behind him. There was no escaping now, no hiding. Besides, she couldn't go back to her normal life never knowing what had become of Mack. Even if it was silly to care so strongly for him. She hadn't seen him in days... Weeks now, really. The fact that he still invaded her mind confused her. But she was sure she was doing the right thing to find him.

Wilkin's mother knotted the thread and pulled the needle loose, shaking it in Clarion's direction. The needle was as tall as she was. "And you, you little harlot. Don't you go giving a man one hundred times your size any ideas."

Clarion staggered back, in part to get away from the needle and in part out of surprise. How did she even imagine Clarion would hope to steal her giant son from her?

The woman pulled back her needle and worked on slipping the thread through the eyehole. Clarion wondered why she didn't make her do it, as the hole was as large as her head.

"I tell you, I'd be glad to see you gone, if only it weren't for this infernal dress," muttered Wilkin's mother. "If it weren't for the fact that the king still remembers you, I'd be rid of you entirely."

Clarion decided to be as quiet as a mouse as she finished up her sponge bath.

The king clapped his hands together and cackled. "Yes! Yes! She looks lovely!"

Clarion squeezed the too-loose fabric that made up her "ball gown" as she flushed under the giant man's gaze. It was like a loose robe of sorts in a pale blue color, pinned and sewn hastily together to fit over her own dress.

"So does the harp work? Let's see you play!" The giant king put a finger on Clarion's back and shoved her toward the harp Wilkin had finished for her. He probably thought he was being gentle, but it took all of Clarion's efforts not to fall flat on her face as she tumbled over her feet.

Clarion stood almost stupidly in front of the little harp and the pin cushion beside it she supposed was to act as her stool. She realized she'd never had a chance to play it or even tune it after Wilkin had finished, and she didn't really know if it would work. It was a rudimentary approximation of her harp back home, rough at the edges and not all that promising.

She wondered if it wouldn't work, if she'd see the king's anger firsthand. But in any case, there was no balking at the prospect now. She settled on the cushion, fixing her skirts around her, and held her fingers to the instrument. She began to play. She decided not to sing as of yet.

It works! Despite the knot in her stomach, Clarion found herself actually smiling as she strung the first few chords of a simple tune. She turned the tuning keys—how had such a large man made such a small wonder?—and adjusted the sound.

The giant man frowned and leaned forward, pointing his ear in her direction. "It's so quiet," he said, and Clarion realized that the harp, being to scale for her size, couldn't project loud enough for the giant man to hear clearly.

She played harder.

The giant king pulled back and rubbed his fingers over his chin. "It *seems* good. But what good is a talented harpist if no one can hear her play?"

Wilkin's mother laughed at that. "Leave it to Jacosa to give you a useless gift."

"My wife rather enjoys the golden-egg hen," said the king. "But Jacosa will have to fix this." He clenched his fists together and stomped his foot, causing Clarion to miss a note, not that he would have noticed. "I won't have it!"

"Your Grace!"

Clarion's fingers slowed as Wilkin appeared, something golden and curved in his hands, but she kept playing.

"I thought there might be an issue," said Wilkin. "So I asked Her Grace if I could borrow this."

He lay the object on the mantel in front of the harp, and Clarion realized it was a speaking-trumpet. The smaller end beside her harp made the sound travel through its echoing metal and project at a far louder decibel.

"Excellent!" The king raised a fist in the air as if celebrating. "Good work, boy." He clapped Wilkin on the shoulder. "And just in time. Excuse me." He bowed toward Wilkin's mother and exited the ballroom to greet the first wave of guests.

Clarion stared at Wilkin and noticed the subtle upturn of his lips as he watched her play. She didn't dare stop or ask him any questions, though, as his mother was still within earshot, even if her attention was drawn to the group of six giants who were making their way into the hall.

"No one's taking their coats?" His mother sighed. "I suppose that's up to me, even if it's a special occasion." She gestured to her dress, which wasn't so fine as the king and his guests' attire, although it was cleaner and newer than anything Clarion had seen her in so far.

Wilkin sidled up to the mantel, even going so far as

to attempt to put an arm down on it until he realized that afforded Clarion far less room.

Clarion kept her voice down and her fingers moving. "How much does the king expect me to play, do you think?"

Shuffling in place, Wilkin crossed his arms awkwardly for lack of anything better to do with them. "Just when he wants to show you off, I'm sure." He nodded toward a small group of giants setting up instruments in the back of the hall. "That'll be the music people dance to."

Clarion flinched at the idea of giants dancing. Even with her daily dose of aloe, she seemed capable of experiencing dizziness as a result of too much giant movement.

She wrapped up her song and watched the entryway for a few moments. More giants were coming in, and the lady of the house—the queen, Clarion was still unused to thinking of them as royalty—had appeared from another room to greet them with her husband. Wilkin's mother took coats and vanished into a back room a few times, reappearing for the next set shortly thereafter.

"When will he bring out his playthings to show off?" asked Clarion as she readjusted her silken dress over her knees. Some of the giants milled about near a large buffet table, and the musicians were tuning their instruments. Clarion was hit with a pang of homesickness as she pictured the springtime ball and the exchange she'd had with Mack that evening.

"When more of his guests arrive," answered Wilkin. He cleared his throat, and Clarion realized that at some point he'd cleaned up and changed, perhaps after his mother had brought her to the king's mansion. That was an uncomfortable ride to be sure. His mother had wrapped her fingers around Clarion and carried her like a stick instead of letting her ride on her palm.

"Clarion," started Wilkin, "if you're hoping to find... That is, I don't think you'll find what you're looking for. I should have forced you to hide until you could escape."

The last bean still lay in a pouch in the pocket of Clarion's normal clothes beneath the fancier ones. "I could have left at any time. I think."

"What do you mean?"

"I have a bean. If I broke it open and threw it down the clouds... Well, part of me was worried it'd land somewhere where it'd hurt someone. Part of me wasn't sure it would even work from such a height. But mostly I knew I couldn't go back. Not without finding out what became of Mack."

"Clarion—"

"Ah, Master Wilkin!" A giant woman with hair so puffed upon her head it resembled a giant beehive approached the mantel. "How are you this fair evening?"

"Good, Mistress Lorica," replied Wilkin, "as good as I'll ever be. You?"

"Well, all right, I suppose." She unfurled a paper fan she'd gripped at her side and wafted cool air at her face. Her eyes darted over the top of the material to look back at the crowd entering and the king and queen who welcomed them. "You know, I was home when His Grace destroyed Master and Mistress Kelby's home the other day. And we're—we *were* neighbors."

Clarion noticed a perceptible bob to Wilkin's throat. "I was sorry to hear about that."

"Weren't we all?" Lorica turned her back on the newly arrived guests. "You're the last of the young men, you know that? Rumors say His Grace did away with Kelby's son, Hearst, along with his parents."

Clarion felt something jump to the top of her throat. Strangely, she'd seen no wreckage of a destroyed house when she'd been on her way to the mansion, although now that she knew about the practice, she could recall plenty of empty spaces between houses where a house might have once stood. For some reason, it hadn't even occurred to her that the residents of the homes would *still be inside them* when the king somehow destroyed them with his bare hands and his mighty anger.

Lorica didn't wait for Wilkin to comment. "And of course, we lost the last of the young eligible women some months ago, thanks to Her Grace and her jealousy." Lorica fluttered her fan at a leisurely pace, like she hadn't just revealed the bloodthirsty nature of the royal couple throwing the party. Clarion had to lean over slightly to avoid the rush of air. "But look at me, prattling on," said Lorica from behind her fan. She held her arm out. "Be a dear, would you, Wilkin, and get me some champagne?"

Wilkin took a step and then paused in front of the horn, rubbing a finger under his nose. "Can I get you anything?"

Clarion laughed. She was picturing Wilkin pulling a thimble out of his pocket and filling it with wine. "I'm good, thank you."

Lorica put a hand to her chest as Wilkin stepped away. "Goodness me! I didn't see you there. Are you that witch?"

"Jacosa? No, I..." Clarion gestured toward the harp. "I play music."

Lorica frowned and fluttered her fan harder. "I didn't realize there were more of you."

Clarion's heart sank. "You haven't seen more of us?"

"I've never seen *any* of you. I know you can talk to us with that herb." Lorica tapped her fan across her palm, folding it. "Norma's told me about the little witch that so fascinates His Grace, but it's not like she'd bring her over to my house for a visit."

Clarion felt her hope bolster. Just because this woman and Wilkin hadn't seen Mack, then, it didn't mean that he wasn't here. She wondered who Norma was.

"I'm so glad Wilkin's returned," said Lorica, apparently not that fazed that her new conversation companion was a stranger and one-hundredth her size. "Norma was a wreck without him."

"Is Norma Wilkin's mother?" Clarion realized she'd

had no reason to ask or any interest in knowing the woman's name before.

"Why, yes!" Lorica pointed her closed fan at Clarion and arched an eyebrow, like she found the little young woman an idiot. "Haven't you been imposing on her hospitality this week? Norma's sure been complaining of it."

Imposing? Clarion would have liked to see what Norma would have considered helpful after all the cleaning she'd put her up to.

Lorica went on, undaunted. "Norma and her husband, well... It was a wonder they ever got together, from what I hear from her. They never did agree on how to raise Wilkin, either. Not that I blame him, really, wanting Wilkin to go with him. If I've told Norma once, I've told her a thousand times." She lowered her voice. "This place isn't safe for children. Now Wilkin is the last member of his generation, and this is definitely no place for him to be anymore."

Lorica drifted into silence for a moment as Wilkin wove his way through the growing gathering of giants to return with a drink.

"Sorry I took so long," said Wilkin, and the way his eyes darted to his diminutive companion, Clarion was sure he was speaking more to her than to the woman receiving the drink.

Lorica flicked her fan open again with one hand. "We were just gossiping."

"Not about me, I hope?" said Wilkin, a smile curling the edge of his giant lips.

Lorica laughed and poked him with her fan in the chest. "Wouldn't you like to know?"

"Has she played for you?" asked Wilkin. "She can make magic out of a harp's strings."

"Oh, no," said Lorica. "I haven't yet had the pleasure."

Clarion found herself blushing, even though she knew Wilkin's compliment was unfounded. She'd barely played, and the horn helped, but it didn't really do the sound justice.

"Ladies! Gentlemen!" As the king guided the queen to the center of the hall, everyone stepped back to make room. For a brief moment, Clarion thought of the contrast between that and the mayor at a ball, how people sought his company but didn't step aside for him, and wondered if her family had once parted crowds before her grandfather had lost his title. "Before we begin tonight's dances, I wanted to show you my latest gifts!"

Clarion stiffened. This was the moment. The moment she'd have to play for a room full of giants to be sure, but more importantly, the moment the royals might bring out Mack.

The king and queen stepped back and gestured toward the direction from which they'd come. A servant walked toward them, holding a pillow with both hands in front of him.

The queen squealed and clapped her hands together. "My little hen!" she said, swooping forward to gingerly snatch the little bird from the pillow with two fingers.

The room exploded into applause. The king laughed and looked down at the pillow as the servant stepped before him.

"Oh." The king poked at the thing still left on it. "I think this one's dead."

Clarion nearly fainted when the king grabbed a man between his fingers and dangled him in the air for all to see.

Chapter 17

 can't." Clarion hiccupped as she fought to swallow back her blubbering. "Don't you see that I *can't*?"

"Clarion, you *must* play," said Wilkin in a hushed voice beside her. "The king has introduced you. The entire town is staring at you right this very instant."

At the sight of the little man in the king's hand, completely lifeless and dangling at an awkward angle, Clarion had gone into shock. She had no recollection of what the king did after he tossed the man back on the pillow, no memory of him introducing her, or of all the eyes in the room shifting toward her.

Wilkin smiled and waved at the onlookers and then turned, making a pretense of adjusting the horn he'd brought in order to step between Clarion and the crowd. Clarion realized he was hoping to buy her some more time to collect herself.

"What's the matter?" whispered Lorica, her fan flapping hard and keeping all but her eyes out of view from the rest of the room.

Wilkin grunted. "She thinks she knew that little man."

"I *did* know him!" Clarion reached up to her cheek to find it damp with tears she couldn't even remember shedding. "How can that not be him?"

"You don't know anything for certain. Not yet. Not now." About to place the horn back in front of Clarion's harp, Wilkin flicked his eyes warily to Lorica beside him. "You came here for a purpose, didn't you, Clarion?"

Clarion squeezed her hands together. "Yes."

"And you haven't fulfilled that purpose yet. I promise you."

"But he—"

"Did you see the man clearly?"

"No..."

"Then you don't know yet."

Lorica flapped her fan harder. "People are starting to get restless," she whispered, and sure enough, Clarion could hear the whispers of the crowd. She took several deep breaths to calm herself, only slightly bolstered by Wilkin's platitudes. There was no way it wasn't him, but he was right, she owed it to herself, and to Mack's father and to Elena and to everyone, to be sure. She'd have to have Wilkin sneak her to wherever the servant had taken that pillow before the night was over.

Wilkin adjusted the horn back into place. His hands rested on the horn an extra moment as he peered down at the little songstress Clarion was becoming.

She tossed back her shoulders, lay her hands on the harp's strings, and nodded up at Wilkin. He stepped back, guiding Lorica by the elbow a short distance away, and Clarion began.

"*They told me you had left for the land above. I told them you would never leave me, my love...*"

"What a fine, fine little thing she is!" The king toasted his wine glass into the air for at least the tenth time. His foot tapped and tapped to the beat of the melody his giant musicians played that had much of the room in motion across the dance floor. "A fine, fine little plaything!"

Clarion would have blushed if the sight of the man who'd pinched Mack's lifeless body between his fingers didn't repulse her so. She clutched the bulky fabric at her lap, chastising herself again silently for singing in addition to playing for her performance. The king seemed more enraptured with her than ever, and she had no intention of staying past this night. If she'd played adequately but not memorably, he'd probably have forgotten her quickly and it'd have been easier to move about his mansion.

"You've said that fifty times already." The queen laughed, but it was more a mocking sound than a joyful one. She snatched the goblet from her husband's hand. "I think that's enough already, don't you?" She passed it to Wilkin's mother. "Norma, take this to the kitchen, would you?"

"Oh, you're *no fun!*" The king stamped his foot a little harder, first in what Clarion thought to be anger, and then back in tune with the beat. He clapped his hands together. "Fee, fi, fo, fum!" It was a singsong tune, not at all like the violent outcry Clarion had heard that day the cloud village shook. He reached for his wife's hands just as she finished passing along the cup. "Shall we dance?"

The queen's eyes widened and she let herself be twirled toward the dance floor for a moment, a sparkle from a shimmering band of golden material at her skirt's hem catching the light, before pulling her hands away and pushing against his chest. "Careful!" she shouted. She looked angry enough to slap him. She patted a small pocket at her chest. "I put my Goldie in there."

The king rolled his eyes and waved at her. "You and that damn chicken. Mistress Lorica?" He held his arm out to the still-fan-flapping woman at the side of the mantel.

"Would you do me the honor?"

Lorica clapped her fan together and curtsied, putting the instrument aside atop the mantel next to Clarion. "I'd be honored, Your Grace."

The queen pointed her nose in the air as the king and Lorica passed. She reached into her pocket to remove the small hen and stroked it tenderly with one finger. "We best get you away," she cooed. "The witch promised me you'd live forever, but I wouldn't trust you to survive that oaf's clumsiness." She passed through the ballroom, smiling and nodding at guests as they called to her, and pausing halfway to the doorway through which Wilkin's mother had left to speak to one fairly animated couple.

Clarion jumped up from her pin cushion seat. She was left alone for the first time in an hour—really, the first time since she'd arrived. But she couldn't find Wilkin anywhere. He must have vanished sometime during her performance because he wasn't there when she'd finished, and no one bothered to explain his absence.

If she couldn't rely on him to take her anywhere—couldn't even convince Lorica, perhaps, to take her to him—it was now or never. The queen was sure to be bringing her hen to wherever the servant had fetched Mack on that pillow.

Clarion bolted for the staircase she remembered was on the side of the mantel, her eyes catching the human-sized basket from which she'd first eaten the aloe that'd allowed her to function in this world. She noted, strangely, that a fair amount of it was gone, leaving only a handful or two. She wondered if Mack had been alive since she'd last been in the mansion, if they'd fed him what remained of the plant to entertain them until something went horribly wrong. A shiver ran down her spine. But now wasn't the time to dwell on that. She tore at the robe-like makeshift dress and ripped one of the seams at her shoulder, stepping out of it as she moved forward to lighten her step

It took too long to get down the stairs—far too long.

She kept checking to make sure the queen hadn't left the room yet, but it was taking all of her focus to keep an eye on her feet as she hurried down the endless steps. By the time she was at the bottom, she was nearly out of breath, but she couldn't spare more than a second to collect it. The queen was still standing there. She could tell even from the floor by the golden shine of the hem on the well-to-do woman's skirt.

The laughter of a man rung overhead as giant footsteps crossed in front of Clarion's path. Despite the memory of her terror at being on the ground with giant people around her, actually experiencing it in the moment was more terrifying than she thought possible.

Am I insane? Clarion asked herself. The music raged on and feet as large as carriages stomped and danced across the hall. The queen was at the edge of the dance floor, but on occasion, a dancing couple still swung dangerously close to Clarion's path.

I have to do this. Clarion took a deep breath, hitched up her skirt and ran forward.

She didn't know how long she ran. It felt like longer than it could possibly be, and her heart hammered so hard, she was nearly drowning in the sound. The giants almost seemed to move in slow-motion around her, which panicked her, but she remembered she'd eaten her aloe that morning, and any difference in perception was probably just the anxiety overwhelming her mind.

She traversed the room unencumbered for more than half the distance. Only when the queen's golden-hemmed skirt seemed within reach, when she stepped back and bowed, about to leave the hall entirely, did Clarion rush forward without properly looking around her.

The sole of a giant boot hovered above her. Clarion didn't even remember freezing in place, but her feet wouldn't move. The boot lowered and lowered almost until she could see nothing else.

Move! she thought to herself. *Move!* For some

reason, a flash of her papa wrestling with the pigs flooded her mind and she found herself free of the danger without even remembering how she got from one place to the next. When she still couldn't move, she panicked and almost fell backward, and she realized the foot had stepped on the back of her skirt somehow—no, it was a piece of fabric from the secondary dress that was somehow still stuck in her waistband. That dress was truly an example of shoddy sewing. She twisted away from it and it tore off, just as the foot lifted and kept on walking anyway.

Clarion breathed hard, the sweat dotting her brow. But the queen had begun moving, getting farther with every moment that passed, and Clarion wouldn't let the opportunity get away.

She ran forward, her arms pumping, darting between legs and ignoring the danger until at last the golden hem was within reach.

She grabbed for it and failed, grabbed for it and failed again. Summoning a strength she didn't even know she had, she ran faster, faster than she ever had before.

And at last she grabbed hold of the hem with both hands, swinging upward as the queen walked and scuffing the floor again as she put her foot down.

Although Clarion was exhausted, she knew she had to get to a safer place, especially as she saw a staircase up ahead. Her arms ached and she thought of the attempted climb she'd made up the beanstalk, but she knew she had to do it anyway. There were no folds in the skirt, but she didn't want to hit the ground each time the woman's foot came down, and there was no hope for switching to her shoe by now. Clarion pulled and pulled, feeling the muscles flex in her arms, until she hung safely off the ground. But even that only lessened the soreness somewhat. Still, as she let her eyes wander and she saw the expanse of a giant staircase behind her, she knew she could never let go, no matter how much it hurt. She squeezed her eyes shut to stave off the dizziness and just focused on breathing.

When the movement finally ceased, it took Clarion an additional minute to realize she could stop breathing so hard. Her ears filled with an off-key tune someone—the queen—was humming somewhere far above her. Clarion opened first one eye and then another and found herself gazing at a giant bed. She collected her senses and started scrambling down the queen's skirt, pausing every few moments to make sure the woman didn't notice her.

"There you are," cooed the queen just as Clarion's feet touched the ground. "Back to your little nest." The woman sighed. "We should really build you a little coop. If His Grace weren't so concerned with Wilkin building that atrocious harp for that little harpy this week, we'd have one already. I do miss having a carpenter in town."

Clarion dashed as quick as a mouse to the leg of the night table where the queen's attention was centered. She wrapped her arms around the leg and tried to get a good grip, but the material was smooth and she slipped down almost immediately because she could find no purchase.

The queen sat down on the edge of the bed, plopping down with such force that even adjusted to this larger-than-life world, Clarion found herself jumping in place.

The woman kicked her foot in the air, her hands balled into fists. "Oh, if only he would tear his own home down in a rage with himself still in it!"

A loud squeaking noise echoed in Clarion's ear and her head spun. A giant mouse—well, she supposed it was giant to her, but just the right size for the giants, which meant it was about Clarion's size—jutted its twitching nose out of a small hole in the wall some distance away.

The queen lay back on the bed and the mouse emerged entirely from the hole. It stared straight at Clarion for a minute and then darted her way. Clarion jumped and ran for the bed skirt, which was made of lace and had plenty of small finger- and toe-sized holes.

She found herself halfway up sooner than she

expected, her heart thumping wildly and a newfound strength coursing through her body, not even fully recovered from her previous exercise. The mouse sat on the floor below gazing up at her, its head tilted quizzically.

Just as Clarion reached for another hole, the top of the bed only a few feet ahead of her—which presented its own set of problems if the queen were to see her, but Clarion had it in her head to make a dash for the pillows she assumed she'd find there—she flew backward, still gripping on to the bed skirt with both feet and one hand for dear life.

"Oh! Disgusting!" The queen had jumped off the bed and peered back at the table. Once Clarion got hold of the skirt with both hands once more, she glanced over her shoulder. The pillow on which the hen and Mack's body had ridden sat empty on the table beside a large box and a lit candlestick. Clarion realized she didn't have time to gawk, as she was easily within the queen's line of sight if the woman glanced back at the bed, so she willed herself to ignore whatever had caught the queen's attention and kept climbing. She did indeed find a pillow on the bed at the top and she ran for it, ducking behind a corner to peer around and watch the elegant, if wan-faced, woman.

The queen reached one hand into the box, her arm trembling, her expression twisted into fear or even contempt. She pulled the top half of a man—his back to Clarion—halfway out of the box and then let it fall, pulling her hand back and clutching it as if it were burned.

Clarion covered her mouth to keep herself from gasping.

"Richard!" shrieked the queen, her shiny shoes clanking against the floor as she made her way quickly to the bedroom door. She opened it, and her voice echoed back to Clarion even as she made her way down the hall. "Richard! You put this foul thing *back into our bedroom*?!"

The door shut and the room fell into silence, but for the rustling whiskers and the quiet chittering of the creature below. Clarion stepped out from her hiding place and her shoulders sagged. She supposed she must see Mack's body at once before the servant returned to dispose of him somewhere she might never find him.

What little hope she'd had that he was playing dead was dashed after seeing the way the queen had tossed him back into the box so carelessly.

She walked to the edge of the bed, only sparing a glance below and finding the mouse now scurrying across the floor, its interest in her diverted. She found herself breathing easier at least at that, but the pain in her chest made her feel like her heart was about to wither.

The gap between the bed and the table required a jump, but at least that pillow was resting there on the other side of the table. Almost like someone had had the foresight to provide for her jump. She thanked the skies for her luck, took a few steps back and ran, her arms flailing as she jumped the distance.

She landed on her feet but tumbled forward immediately, managing to twist into a sideways summersault so she'd hit the pillow with her back instead of her neck. She lay on her back on the pillow and caught her breath for a moment, gazing up at the flicker of the flame that was larger than her torso. There was a smaller box nearby, and she thought she saw a small—her size—pair of trousers hanging out from over the top of it. She thought about looking closer, but she sat up with a start as she heard something—the door opening—and she panicked, sure the servant would take Mack away before she saw him. She ran across the pillow, heaved herself up the ledge of the box, and stood atop the ledge, frozen, as she gazed down.

The inside of the box looked like a single-room cottage, complete with a bed for a person and a pile of hay on which the little hen huddled, snoring. The light from the candle illuminated the small cottage quite clearly, almost like how the dying sunlight from a sunset would shine through a skylight.

The door closed, and Clarion couldn't see where

whoever had entered had gone, but she had no time to waste. She dropped down into the little home and searched everywhere for the body—finding it bent at an awkward angle, half sticking out from under the table that was properly her size.

She darted for the table and slid under it, reaching to pull the body fully beneath it with her.

She willed herself to breathe slower, to breathe more quietly, but she found herself heaving regardless. Her back muscles strained as she pulled Mack closer to her and flipped him over so she could see his face.

His eyes were lifeless, his skin tinged in yellow. His neck bent at an unnatural angle.

But it wasn't Mack.

Chapter 18

"larion!" hissed a man from somewhere above her. "Clarion! Tell me you're in there!"

Clarion pulled her hands away from the dead stranger, feeling guilty at the wave of revulsion along with the feeling of relief that washed over her. *Just because you don't know the man doesn't mean it's not terrible he's dead.*

"Clarion!" The voice got closer, although it was hushed.

Clarion had no time to wonder where the man had come from. "Wilkin?" she whispered loudly, her eyes looking up as she crawled out from beneath the table.

She found a face looking down on her, but it was far smaller than she expected. The corner of his lips turned up in a smile, his light-colored eyes twinkling over the top of his long nose.

"Mack?!" Clarion crawled out from beneath the table and stood, her legs shaking. Mack heaved himself up over the edge of the box and jumped down, slapping his palms together.

Mack and Clarion stared at one another for a moment in the flickering candlelight, no sound but for the clucking of the hen, who came over to investigate and dash between their legs.

Clarion reached over and wrapped her arms around him, burying her face into his shoulder. "I thought you'd died!"

Mack hesitated and then placed his arms around her, enfolding her in a gentle hug, rocking her back and forth slowly and placing his cheek atop her head. "I'm sorry," he whispered.

Clarion couldn't believe how natural it felt to be held by him, how loud his heartbeat could be in her ears. She wasn't unaware of how little she truly knew him—she wasn't over the remorse she felt at ending her first romance with Elena. She hadn't forgotten what his rash actions had put her through, nor had she put the poor dead young man behind her entirely out of her mind. But for just one small beat of time, she felt warm, and she felt safe. It was probably the only time she'd truly felt that way since her papa had died, even if her loved ones had tried to comfort her in the days and weeks after.

But the moment couldn't last forever. She pulled back and grabbed him by the shoulders, shaking him roughly. "What were you thinking?" she hissed.

Mack let his hands fall from Clarion's back and smirked. "I deserve that."

Clarion shook her head and studied him closer. "What are you wearing?" His clothes—now that she thought about it, she was pretty sure the dead man was wearing the outfit she'd last seen Mack in—were plainer than she'd ever seen him wear. But also cruder with wide, bulky stitches, like a giant had made the outfit for him, just as Wilkin's mother had made her the crude eveningwear she'd left behind downstairs.

Mack stepped back and held his arms out to either side as if to give her a better view. He laughed when Clarion just stared blankly at him and took both of her hands in his. "We haven't seen each other in days, we're in a land of giant people that rests atop the clouds, and that's what you find important to ask?"

Clarion frowned and took one of her hands away to point behind her. "When your clothes are on a dead man, I'd say it's certainly part of the mystery that needs explaining."

Mack's face fell as he brushed past Clarion to crawl under the table. Less than a minute later, Mack was dragging the poor young man out from beneath the table, his hands looped through the man's armpits.

Clarion jumped back. "What are you doing?" She covered her mouth, not sure if she was imagining the stench.

Mack dropped the body at her feet. "The queen told her servant to come dispose of him, right? Do you really want him to not be able to find the body and then poke around this box until he uncovers the both of us as well?"

"How did—" Clarion was unable to complete her sentence as Mack grabbed her hand, hushed her, and tugged her after him beneath the table just as the giant-sized door to the bedroom swung open.

Mack and Clarion shifted as quietly as they dared beneath the table onto their stomachs, peering out just a little without bringing their heads too close to the edge.

A giant finger lowered into the box, poking the man wearing Mack's clothes. When the man didn't stir—Clarion had no idea how anyone could think he would after seeing the tilt of his head—the hand unclenched and swooped him up out of the toy cottage box. The gold-laying chicken scurried mere inches past their faces, bawking, causing Clarion to cry out.

Mack's hand whipped out to cover her lips, but it was too late. The servant paused, the body only halfway lifted out of the box.

The table lifted from above their heads, and Clarion could feel her body shaking as a giant man lowered his bulbous eye toward them.

"Little harpist?" he said, righting himself. "Master

Wilkin? What are you doing here?"

Clarion kept her arms clasped tightly across her chest the entire ride on the pillow. Once in a while, her eyes flicked toward Mack, who sat curled up with his thighs clutched to his chest and his forehead on his knees, but then she'd see the body of the dead man in Mack's clothes laying there, his arm bent backwards, and she'd shudder and turn away.

"I'm sorry I didn't tell you," Mack mumbled from beneath his arms. It was the first time he'd bothered to speak since the servant had picked them both up one at a time to place them on the pillow he now carried down the hallway.

Clarion didn't know what to think. She'd thought the servant had misspoken, but from the way Mack was acting... "What did he mean, 'Wilkin'?"

Mack took a deep breath and raised his head. "Wilkin Magnus Destriansson. That's my full name. Mother likes 'Wilkin,' and Father prefers 'Magnus.' Skies forbid they can agree on anything, even what to call me. So I like 'Mack.'"

Clarion felt her blood run cold as the servant began descending the steps. Her hands shot out to either side in order to keep steady. "You're Wilkin? I mean—you're WILKIN?"

"Oh." Mack wore a faltering smile. "Should I have kept pretending otherwise? I thought he gave me away." He nodded backward at the giant carrying them, and Clarion craned her neck to see what she thought was the arching of an eyebrow on the man. She'd almost forgotten he could hear them clearly, assuming Mack had taken his aloe.

If he even needed it. "But how?"

155

Mack pointed at the dead young man beside him. He was practically still a boy, now that Clarion studied him. She felt terrible for having felt relieved. "He was born gigantic, too."

"So... You're a giant grown small. Not a... human... grown big?"

"We call you all little ones and tend to think of ourselves as the humans." Mack grunted and rested his chin on his knees. "But then again, I know there are more of you than there are of us, so you're probably the default, and we probably are the giants. You're just... Englishmen."

"There are probably more mice than *Englishmen* where I come from, but that doesn't mean they're the default, either," said Clarion, sighing. Her insides were such a hodgepodge of emotions.

The servant reached the bottom of the stairs. Instead of turning toward the laughter and the glow emanating from the still-occupied hall, he went the opposite way. Clarion clutched handfuls of pillow and stared up at the man. "How?" she asked, more to Mack than the servant she was staring at. "How can you really be that big? How can you..." Her tongue twisted, her mind racing. "How can you be small now?"

Mack shrugged as the servant took them through the kitchen, where a number of giant women scurried about. "I don't know if I ought to be by rights. I was born big, but my father really is a little... He really is human. He ate the tarragon to grow big when he first came here and well..." His face darkened and he buried it under his arms again. "He liked my mother for one night at least."

Clarion rolled her eyes, not believing the young man beside her—the boy, really—was the same confident, suave young man who'd burrowed into her thoughts from the very moment she'd spotted him. The servant exited out a back door and put the pillow down atop a pile of boxes. He extended a careful hand and grabbed the dead boy gently between two fingers, as if he might crush him. *As if he needs gentle care now of all times*, thought Clarion.

The giant servant stepped toward a heaping pile of something some distance away from the grand house, and Clarion gulped as she realized it was a pile of muck and feces and waste.

"Wait!" she cried, but the servant didn't hear or didn't heed her.

Mack peeked out from behind his arms. "What is it?"

Clarion clutched his arm. "He's throwing him out in the *garbage!*"

Mack sighed. "There's nowhere else to put him. We don't have soil like you do beneath the clouds. If we dug a hole big enough, he'd just fly back to the earth."

Clarion opened her mouth to ask how they grew any of the food, fed any of the livestock she assumed they ate, without dirt, but wondered if it was the most important question to ask at this moment. Besides, she'd seen so much else that was inexplicable.

"Our plants grow out of the clouds," said Mack, reading her thoughts. "Though no one but your witch has been able to grow plants that do... magic."

No one else can grow magic plants where I come from, either, thought Clarion.

The servant dropped the little man and slapped his hands together a few times, a dirty job done.

"Father's going to kill me for losing that suit."

Clarion glared at Mack and he flinched. "Sorry. That was insensitive. But that man—Hearst—well, he wasn't a very nice kid. Not that he deserved what came to him. No one deserves that."

"How... did he die? The king seemed to expect to find him alive."

"Lorica mentioned it before. The king was angry with Hearst's father, and his father begged the king to give his son some of the tarragon instead of killing him." Mack stretched his legs out as the servant grabbed a shovel leaning against an outbuilding and used it to mix up the mulch. "The king agreed he'd make a fine addition to his collection, so I lent him my suit and he survived the king's anger. I don't... know how he died since then, really."

Clarion imagined a too tight grip as someone scooped a living person in and out of a playhouse. "I don't think the king and queen are as gentle with their playthings as they claim to be." She bit her lip. "But I don't understand. The king would turn one of his people into a little plaything? And you'd go along with it?"

"You might think you have an idea of the full power of the king's anger, but you don't."

"If you say so." Clarion shook her head and let her eyes stray from the servant. She studied the back of the house, mentally calculating how long it'd take her to run to the front, how long it would take her to run from there to where she knew the beanstalk last stood. She fingered the bean, still in her pocket. She'd be willing to risk that throwing it down would grow another, but there was no way she'd make it there before a couple of days had passed. Not without a giant carrying her. No wonder the servant seemed so unconcerned about leaving them unwatched.

"Can you turn back?" asked Clarion. "Into... a giant? Just long enough to get us to the beanstalk?"

"It doesn't matter if I could. The beanstalk is gone," said Mack. "I'll have to hide you until Jacosa—"

"I have another bean."

Mack's eyes lit up. "Of course! I almost forgot."

"Oh. Right. I... guess I told you that. When you were... huge."

"Why didn't you use it?"

Clarion ran her fingertips lightly over her throat. "I wasn't going to leave without you."

A ghost of a smile danced across Mack's lips. "I can't leave."

Clarion felt herself leaning away from him. She didn't understand who he was. Was he the timid Wilkin or the suave Mack? "Why did you come here in the first place? I thought you were in awe of the magic, curious to know where the beanstalk might lead, and yet now I see you knew all along. I suppose your father knew, too, and his desperate search and disbelief at my story was just a cover to keep more people from following you."

"It was no act." Mack stood and walked a few wobbly steps across the cushiony surface to sit beside her. "Father was no fan of this place, and he asked Jacosa some years ago to make him forget. He came across your town long ago while traveling, and he came up here and, well... He left once for a time, but he came back for me. But this time, he was determined to forget all about it. He... wanted me to forget all about it, too."

"Is that how the mayor knows him, I wonder?" Clarion leaned closer to Mack, not sure even herself if it was intentional. "Did you remember when you came to my town?"

"Not at first, no. I never imagined..." He gestured at everything around him. "All of this." The giant servant whacked the pile of filth again and Mack laughed derisively. The vision in front of them wasn't actually matching up to the wonder in his statement.

"Then why did you come back?"

"When I arrived, that first night, I went for a walk. That witch found me."

"Jacosa."

Mack nodded. "She said she was looking for me, that she had answers. Why I couldn't remember my mother or much of my childhood. Why my father was so distant. Why I never felt... whole."

Clarion wondered at 'feeling' whole. She'd never felt less than complete when her papa was still alive. When she could look at Elena with nothing but love in her eyes. But thinking that she wasn't whole after her papa had died, that something was 'missing'... That was a good way to put how she felt.

"Of course, I thought the woman was crazy." Mack ruffled his hair and laughed, and Clarion felt for a fleeting moment that sense of wholeness once more. "*Especially* when she shoved some dried rosemary and tarragon leaves at me and said, 'Eat the rosemary to remember. The tarragon to grow.' and hurried down the alleyway without further explanation."

"So you ate...?"

Mack shook his head. His hair seemed wavier without the hat atop it. "I can't say I've made a habit of eating dried grasses from strange ladies, no. I've heard tales of what such things can do to you. But I did... I pocketed them. By the time of the ball, I'd nearly forgotten, but then..."

"The quake. And the beanstalk."

"I didn't know what I was doing when I climbed, I promise you. I just felt..." He shrugged. "I felt like those *answers*, whatever it was that would make me whole, might be at the top. I knew it was a stupid idea. I had no idea how long a climb it would prove. But my desire—my *need*—to know kept me going."

Clarion wondered at how he could have been so lost, when it was his confidence and his poise that had drawn her to him. He'd seemed *safe*. Comforting, even. Someone who knew the best life had to offer and was happy to share it. But it was all a mask. Maybe this man was just as broken as she was beneath it all. Hadn't she viewed her attraction to this man, this adventure to save him, as her salvation? Hadn't she thought she'd finally found... purpose?

"When I broke through those clouds and saw... This place in the subtle glow of the rising sun... I remembered what the woman had said." The corner of his mouth twitched. "If it was all a dream, then hallucinating some more might not matter. The rosemary gave me my memory back and the tarragon made me grow a hundred times in size." He laughed, some unshared insight making him think of the memory fondly.

Clarion put a palm down on the soft cushion beneath her and moved her fingers closer to his foot. "But now that you've been here, now that you know... Why won't you come back?"

"Because I remember my father took me away without my mother's permission." Mack swallowed, ignoring the closeness of Clarion's fingers. "Because I'm all she has."

The servant placed the shovel back against the wall.

The moment gave Clarion time to think. She wanted to say she didn't like his mother, though she didn't like his father, either, from what little she knew of him. But did that matter? He barely knew Clarion. He might not take such a comment against his mother well, despite her good intentions. "What about the king?" she said instead, her voice low. "You told me yourself how dangerous the king is."

It was the right tactic. As the servant approached, Mack leaned in closer to whisper, "I'll get you back. I promise. Now that you know I'm fine, I hope you'll be willing to go."

Clarion wondered if that was what he intended to achieve by shrinking himself back to her size and showing up beside her in the king and queen's bedroom. He likely planned to skip the part about him being a giant, as if he could possibly convince her to leave him behind if she thought he was just the king's plaything.

The servant scooped up the pillow gently with both hands, and Clarion fell into Mack, their shoulders touching, her hand on his chest and his arm darting out behind her back to keep her from tumbling over.

They gazed into each other's eyes. Clarion didn't know if it was love, the stirring she felt in her belly, the rush of heat to her face. But she did know one thing. She would get him out whether he wanted to leave or not, and she would see him safe—even if he didn't forgive her and he left her town without her, he would be back home, back on the ground. And then she would visit with Elena, to make sure she was all right—and see Krea and her mother and everyone. She would leave the insanity of this world in the clouds behind.

She was tired of other people making decisions for her. This time, she knew she was right to make the decisions for other people.

And she suddenly had an idea how they could manage it.

Chapter 19

larion clutched the basket in which she'd first found the aloe along with Jacosa's note to her chest. She stared up at the towering king and queen from the mantel, doing her best to seem confused and out of place.

"What do you mean, you have no more of that stuff that lets the little ones talk to us?" the king said, pacing back and forth and flinging his hands so wildly, he almost hit Wilkin's—Mack's—mother in the face. The party was dying out, and the king's loud voice made even more people scurry toward the entryway. Clarion watched as Lorica flapped her fan wildly and left without so much as a goodbye to her host and hostess.

"The witch didn't leave enough of it." Mack clutched one fist to his chest and bowed slightly as the king paced by. It looked silly, a tiny man bowing to a gigantic king.

The volatile ruler stopped abruptly and slapped a palm against his forehead. "Then what are *you* using?"

"The last of my own personal stash."

The king tilted his head back and forth, his face screwed up, his voice condescending. "'*The last of my personal stash.*' Then why didn't you save it for *her*? What did I need *you* small for anyway?"

Clarion noticed the twitch of Mack's eye, the way his fist against his chest trembled slightly. "I thought there'd be more aloe," he said, curtly. "And I know Her Grace enjoys having a little man, and after I saw Hearst had died..."

The king stared at his wife, letting loose invisible daggers from his eyes. "Did you tell him to shrink down, woman?"

"No!" The queen rested her fingers at her collarbone, affronted. "I'd never do such a thing without your permission." She pinched her lips. "And skies above, we all know we're running dangerously low on young men. I wouldn't ask the last of them to shrink to play around with *your* little *songstress*." She spoke the word "songstress" like it was equivalent to a fallen woman.

"I took the liberty upon myself..." began Mack.

His mother stepped forward and stood between the mantel and the king, her arms spread wide as if to shelter her giant son from the man's anger, not her diminutive son. "Wilkin's been through a lot the past few years," she said. "His father shrunk him too long, and he hasn't been right since he got back." She looked over her shoulder. "And I think there's something about having that young woman here, even if she's small. He's got no one else to catch his fancy, and—"

The king's face leaned closely to hers. "Are you saying he's *in love* with that little thing? Don't be disgusting, woman!"

"Why not?" said the queen, scoffing. "Just give her some tarragon and make her your mistress, why don't you?"

"I would never!" The king stepped away from Mack's mother to wag a finger in his wife's face, but she didn't flinch. He settled for waving his hands in the air. "And what would be the point of having a tiny songstress if she. Was. No. Longer. Tiny?!" His voice grew louder and louder with each word, and Clarion found herself covering her ears. She knew it would go unnoticed, not just because no one but Mack was bothering to even look at her throughout this discussion, but also because even if she couldn't hear them—especially if she couldn't hear them—surely, they'd expect her to react when he shouted like that.

"Your Grace," said Mack's mother, licking her lips and rubbing her hands on the front of her skirt, probably used to finding an apron there, "if I may..."

The king raised a hand and Clarion was certain he was about to strike the woman. Despite her distaste for her, Clarion was terrified for the woman's sake. But the king caught himself, and the redness faded from his face as he gently lowered it down. "You may... Assuming you have a solution to this mess, you may..."

Mack's mother loosened her shoulders. She'd stiffened in anticipation of the blow. "Wilkin told me he has a bean that can grow a stalk back to the lower world."

Clarion knew he'd told her as much before they started this whole conversation. She didn't see the need to let the king and queen know they were leaving themselves, but Mack had refused to leave his mother alone to convey their message and Clarion had refused to go without him, so they were stuck at this dangerous impasse.

"A bean?" said the king, crossing his arms hastily against his chest.

"Yes, a bean." Mack's mother smoothed her skirts. "And seeing how the lower world has no shortage of young people... The two of them could go back, stock up on all the herbs they need, and bring back more young people we can grow to our size with tarragon."

"What?" the king said, his voice booming. No one moved for a moment and then the king let out a throaty laugh. "What? Are you serious? Have you gone mad, woman? Don't answer that. I know you went mad when you accepted one of them as the father of your son..."

Mack's mother winced. "It would solve some of our population problems."

The king sneered. "Population problems? *Problems*? Is it a problem that I get to decide who gets to live in *my* domain?"

"No! No, of course not." Mack's mother's voice was shaking.

The queen rolled her eyes. "But at the very least, if that little witch isn't returning despite your obvious need for her... Send Wilkin back with the little songstress. He knows the lay of the land, and he'll make sure they return promptly." She nudged Mack's mother aside and held a long finger out toward Mack's head, patting it like she might her little hen's. "Won't you?" She smiled.

Mack didn't show any sign of being repulsed by her gesture, although he bowed to force her to stop petting his head. "Of course, Your Grace."

"Fine, fine!" The king paced away. "Do what you will! Fine!" As the king left the ballroom, his booming voice echoed, "Fee, fi, fo..." before he vanished from view.

Mack's mother scrunched up her shoulders and squinted her eyes as the man's nonsense echoed throughout the hall.

Clarion opened her mouth to speak, to ask if Mack was okay with this change in plans to have Mack leave with Clarion—a change his own mother had come up with for them, probably because she didn't want Clarion to ever come back, but that suited Clarion, who couldn't have planned it more perfectly—but Mack put a finger to his lips and Clarion snapped her mouth shut, remembering she wasn't supposed to talk for fear the queen would discover her lie about the lack of aloe.

"Mother?" asked Mack, holding a hand out to Clarion for her to take. "If you please?"

His mother grumbled and held her palm out toward her son. Clarion didn't fail to notice that she offered to carry *him* more comfortably. She dared to spare a glance at the towering woman's face and noticed something approaching a snarl as she and Mack strode upon her palm hand-in-hand.

"Be quick," said Mack's mother, her voice sharp. "For

our sakes as well as yours." She bowed her head toward the queen, who simply raised an eyebrow, and they exited the ballroom. "And don't you dare get caught up in... distractions," continued Mack's mother. "If your father tries to keep you there, I'll come find you both myself." She grunted. "And I have no intention of eating tarragon before I do."

⁂

Clarion clutched the beanstalk for dear life, the feeling of Mack wrapped tightly around her from behind the only thing that offered her any comfort.

"We're lucky that worked!" Mack breathed into her ear. It was hard to hear him this high up in the sky. "Although who knows where that bean landed..."

It wasn't the first time Mack had made that comment since he'd tossed the bean she'd given him down the hole through which she'd arrived in the cloud kingdom. She was sure to remind him to break it with his teeth first, in case that at all proved necessary to the plant's growth. She almost thought it hadn't worked, but before too long, there was no mistaking the grumble from below them and sure enough, the top of that vile giant beanstalk had poked through the clouds after just a few minutes.

"I can't... think about that... right now." As Clarion slowly lowered her foot to the next bean sprout, her teeth chattered.

Mack laughed, and Clarion could feel his chest rumble against her back. More confident than Clarion about the climb, he'd offered to do it by embracing her from behind, his arms threaded through hers. "True. Sorry." He lowered his arm to grab another sprout.

"At least... going down... is easier... than going up,"

breathed Clarion heavily.

"You'll get no argument from me there." Mack spoke so casually, with such poise, Clarion couldn't help but be jealous of his confidence. She was still shaking at the thought of falling, even though she knew he'd have to lose his grip as well for that to happen. But Clarion wasn't confident enough in her climbing or descending skills to be sure she wouldn't somehow summon the power to knock him down with her.

She heard a loud noise from behind her and felt the loss of Mack's comforting presence against her back. Her heart thudded almost out of her mouth as she gripped the shoots so tightly, she could feel the juices oozing between her fingers.

Mack laughed. "We're on the ground, Clarion. Jump down. I'll catch you."

Clarion opened a tightly-clenched eye. Mack was on the ground all right, his arms out upward toward her. His head was tilted slightly, his lips curled in an echo of a smile. Even though he was wearing peasant clothes, he still carried himself with the air of a lord. (Were those really the clothes he'd had on as Wilkin, or had he found a stash of small clothes at the king and queen's toy cottage? The thought that he was likely naked before she saw him then for a few minutes caused something hot and burning to race across Clarion's body.) Clarion wondered if he really was one by rights, or if his father had made that up for them along with a made-up past. He was so different on the ground.

"Come on!" said Mack, beckoning her near with a long-fingered hand. "You haven't long now!"

Clarion loosened her grip to slide down a few more feet before she finally let go. She felt Mack's arms back around her almost at once.

"That wasn't so bad, was it?"

Clarion willed her limbs to stop shaking and looked up. Her nose practically touched Mack's smooth, round chin as she anchored herself in his pale eyes.

"I didn't recognize you," she admitted. "When you were... bigger."

"I imagine it's hard to see all the details when you're about the size of my nose." Mack shifted his hands from around her stomach to clutch her elbows gently.

Somewhat reluctantly, Clarion pulled away and spun to face him better. "Do you mean to keep your word? About bringing young people back from..." Her jaw slackened. "Where are we?"

Mack's brows furrowed as he tore his face from Clarion's to follow her gaze. "Somewhere... dead?"

Clarion put a hand gently on his shoulder as she passed by, almost tripping down the hill. She stared around her. It looked familiar. When she let her eyes pass over the upturned dirt and rubble, she started seeing familiar landmarks: trees in fields, smoke coming from cottages just dots in the distance. "This is Jacosa's garden!" She moved forward, stumbling, searching for anything she recognized. She fell forward and her hand clutched a piece of wood standing upright. "Her cottage was burnt down!" She stepped back and gestured around her. "Her entire garden was scorched!"

Mack moved closer, nearly falling over himself as he waded through the mess. "Who would do this?" He saddled up beside Clarion, clutching her arm as he stumbled some more. "We didn't actually need more aloe or tarragon, but... Now we probably really do. What little we have won't last."

Clarion stepped back so Mack could no longer hold on to her arm. "Why would we? We're not going back!"

Mack swallowed. "*You're* not going back..."

"Why for all that is good would *you* go back?" Clarion looked around and spotted the ax, its charred handle still attached to the blade propped up near some rubble nearby. She had no idea which plant brought out those creatures that would eat the stalk—and if there was even any of it left anywhere—so the ax would have to do.

"Clarion, don't." Mack positioned himself between

Clarion and the hill leading back to the beanstalk. "Don't. It could be the last bean."

"Good!" Clarion placed her feet carefully through the mud and rubble to walk around Mack. "Then there's no more danger of those giants making us their playthings!"

Mack darted closer to her, putting a wary hand on her forearm to avoid the ax's blade. "It's not as simple as that."

As she gazed into Mack's eyes, Clarion felt the tension let out of her shoulders. She didn't know what to feel. Could she stand it if someone kept her from her hometown, from her mother, even if she didn't get along with her all of the time? But Mack's mother was even worse than Clarion's. And if it meant keeping others safe from a strange crazy giant tyrant who put his own people in danger...

A sudden thought occurred to her. "Elena!" The ax slipped from Clarion's fingers to the ground, and Mack shouted a little as he jumped back out of the way.

"Careful!" he said, but Clarion was already heading for the gate. Or where the gate had once been. It hung halfway off its hinges, singed and cracked.

"If this happened right after Elena and I rose to the kingdom in the sky, Jacosa might not have been able to save her—"

"Elena was with you?" Mack jogged and stumbled to catch up to Clarion. "Up there?"

Clarion realized with a pang of guilt she hadn't explained that to Mack yet. She hadn't thought of Elena enough, really, since she'd been up there because part of her was confident Jacosa had seen to her.

"Yes, briefly. She got us up there by taking something that made her float." She raised her leg high to cross over the jumble at the gate. "She got sick. And she did it for me. I need to know she's all right."

"Okay," said Mack, following suit and nearly falling flat on his face. Clarion didn't stop to wait for him as she

170

headed down the path, grateful it seemed unmolested, if a bit kicked up and dusty. So a lot of people had been this way, but it looked as if Jacosa's garden had been the only victim of their ire. The houses she expected to see at the edge of the village were clearly unscathed.

"Clarion, wait!"

Clarion felt herself being spun around. Mack's eyes searched her face wildly. "No. Nothing." The lump on his throat bobbed as he took her hands in his. "It's nothing. Let's go find her."

"Clarion?"

Clarion turned around to see Jackin climbing up over a dip in the road toward them. "Where have you—oh! Him."

Clarion and Mack both stared at their hands, still clasped together, and dropped them.

Clarion practically shook Jackin by the shoulders. "Where's Elena?"

Jackin's eyes grew glazed. "You wouldn't know, I guess. She's sick. She hasn't woken in days." He nodded over Clarion's shoulders, at Mack or at Jacosa's garden some distance behind him. "Without the witch, Father thinks she's as good as dead."

Chapter 20

"Where is she?"

"Clarion?" Eustace peeked out from the hallway leading to the kitchen in the mayor's mansion, wiping her hands on her apron. "Clarion, is that you? Where have you—"

Clarion left Jackin and Mack to explain things to her mother, shoving down the pang of guilt that ate at her as she reached the top of the stairs.

A door swung open and Clarion came face-to-face with one of Lord Destrian's servants. She stared at him a moment, wondering if the man was once a giant, if he knew about the land in the clouds at all, and if he, too, had taken something to forget the place. But she didn't have time to worry about it. She brushed past him as he made his way to the stairs, not a word passing her lips.

"Lord Magnus?" The servant's voice rung out loud and clear behind Clarion as she grabbed for Elena's door handle. She didn't wait to hear the rest of the exchange, though, and she pulled it open to find Krea at Elena's bedside and Mariah a few feet away, wringing a cloth above a bowl of water that sat on Elena's vanity table.

"Clair?" said Krea, her mouth agape. She jumped up

and embraced her, nearly squeezing the breath out of her friend. "Where have you been?" She pulled back and put both hands on Clarion's cheeks as if she were a beloved pet returned after having strayed.

"I... found Mack. Magnus." Clarion peered around Krea's shoulder, her stomach twisted. "Is she...?"

Krea stepped aside so Clarion could get a better view. "She's been ill for days. Jacosa brought her here the day after we last saw you. She was awake then, but moaning..."

Not waiting for her to finish the story, Clarion rushed to take Krea's seat at Elena's bedside and took Elena's pale hand in hers. "Elena? Elena, it's Clarion..."

"She won't hear you." Mariah leaned forward, putting herself between Clarion and Elena to place the damp cloth atop Elena's forehead. "She hasn't responded to anybody."

Clarion leaned back to give Mariah space but didn't drop Elena's hand. She looked to Krea for answers. "Jacosa was supposed to heal her!"

Krea and Mariah exchanged a glance as Mariah stood back up. "You know what happened to her, then?" asked Krea. "Jacosa... She wasn't generous with answers, I tell you."

Clarion placed Elena's hand against her cheek, leaning into her soft skin. It was cold, and Clarion wondered if she was still breathing. She noticed the rise and fall of her stomach under the blankets... But it wasn't the movement that concerned her.

Clarion shot up, kicking the chair back. She didn't even flinch as it crashed to the ground behind her. "What's happened to her stomach?"

"Yeah, we wondered." Krea grimaced as she righted the chair. "Ma says there's no way she's so pregnant, not after we all saw her fit into a tiny little thing of a dress just a short time ago..."

Clarion flung back Elena's heavy and luxurious

173

blankets so she could look at her stomach more closely. Mariah gasped and leaned in, grabbing the edges of the blankets and attempting to set them right again. "She's cold. And don't go flinging her bed sheets like she's some commoner! *Whatever* was going on between the two of you doesn't give you the right..."

"So it's true?" asked Krea. "Jackin told me, but I didn't believe... Clarion, are you two sweethearts? I thought you was sweet on Jackin once, but he told me as much as he wanted it, it could never be, that you and his sister..."

Oblivious to the discussion around her, Clarion stared at Elena's abdomen, which the thin nightgown revealed to be monstrously bloated. It did look like she was about to have a baby.

"She's not pregnant," she explained, cold sweat dotting her forehead. "She ate something from Jacosa's garden that she wasn't supposed to. She floated for a while. She... flew."

"I knew she couldn't be pregnant," said Krea, matter-of-factly. "Who'd she be pregnant with? She never showed no interest in any of the village boys, and she just met that fiancé of hers a couple of hours before he vanished."

Clarion didn't move as Mariah tucked Elena back in. "Well, whatever the cause," said the maid curtly, "we've no hope of treating her now."

"Why?" asked Clarion. She thought immediately of the ruins of Jacosa's garden and her palms grew clammy. "What happened to Jacosa's herbs?"

"The same thing that happened to the witch herself," said Mariah, standing straight again. "Burnt to a crisp."

"Mack!" Clarion rushed down the hallway of the second floor of the mansion, wringing her hands together. "Lord... Magnus!"

"Oh! Goodness me! You scared me. Clarion." The mayor came upon Clarion as he crested the top of the stairs. "Magnus told me you'd brought him back, but I'm sorry. I'm so distracted as of late, I'd nearly forgot and chalked you up for still being among the missing."

Clarion stopped, finding as good a target for her questioning as any. "Krea and Mariah told me... That is, I saw... Is it true, Lord Destrian and his men killed Jacosa?"

The mayor ran a weary hand over his face. "So you've heard. They set fire to her place the day after you'd gone missing, the night Jacosa brought Elena here like that..." He stared off over Clarion's shoulder, distracted a minute, before shaking his head. "They said she was there when they did it, and that she refused to leave her home. That they... let her burn inside it."

"But... why?"

"They told me she'd cursed Elena." The mayor swallowed. "That she caused the earth to shake. That she was responsible for your and Magnus' disappearances, that if we didn't rid our town of evil, there would be more disaster..."

"And you believed that? Jacosa has lived here since before I was born, probably since before *you* were born, and you attribute a few disasters only recently to her on some *stranger's* say-so?"

The mayor's head hung low. "I didn't know what to believe. I was beside myself when she brought Elena here. I didn't *tell* them to go do that."

Clarion let out a grunt. "But you didn't try to stop them, either."

"I didn't know that's what they were doing. They confronted Jacosa before they left. I heard whispers and shouting and... I don't know. I was at Elena's bedside and before I knew it, they'd all gone."

175

"Jacosa was going to *save* Elena!"

The mayor looked about to keel over. He reached for the top of the banister to steady himself. "I know she was the only one who might have had something to treat her with—"

"She *did*! She told me she could heal her." Clarion's anger caught in her throat as she considered what might have happened. Jacosa and Elena should have arrived in Jacosa's garden, and she could have given her whatever herb she needed right then and there. Why did she take her back to her house untreated? Clarion massaged her forehead. The more she thought about everything, the more confused she got.

She thought of her papa for the first time in what felt like days, although she knew it hadn't been that long. He was always there when she couldn't get her bearings. *Breathe, little one. Clear your head and just breathe.*

But now that Mack was safe—at least for now—Elena's health was the only important thing. "The poppy!" Her last conversation with Jacosa fluttered through her mind. "Maybe... Maybe Jacosa already gave her it. I'd forgotten... She said Elena would be out for days after."

The mayor clutched Clarion's shoulders. "So there's hope? She's just... resting?"

"Mayor!"

The mayor stepped back to see who approached them from the stairs. Eustace trailed up after Mack and Mack's servant, her face ashen. "I couldn't get Lord Magnus to sit still..."

Mack snapped to attention in front of the mayor and Clarion, his hands clutched behind his back and his pointed nose just a touch in the air. "Where's my father?"

The mayor glanced from the servant to Eustace to Mack and back again. "They didn't tell you?"

"I wanted his lordship to rest, so I brought him to the kitchen, where she"—the servant nodded at Eustace—"and the housekeeper tried to ply him with food, but he wouldn't be appeased."

Mack waved a hand sharply in his direction. "Because I'm not getting any answers."

Glaring at Mack's servant, Clarion stepped forward. "Your father and his men burnt down Jacosa's garden. With Jacosa still home."

The servant gulped audibly. "We tried to get the witch to come out beforehand—"

Mack balled his hands into fists. "You and Father *killed* a woman? You killed the village's *witch* at that?"

"We were only protecting the village." All heads turned as Jackin appeared at the top of the stairs, taking a vicious bite from a pear as if it might bite him back. Which, if he'd purloined it from Jacosa's garden before it burnt down, it just might. "She'd lost her wits."

"You were a part of this?" Clarion snatched the pear from Jackin's hand as he stood beside her. She didn't know why it bothered her so much. When Jackin didn't answer—just stood there dumbfounded, his eyes refusing to meet hers—she continued. "And where's Lord Destrian now?"

The servant spoke up. "I was trying to prepare Lord Magnus for the news—"

"What *news*?" demanded Mack.

The servant's shoulders stiffened, and he bowed slightly as he clutched a fist to his chest. "His lordship *did* try to save the witch from the burning. He assumed once the flames started, she'd be driven out..."

The color seemed to drain from Mack's face. "What are you saying?"

Although the anger had gone out of Mack's voice, the servant shrunk back. "His lordship... died. He never came out from the cottage, and I'm sorry to say we could find neither he nor the witch."

"I'm sorry, dear," said Eustace, as if she had anything to do with it. She shuffled forward to put an arm around Clarion, and she squeezed her, saying quietly, "I'm so glad to have you back with us. I was worried sick."

But Clarion didn't—couldn't—answer. She saw Mack's heart torn into pieces in front of her, saw the shade of the man she'd first thought him to be fade away into nothingness, the lost and quiet boy that was Wilkin all that was left behind.

"So he's gone?" asked Mack, quietly. "I... So my life here is at an end." Clarion wondered if anyone but her could have imagined what he meant.

The servant put a hand on Mack's shoulder. "Charles and Henry as well; they went after him and they weren't so lucky. I saw them burn before they even reached the cottage, buried their bodies the next day." Tears welled in his eyes, and Clarion realized he must have been referring to Lord Destrian's other two servants. "...If I wasn't told expressly to run back for help, I would have..."

Although he spoke to the servant, Mack's gaze flashed hotly toward Clarion. "There were bodies for your fellow servants, but none for Father and the witch?"

"No, but there was so much rubble..."

Jackin crossed his arms. "There was no way they survived." Flustered, Clarion searched Jackin's face for some sign of remorse, of empathy, for the loss of the witch and several others, but he caught her eye and seemed only angry.

Mack ignored him, towering over his servant, and Clarion thought of a giant staring down at a tiny person. "And what did you hope to accomplish by burning down a garden with magical properties?"

"My lord, that is..." The servant took a step back. "He was so upset at your loss. So stressed. Then when he saw the poor young woman, he... changed. He said he remembered, and that the witch was to blame for everything, for both giving and taking away..."

"He remembered what?" asked Eustace. Clarion had almost forgotten whose hand rested on her shoulder.

"I... I don't know. He'd been here before, almost twenty years ago. It was from somewhere around here that he fetched Lord Magnus when he was about ten." The servant was sweating so much, he actually glistened. "I didn't ask. I *never* asked. But he was certain the witch knew where Lord Magnus was, and that she had had something to do with everything gone wrong since our visit."

Mack grabbed the man by the arms. "Tell me *exactly*—"

Before he could finish, the ground shook, and the air above them roared. It was as if a ceaseless, impossibly robust wind had blown from one edge of town to the other, the ground turned to liquid as the thunder echoed in everyone's ears.

The half-eaten pear slipped from Clarion's fingers, the moist exposed insides caressing her fingertips as it fell to the stone floor just as the servant slipped from Mack's hands and fell backward down the marble stairs.

Chapter 21

"Grimey, that was a bad one!" Krea peeked her head out of Elena's room once the shaking had finally stopped.

No one said anything in response as they gazed down at the man below them, red spilling out in every direction to stain the pale bottom step.

"Well, come on! Someone do something!" Eustace sped past her daughter and the still-frozen Mack at the top of the stairway to scramble down, taking the steps two at a time. She crouched beside the man and tried to touch him, drawing back, then reaching out again, as if attempting to determine whether or not her touch would make it worse.

Clarion knew it wouldn't matter. The man's eyes were open, but he was as twisted and as lifeless as that man she'd mistaken for Mack.

"Mayor?" came Mariah's stiff and soft voice. "Elena's moaning. She's taken a turn for the worse..."

The mayor cried out and disappeared behind them, dragging Jackin by the arm after him. Clarion stood, transfixed, one foot pointed down toward her mother and the dead man, the other toward Elena and the rest. She stared at Jackin, and he at her, as the mayor dragged him away. At the doorway, a sullen Krea stepped in where the mayor had been, sliding her own arm through Jackin's as the mayor disappeared inside. She leaned her head against Jackin's shoulder and Jackin spared one last glance at Clarion before straightening himself rigidly and walking inside with Krea.

Clarion didn't even realize until that moment that her hand clutched Mack's tightly, her fingers woven through his.

She turned to go check on Elena.

"Don't." Mack tugged her back. "You can't help her."

"But I have to at least..." Clarion stared at Mack. Sweat dotted his forehead, much like it had the fallen servant's. He looked ashen. Ill. "You think they're back in the land above, don't you? Your father and Jacosa."

"They have to be."

"I think we would have noticed if they'd grown another beanstalk before ours... But if they'd used the same one we did, we would have seen them when we climbed!"

"Not if they didn't want to be seen." Mack looked down at the man who had slipped from his grip and at Eustace and Gytha, who had come out to see what had happened and who crouched beside the body along with Eustace. "If Elena needs something more, Jacosa has it."

Clarion stared back at Elena's room, and the still-open door. She didn't want to go back to the giants—she didn't want Mack to have an excuse to go back there. But she needed Jacosa and whatever little herbs there may be left.

And Elena had her family. She had Krea and Mariah, and even Eustace and Gytha.

If she and Mack delayed too long, there might be questions when they eventually disappeared.

"All right," said Clarion. "But only to get Jacosa back." A sharp pain in her abdomen made her question her decision. *Elena needs me,* she thought. Only she couldn't decide what would be better, to be at her side or to go get the one woman who could help her.

But she couldn't trust Mack to go off on his own and ever come back.

"Clarion! Clarion, wait!"

Clarion and Mack had gotten as far as the front step of the mayor's mansion before Eustace trailed out after her. There'd been no avoiding passing her and Gytha—and the dead man—on their way out, but she'd made her steps light and careful and had hoped the stress of the situation might distract her mother long enough for them to pass by unmolested.

Mack tugged on her hand. "We have to go. Quickly. Before that last stalk is destroyed."

Clarion ground her foot into the earth and tugged back. "Just wait. *Wait* for me." She turned toward her mother. "Mother..."

"Where are you off to now?" Eustace grabbed her by the elbow. "You're going to vanish without a word again? Now of all times, when we have another dead man in the mansion and your dearest friend needs you?" She stared over her shoulder at Mack, her eyes narrowing.

"It's not... that," said Clarion, guessing her mother assumed she fancied herself a lover running away from it all. "We think we know where Jacosa is."

"Jacosa's gone," said Eustace. "It's just as well. We can't keep relying on her forever."

Clarion frowned. Her mother was awfully cold about a woman she presumed dead—not that that was surprising, considering her feelings toward the witch. "We can rely on her now at least. When Elena needs her."

"What can *she* do?" A shimmer danced over

Eustace's dark irises. "She's not a miracle worker, Clarion."

"Yes, she is!" Clarion tugged her arm away from her mother. "You've seen what her plants can do!"

"Trifles. Tricks." Eustace's lips trembled.

"That's not true!" said Clarion, realizing her mother had never seen the beanstalk, had never held tightly to her best friend while she was floating in the air.

"Oh, then where was she when your father got ill?" said Eustace. "Where was she when he was dying? What good her plants did then!"

Clarion's throat tightened. They'd gotten plants to ease her papa's suffering, but that was all Jacosa could offer. *"He's beyond my saving,"* the witch had said. "That was different."

"How so? Because I dared to not help in her stupid garden?" Eustace clutched her fists together. "Because she knew I'd once loved another?"

Clarion felt as if her mother had kicked her in the stomach. "What are you talking about?" *And why are we discussing this now?*

"When I was your age," began Eustace, rubbing her palms on the front of her skirt, "I asked her for a love potion."

Clarion's brow raised. Krea and Elena had gossiped about love herbs in Jacosa's gardens, had giggled about relying on them to win someone's heart. Krea changed her mind every other day about the boy to whom she'd most wished to feed them. Elena had been coy about revealing whom she'd give them to and had told Clarion later she'd wanted to give them to her. But that she was much happier knowing she hadn't needed them. But neither had asked the witch for the herb, assuming such an herb even existed. They didn't want a love they didn't truly earn, a love they'd always doubt.

"I wanted a life of comfort," continued Eustace. "My mother was widowed young, and the two of us, we grew up poorer then than you and I are now.

183

"When Mother passed when I was just your age... I had no one to turn to. I had to marry." Eustace took a deep breath. "I fancied the young mayor, thought to be his wife, even though he had designs on a lady from another town." She straightened her back and jutted her chin out. "I asked Jacosa to help me make the most important man in the town fall for me."

"And you're saying... Papa fell for you instead?"

Eustace guffawed bitterly. "Jacosa gave me some herbs to eat, told me what to think and say to get it all to *work*. The mayor didn't give me the time of day, but your father, a *pig farmer*... Well, the mayor announced his engagement within days and I figured it was the pig farmer or no one."

Clarion laughed, but it wasn't jovial. "The magic worked."

"No, it didn't," said Eustace. "Don't get me wrong, Clarion, I was satisfied with our life in the end—"

"No, you weren't, and yes it did!" Clarion rubbed her temples. "Papa would have been the lord of this village, you know that, if the mayor's grandfather hadn't seized power from Papa's."

"So it was just Jacosa's sick joke?" Eustace scoffed. "Yes, our family was real important. In between the layers of mud and pig feces, you could almost even see there was a family living in that hovel."

Clarion burned inside from her fingers to her toes. "I *loved* it there!"

"Clarion, you were meant for greater things." Eustace stepped forward and rested a gentle palm on Clarion's cheek. "Your songs, your talent..."

"Greater things?" Clarion stepped back, out of her reach. "Like being someone's servant and scrubbing pots and pans? Those greater things?"

"Clarion, I'm going to marry the mayor."

Clarion chuckled. "You keep on dreaming of that, Mother. Maybe once I *find Jacosa*, I'll ask her if she has any of those love herbs left and you can try again now that there's no male left in the true lord's bloodline."

"No, I mean it." Eustace threw her head back. "He's asked me to marry him. That was my true intention in accepting this job, in getting rid of everything from our old life. It was why I felt justified in asking him to buy the harp. I hoped it'd be yours once more; I just didn't dare express that hope in case it didn't come to pass."

Clarion's gaze flicked to the mansion behind her mother, to the opulence and the grandiosity that her papa had never once envied.

"Bricks and more bricks, my little one," he'd said. *"Ghosts from our past. Nothing more."*

"I'd hoped to make a match between you and the mayor's son..."

Clarion stumbled. Her mother had all these plans for her, and she'd never once asked what *she'd* wanted?

Eustace wrung her hands together. "But then there was that night at the ball, and how you and Lord Magnus... Well, I thought that'd be an even better match for you, but I worried Judd wouldn't be in an amenable mood if he lost the match for his own daughter. But in any case, Jackin settled on Krea while you were missing."

"Jackin and *Krea?*" Clarion looked back at the mansion, as if she were staring at the surprising couple herself. At least Krea would be happy. She hoped Jackin could make her so.

"I know. Judd isn't entirely settled to that match. I'm thinking he might disown Jackin if he marries her. I don't know why the boy is being so stubborn. He doesn't even seem that in love with her."

Clarion thought of the way he'd looked at her as he took Krea's arm and wondered if it was supposed to be meant to hurt her, as if she'd care if she lost Jackin's favor. Although she did care if her friend was going to be stuck in a loveless marriage because Jackin wasn't man enough to admit the truth. But that wasn't a problem to worry about just now. She'd just have to talk Krea out of it when everything settled. She turned to go. "Weddings all around, I see," she said. "But right now I care more about Elena being able to go to them than anything. Mother, I'll be back..." She froze.

Mack wasn't where she'd left him.

Ugh, he's infuriating! screamed Clarion in her head.

"He left a few minutes ago without you," said Eustace, drawing up beside her daughter again. "Clarion, can't you just trust the boy to do whatever it is himself? What can you possibly do to help? You've nearly given me a conniption twice in the past month, I've been so worried about you. You've always been frail, you know that. Come back inside with me..."

Clarion spun on her heel and ran down the road after him.

Chapter 22

 he beanstalk was still standing—the sole vibrant green sign of life in what was once a flourishing garden—but there was no sign of Mack anywhere.

"He went without me! He *climbed up without me!*" Clarion didn't care that there was no one to hear her frustration. In fact, it made her feel freer than ever. She kicked the beanstalk for good measure, not even caring that her toes hurt in response.

She gazed up. There was no way she was going to be able to climb the beanstalk. But she couldn't trust Mack to send Jacosa back—she wasn't even sure he was right that she was alive and up there. Did the fire burn the last of the beans that grew these stalks? Did Jacosa and Lord Destrian have to wait for another beanstalk—the one Clarion and Mack had grown—to appear? Would they have worked together after what he'd done? Why didn't the groups see each other as one climbed up and the other climbed down?

She didn't trust Mack to come back himself, either. But at this point, she was almost upset enough with him not to care. Almost.

Clarion sighed and looked around. Were there any plants left? Could she even risk taking the one that made

Elena float after seeing what it'd done to her? She couldn't even remember what it was. Besides, she knew she wouldn't be able to control her floating once she got there. Perhaps, though, there was something for healing left in the rubble of the cottage. Given something new to focus on, Clarion trotted down the hill carefully, dragging her toes now and then in the dirt to see if there was any green left beneath the scorched earth and rubble.

She was almost to the pile that had once been Jacosa's cottage—a back corner of the cottage still stood, there might be hope of finding an unburnt cupboard there—when the ground shook again.

It was loud, like the skies were cracking in two. It seemed even louder and more vehement here than the last one, unless it was just magnified by her proximity to the beanstalk and the gateway to the world above.

Because now she knew what had caused these disturbances all along—the giant king acting out in anger against his own people.

When it finally stopped—Clarion was certain she heard that strange sound, "FUM," on the air—Clarion righted herself and came face-to-face with Mack, his hand clutching something pale green.

"I thought you left!" Clarion's fist shook at her side, and she wasn't sure if she was trying to stop herself from slapping him or hugging him.

Mack looked sheepish. "I planned to, but I thought..."

"You thought?"

"I wanted to wait for you. And see if the witch had anything left that might help. Anything at all."

Clarion wasn't sure if she believed him about waiting as she stared down at the pile of dried plants in Mack's hand. It was wavy and crackly, almost like hair. "That's all?"

"It's tarragon," said Mack. "The stuff that makes giant people small and small people giant."

Clarion bit her lip. Of all the plants to have survived the fire, what use would they get from that? Then she thought of one. "Is this for your mother?"

"What do you mean?" asked Mack.

"To make her our—my—size. To bring her back here, away from that madman ruling over your cloud town."

Mack stared up and chewed his bottom lip. Clarion found herself strangely compelled to trace her hand on his cheek.

Then she realized she was.

Mack rested the fingers of his free hand atop Clarion's at his cheekbone. "Clair," he said, referring to her with the nickname only her longtime friends used. He turned his face into her hand, and Clarion could feel the light prickle of his stubble massage her palm, such a different sensation from touching Elena's smooth and soft cheek. "You're right. I should take her down here, instead of offering to stay with her, but I'm afraid she won't come."

"It's not safe for you... for her. For anyone."

"I know!" Mack grabbed her hand, clutching it tightly. "I... I'll prioritize getting the witch to come back for your friend, I promise you. No matter what. And then I'll decide what to do."

Clarion wasn't sure why she felt the need to say it, especially right then. "Elena isn't just a friend. I loved her."

"*Loved?*"

"I mean, I love her still, of course I do." Clarion almost choked on her words. "As my dearest friend. But until recently, I thought I really loved her. Like I love you."

"You love me?" Mack smiled, and it was like a wet brush stroke had rippled through a canvas, changing the picture entirely.

"Well, I..." Clarion took a step back, but Mack gripped her hand tighter, pulling her closer. "I'm attracted to you."

Mack's pale eyes danced back and forth as they examined her face, and Clarion could feel heat bursting throughout her body. "Father thinks me a flirt," he said. A lock of hair fell over one eye, but he didn't even flinch, didn't take his gaze off of Clarion. "But the truth is, I've never actually been in love. Never spent more than a few hours in this or that girl's company."

As she swallowed, Clarion found herself staring down at the tarragon in Mack's other hand. "I don't know if we ever really spent more than a few hours together. Most of the time I was scrubbing, for what good it did. And you were making my new harp." She faced Mack. "I'm surprised you have such talent. That you knew how to make one, crude or not."

He laughed. "Crude, huh? I didn't know exactly... When I was younger, when I still lived up there with Mother, I apprenticed under a few of the tradesmen in town for a while. With Father gone, Mother was eager to find me some kind of paternal figure to look up to. Our carpenter made instruments on occasion, but I'd be lying if I said I committed harp-making to memory." His face inched closer to hers. "But I thought of you playing and singing, and it was like the skies themselves made those memories stronger and filled in the details, showing me how to make it so you could play and sing again."

Clarion opened her mouth slightly to ask more, but Mack had leaned forward, pressing his lips against hers. It was soft, yet hard somehow, too. He pulled back just the tiniest bit, but before Clarion could even think to close her mouth, he pressed forward again, dropping her hand and placing his at the small of her back, pulling her closer, pressing his lips against hers again and again and again. His lips moved hers, open and shut, open and shut.

She wrapped both arms around his shoulders and pulled as hard as he was pulling her, pressed her lips as hungrily against his as he did against hers.

She didn't know how much later it was that she pulled back, gasping for air, wondering if she'd even remembered to breathe.

Mack grinned. "So... You fell in love with girls?"

The moment soured and there was a pain in Clarion's stomach as she inched back just slightly. "Just one girl."

"But no other boys?"

"No." Clarion ran her tongue over her bottom lip, fighting the urge to kiss him again. "I didn't think I even could."

Squeezing her tighter with the one arm he had around her back, Mack laughed. "Maybe you just *thought* that. Maybe you hadn't met the *right* man yet."

Clarion felt ill. She pushed one hand against Mack's chest, trying to put more room between them. "You don't understand." Elena hadn't understood, either, although at least Clarion knew her heartbreak was at least partially to blame. The heartbreak that *she* had caused. Partly over this flirtatious young man who didn't even *know* her. Who didn't understand.

"I want to," said Mack, every trace of mischievousness gone from his face.

Clarion paced back and forth over the small section of dirt beneath her feet that wasn't littered with rubble and cinders. "I suppose I hadn't met the *right* man—the man who would make me feel something, anyway. But that doesn't mean that what I felt before wasn't..." Clarion trailed off, not even sure she'd ever felt madly in love with Elena. She loved her, like she loved Krea, only with Elena, she'd wanted more. She'd wanted to kiss her, to hold her... But that had died with time, with grief. That was why she'd ended it between them in the first place. However, that didn't mean that her feelings for either Mack or Elena were wrong, that one negated the other.

"All right," said Mack, clearing his throat. "I'm sorry. I am."

Clarion stopped pacing and Mack ran his free hand over the back of his scalp. "I really messed up a good thing there, didn't I?"

Shaking her head, Clarion grabbed Mack's other hand, the one holding the tarragon. "It doesn't matter. Now is hardly the time for this." She coaxed his fingers open and spread the tarragon stalks out on his palm. "How many do you need... to change?"

Mack removed one stalk from the pile of six or seven and held it out between two fingers. "Just one."

Before he could react, Clarion snatched two of the stalks and held them out in front of her. "Then I know how I can make the climb."

Mack stepped toward her, his face draining of color. "Clarion, I don't think you'll like it, and besides, no one's ever grown to the size of a giant while still—"

But Clarion had already popped a stalk into her mouth and swallowed it.

Chapter 23

t was foggier up here than it was last time, or maybe her size made the difference. Maybe it seemed clear when she was little because she wasn't tall enough to reach the fog. Clarion shivered, rubbing her hands up and down her bare arms for what had to be the fiftieth time since she'd made it to the cloud kingdom. The fine little hairs on her forearms—she laughed thinking of them as little, wondering if each was now about the height she used to be—stood up straight.

But at least she'd managed to scale the beanstalk in just about ten footholds.

"This," said Mack as he clutched both hands in front of his groin, his shoulders shaking and his teeth chattering, "is partly why I wanted you to think this through. Clothes don't grow or shrink along with the bodies. I only had something to wear in the king and queen's toy box because they had that outfit in the right size there. I kicked the other clothes under the bed." Clarion supposed she ought to think of him as Wilkin, now that he was a giant, but since she was a giant as well, he really did just look like Mack.

"Then how did you salvage the clothes you wore the night of the ball? The ones you gave to that poor dead man..."

His face flushed. "I might have removed them before I ate the tarragon."

"You removed your clothes. After you climbed the beanstalk. And realized giants were real."

"I took the rosemary first," he said, "and I remembered how this all worked. That, and they were quite sweat-soaked at that point anyway."

Clarion wasn't going to ask if he'd really removed the clothes before or after he'd gained his memories, as his sheepish smile seemed to say there was more to the story he wouldn't be telling her. His shame suddenly reminded her of her own. She stopped rubbing her forearms to make sure her wrists were lined up at just the right part of her chest. She squeezed her legs together tightly but didn't have enough spare arms and hands to cover it all. Besides, she hadn't waited to see Mack's reaction after she grew. She'd just climbed. And since he arrived shortly after her as big as she was, she reckoned he'd gotten an eyeful. Part of her wanted to die of embarrassment and the rest didn't have time for that.

"Come on," said Mack, hunching over and running in front of her. "My house is first. You can wear one of Mother's dresses and I can grab one of my outfits. If we're quick enough, no one will even see us..." He stopped.

Clarion, who'd been running behind him, the soles of her feet tickling beneath her, almost ran into his back and had to look away quickly so as not to stare at his sharp, defined bare buttocks. They were almost angular compared to a woman's, and Clarion couldn't believe she was yet again thinking about such things at such a time. Especially since she wasn't even sure she'd forgiven him for being so confident in himself just a few moments before.

Mack's voice came out slowly and he stood straighter, his shame forgotten. "What has he done?"

Clarion tore her eyes from his rear—which she just realized she was *still* staring at—and leaned to look over

Mack's shoulder. A house—Mack's house, she thought—was still there a few feet in front of them. But there was only one other house down this cloud road that led to the king's grand estate. Actually, now that she had a better vantage point, the king's place wasn't a mansion like the mayor's mansion at all. It was a castle.

But that made sense. He was a king, not a lord. A tyrant king who lived in an actual castle.

Still, the disappearance of the other houses was more disconcerting. "He... destroyed them all?" Clarion asked, her voice trembling more from fear than cold.

Mack's brows furrowed together as he grabbed Clarion by the wrist, pulling her toward his home. Clarion almost protested, knowing it left her chest exposed, but Mack never glanced over at her as he pushed the door open. "Mother?" he called. His voice echoed into the darkness. A trickle of light from the open doorway and a single window showed that no one was inside.

Mack let go of Clarion's arm and strode to a chest at the foot of the two beds pushed up against one corner of the small cottage. "Let's get dressed."

Clarion went back to covering her chest and looked about the place. It was so small—so homely—from her current vantage point. The workbench on which she'd had a makeshift area to herself was so... ordinary. That darned sink with its endless supply of dishes seemed so inconsequential.

Mack appeared in front of her, pants on, but his chest still bare. He held out a faded yellow dress. "From when Mother was younger," he said. "I don't think she wears it anymore."

Clarion drank in the sight of his chest in the sliver of light. It was pale but covered with wisps of dark hair. Although he was thin, his muscles were alluringly defined.

Mack cleared his throat, and Clarion snapped out of her thoughts, just managing to catch Mack's eyes traveling from her own mostly-exposed abdomen and chest to somewhere above her head. A flush dotted his cheeks and Clarion snatched the dress away from him, shoving her arms through and scrambling to pull it down over her head.

The lump at Mack's throat bobbed and he stepped back, clapping his hands together a couple of times. "Good. Good. So... yeah." A loud scraping noise echoed in the darkness and he jumped, but he turned around only to find that he'd backed right into a chair. "I'll get a shirt," he mumbled, and he vanished back to the foot of the bed.

Clarion took another few steps inside, her fingers tracing the path she might have once walked across the table's surface. "Do you still think they're here? Jacosa and your father?"

She heard a clunk as Mack shut the chest. Like proper tidying up was important when the vast majority of your neighbors' homes were reduced to rubble. "I don't know. But if they are, they're with His and Her Grace."

"What made those two king and queen exactly?" Clarion asked. Was it a blood right, like the lordship of the town had been her father's? But even that was changeable. Even that could crash down, and lords could be made paupers. There'd been little reason for her family to lose that right. Here, there was all the reason in the world and yet...

"What do you mean?" asked Mack, tugging at the bottom of the white shirt he'd put on. "He's the king... Like his father before him. No one's questioned that."

"Even when his anger causes him to destroy homes? To kill people?" Clarion took hold of Mack's elbow. "Is everyone in your town... dead?"

Mack looked around the room, as if searching for signs that his mother was hiding somewhere. "I hope not. But... I don't know." He unfolded his fist. The few strands of tarragon left had grown with him and looked much the same on his palm as they had before. "These grow or shrink in the hands of someone who ingests them. Otherwise I don't know how we'd hold them when we're this size."

196

"Oh!" cried Clarion, who looked at her own hands. "I... I dropped it. My other piece."

Mack tucked his remaining pieces into a pocket on his shirtfront. "I figured you would, in the panic of the transformation." He frowned. "But it's all right. I have enough to get you back. And maybe Mother and me also."

"Maybe?" Clarion's breath caught in her throat. *After everything, 'maybe'?*

"Clarion, I don't know." He swallowed. "But I'll get you back. I promise."

"I'm not some plaything to be protected." Clarion tossed her head back, not used to her long hair tumbling over her shoulders without a bonnet to keep it in place. "I wish people would stop acting like I am."

Mack laughed. "I don't think you are. You came up here to find me, a man you hardly knew—after I willingly climbed up here and started this entire mess? No, it's just a matter of me making up for my mistakes. Me making sure you and your friend don't have to suffer anymore for my problems."

Clarion cocked her head, studying Mack. He was possibly the first person to say she didn't need protection, the first person to treat her like she wasn't brittle and fragile because she'd experienced loss. Although to be fair, he could hardly know how much that loss had hurt her, and he hadn't even known her papa.

"To the castle?" she asked.

"To the castle."

They met no one on the cloud path to the castle, saw nothing stirring from the piles of broken houses.

"Where'd the rubble go?" Clarion pointed to an empty patch of cloud where she'd expected to see the remains of the first house she'd seen destroyed.

"It does that. Disappear. And we don't know where it goes," said Mack. "I hope not down to the land below, but that would be kind of hard for you all to miss. In time, whatever the king determines is unwanted sinks into the cloud below."

Clarion stared at the white fluff beneath her feet as she walked forward, unsure how it supported her and everything around her. Jacosa's spell-infected garden seemed so mundane next to the impossible things she saw here.

Clarion felt Mack intertwine his arm through hers.

"Wilkin!"

Clarion looked up to see Mack's mother and Lorica—the fan was a dead giveaway, even if the face looked less warped to Clarion now—spilling forth from the open castle door.

"I thought you'd never return!" Mack's mother clutched his shoulders, not seeming to notice how she elbowed Clarion in the chest as she did so. "His Grace has gone mad! Mad!"

Mack wouldn't let Clarion go, though. "What's happened?"

"He's destroyed everything! Everyone!"

"Be glad he was gone, Norma." Lorica flapped and flapped her fan. "It kept him safe."

Mack's mother stared at Clarion, her face souring. "Who's—"

"The little songstress!" Lorica's eyes widened as she folded her fan to give Clarion a closer look. "She grew... big."

Although Clarion hadn't even thought it possible, Mack's mother seemed even angrier to discover the identity of the young woman on her son's arm. "Why just her? Why would you bring her back *like that*? Oh, Wilkin, you never listen to me. You've *never* listened to me—"

Clarion couldn't help but notice the slight tremble in Mack's hand. "Mother, this is hardly the time," he said.

"What's happened? Is everyone really..." He couldn't bring himself to finish.

"Dead." Lorica whacked the fan open again. "Everyone but us, Her Grace, and one of their servants."

"Why?"

Mack's mother took a step back. "The little witch came back," she said. "And she didn't come alone."

Chapter 24

ack hadn't thought it the smartest idea to waltz straight into the castle through the front door, but once Mack's mother told them that Jacosa was on the ballroom's fireplace mantel, Clarion refused to go anywhere else.

"But if you shrank back down at least—" protested Mack.

"We don't have enough tarragon to spare," hissed Clarion, not entirely unaware that Mack's mother kept an eye on them as they ascended the few steps to the castle door. "I won't risk it. Besides, I feel safer being the size of the madman."

"We're not safer at all." Mack pulled Clarion toward him. "No one is safe here."

Clarion wondered, as she examined Mack's wan face in the candlelight from the chandelier above them, if she could finally count on Mack leaving it all behind. But she was certain he wouldn't consider anything unless his mother consented first.

She wondered at his lack of comparable concern for his father, whom he insisted would be here with Jacosa—although after learning of what he and his men had done, she couldn't help but feel she wouldn't be so concerned with him either in Mack's position.

A booming voice echoed throughout the castle, a guttural rumbling that made Clarion's blood run cold.

Just before they were about to enter the ballroom, Mack's mother stepped in front of them. "Wilkin, you should know something..."

Lorica, her fan tucked under her arm, put a finger to her mouth and shook her head, guiding the group inside.

"Fi! I don't see how this will work! I think you're just *lying* to me. Trying to buy *yourself* some time." There was no mistaking the anger. The king walked back and forth in front of the fireplace, flinging his arms all about him.

His wife—her face overly powdered, her features pinched—stood a few feet away. "Well, you're not taking my chicken." She traced delicate fingers over something tiny in her palm.

The king stormed over to her, his face red. "Why would I want to? It shits out gold, doesn't it? That's more than you do."

The queen moved her fingers to her throat. "How crass!"

The king leaned over, pulling back his hand into a fist and shaking it dangerously close to the queen's face. "I'll show you crass! Fee, fi—"

"Stop! It wouldn't work with the hen anyway. It doesn't work with animals. And the hen is hardly my enemy."

Clarion searched for the source of the voice and didn't find it until the king swung around to face the mantel.

So that was how strange it felt to hear a tiny person speaking as if she were a hundred times taller.

"It has to be a human," said Jacosa, who stood at the edge of the mantel with her hands clutched together. "And even then, I can't guarantee it'll work..."

"Of course you can't guarantee!" roared the king.

201

"All you have are excuses!"

A man appeared from behind Clarion and Mack, making Clarion jump. It was a servant—probably the man who'd carried them on a pillow before. "Your Grace," he said, his voice shaking as he moved closer to the king. Clarion was reminded of the poor dead servant of Lord Destrian far, far below them. "Our crops are gone. I don't know how the gardeners did what they did—"

"You don't *know*?" The king rounded on the man. "They didn't know, either! They weren't growing things fast enough to suit me, so I turned their homes to rubble!"

Clarion remembered her own questions as to how they grew anything from a cloud, how they managed to have any giant livestock. Mack had insisted they just *could*, they just *did*, but Clarion wondered...

The king stomped his feet like a child throwing a tantrum. "I told you you were to take over the growing of food, or you'd be sorry!"

The queen held her hand out to the mantel, and Clarion spotted a small white dot—the magic chicken—crawling over to her former master. The queen tossed her head back, picked up her skirts and stormed over to her husband. "Well, maybe if you hadn't *insisted* we throw all these parties, we wouldn't have eaten all the food."

"I insisted? *I* insisted? If I didn't keep you in your cups, I wouldn't even be able to stand a minute beside you!"

The queen paled and backed away. "Now wait a minute. You've already destroyed most of the town. You can't—"

"FEE, FI, FO FUM!"

"Your Grace!" The servant stumbled backwards, tripping over his own feet and falling on his backside. "I can make it work somehow; I just need *time*."

But the king had already swung his arms and taken a great big leap, landing where his wife and servant had been and opening up a hole in the ballroom floor. Debris went flying upward in every direction, and Clarion screamed, unable to move. When she could think again, she found her face pressed into Mack's chest, his hand clutching the back of her head. Her feet couldn't find purchase. They kept slipping on the tiles, shaking like she wasn't even in control of her own body.

Then, after the last rumble, the last roar of the king's strange call, there was silence.

Clarion pulled back from Mack's chest, her whole body weak.

Lorica was flapping her fan like mad, one hand pressed against the arch of the doorway to lift herself up, strands of her hair fallen out of place.

Mack's mother lay on the ground in front of them and Mack, after touching Clarion's shoulder lightly and exchanging a look with her, went to help her up.

The king stood up straight in the middle of the hole, smug as he looked around. There were splashes of red liquid on his shins and even as far up as his thighs.

The queen and the servant were nowhere to be found.

Clarion ran to the mantel to check for Jacosa and stifled a gasp as she discovered the flustered witch getting to her feet, clutching on to a man tied with rope at the ankles and the wrists. The witch righted him back atop the cushion on which Clarion had once sat to play the harp.

"Lord Destrian?" said Clarion, her eyes darting to the little fallen harp. It looked so small and simple, like a child's plaything. But there were more important things to concern herself with.

Jacosa raised her eyebrows. "Fancy seeing you here. And so big."

"What is this?" boomed the king from behind Clarion. She spun around to find the madman headed her way. "Who are you?"

Clarion wondered why he hadn't noticed her come in earlier, but he *had* been in the middle of a raging rant.

Clarion's eyes darted over to Mack, his mother and

Lorica. Mack shook his head "no," but she didn't know what he didn't want her to say. She wasn't sure what the best thing *to* say would be.

So she curtsied, avoiding the king's madly roving eyes. "It's your harpist, sire. We couldn't... That is, there was no more aloe for me to take so I could sing for you. So we decided it best that I grow to a size where you could hear me."

Crossing his arms tightly across his chest, the king laughed. "And do you see a harp for a woman this size?" He flung his hand in the air. "What use have I for a huge harpist? I wanted a tiny plaything that performed." He leaned forward, his red face close to Clarion's. "What's so special about you now?"

"Your Grace," said Jacosa, and Clarion gratefully stepped aside to let her receive the king's attention, "if I may continue."

Jacosa's words seemed to drain some of the vibrant color from the mad king's skin. He took a deep breath and straightened, not at all upset by the fact that he'd just killed two giants—including his own wife.

His voice boomed. "You may."

Jacosa looked around the mantel until she spotted a tiny golden cup that had fallen over, a cup in which the little gold-laying hen poked its beak. It was made for small hands like hers. She picked it up and walked back to her tied-up captive, pulling something out from her waist. It was a small dagger.

Clarion had never known the witch to carry a dagger.

"Without the seeds of my dear children, I cannot grow another crop of plants to aid and heal, to craft miracles for those in need." Her eyes flickered toward Clarion briefly, and Clarion wondered if she knew what was wrong with Elena, if she was telling her to give up hope. "My family has managed to grow seeds for generations. It's been a long time since the magic had to be renewed." She cleared her throat. "My family's magic starts with sacrifice of a specific sort."

She raised the dagger above her head and turned toward her bound captive. Clarion wasn't sure if she just imagined the flicker of light that flashed over her eyes. "To start anew, I'll need the blood of an enemy, of one who took it all from me."

As she lowered the dagger, Clarion couldn't hear her own gasp over the hollow laughter of the mad king beside her.

Chapter 25

ack was at the hearth in an instant, but it was too late, and the king wasn't having anyone interrupt the little witch again.

He struck an arm out that landed with a thud against Mack's chest. Mack grunted and crumpled, and Clarion rushed to ease his fall. She wasn't even sure she'd find him in one piece after she'd seen what the king's strength was capable of.

"Fa... ther." Mack grunted between syllables.

Clarion ran her fingers through his hair, grateful he was still speaking.

"This blood will grant my wish!" chanted Jacosa, far louder than her tiny size allowed. She held the cup up over her head with both hands, the dagger discarded. "This blood will renew my magic! From it, I undo the wrong that was done to me, and do as I please!"

Clarion knew she wasn't imagining the light that surrounded Jacosa's entire body. The air around her seemed to crackle, and her hair stood up in all directions.

Despite his pain, Mack shot up to his feet. Stunned, Clarion was slow to react, but she saw what had caught his attention: Lord Destrian slumped over on the cushion, his arm dyed red. Jacosa might not have killed him to fill her cup, but the bleeding might.

"THIS BLOOD!" shouted Jacosa. "This blood is my power!" She drank from the cup, just as Mack came to a stop at the mantel, his roundabout path there taking him far out of the king's reach this time.

Clarion didn't remember following Mack, but she found herself behind him, the king's thunderous roar echoing in the ballroom as Mack gently scooped his small father into his open hands. The man's head lolled, but his eyes flickered open and shut.

"Away with you!" said the king. "Away with you both! The little witch has promised me—"

But before Clarion could hear the rest of what the king had to say, she'd snatched Jacosa into her own hand, letting the cup clatter to the floor, a small splash of red dotting her fingers. She ran. Ran past the king before he could launch himself at her. Past Lorica and Mack's mother, leaving Mack and his father behind.

She hoped Mack could fight to save those he loved without her.

She needed Jacosa for Elena, and she owed Elena that much.

To Clarion's surprise, Jacosa didn't squirm or fight her as she scurried down the stairs. "To Norma's," said the little witch. "Quickly. We won't have much time, as there aren't many places to hide."

As Clarion ran down the cloudy path past the sinking rubble of the remaining cottages, she knew what Jacosa meant. "I need you back home," she said, not planning on stopping until she reached the beanstalk. "Elena needs you."

"Elena will be fine," snapped Jacosa. Her hair still stuck up at all angles, but the light had faded. "But no one will be fine forever if I can't re-grow my garden. If we're leaving this place for good, I need to stop at your young man's cottage."

They were nearing Mack's house, and Clarion could just make out the green top of the beanstalk among the clouds a short distance farther. She didn't know whether to trust the witch or not after everything—and witnessing her drinking human blood didn't help her case. But she knew for a fact that almost nothing was left of the beans and herbs that only brought miracles to life when grown in Jacosa's garden, and maybe she did need something she'd left in that cottage to re-grow it. Who knew how long the place would keep standing.

Clarion had no choice but to stop as the soft cloud street started quivering beneath her.

"FEE, FI, FO FUM!"

It was more of a shriek than a threat this time, more a roar than a man's voice.

"What *does* that nonsense even mean?" said Jacosa casually from Clarion's hand. "All these giant people say it whenever something doesn't go their way."

Clarion was about to snap that Jacosa would clearly know more about these people than she would when the door to Mack's cottage burst open.

Clarion first noticed the bare pale shoulders, the way the oversized dress sagged on the woman.

"Clarion?" The woman embraced her, and the only reaction Clarion could muster was to raise the hand carrying Jacosa quickly in order to ensure the small witch's safety.

The woman pulled back—it was Elena. Giant, beautiful Elena.

"Inside! Now!" hissed Jacosa, and Elena grabbed Clarion by the shoulders, pulled her in after her, and shut the door.

Jacosa latched on to a pin cushion twice her height with both hands and tossed it aside with a great big bellow. She immediately dug into a hidden compartment, pulling out greenery and seeds and stuffing them into a satchel at her hip.

Clarion could barely pay attention, though, as she was still taking in the sight of a giant—and apparently healthy—Elena.

"How?" asked Clarion, not unaware of the sounds of the mad king's anger, and the danger Mack could be in at that very moment. But Elena standing there before her made it all seem like a dream.

She didn't even realize she'd grabbed hold of Elena's elbows, had drawn her closer as if to verify she was really standing there.

"Krea and Jackin told me what had happened... since I was asleep." Elena stepped back and lay a hand on her stomach. "The weird side effects of that herb I'd taken, what had happened to Jacosa's garden, that you had come back with Magnus in tow."

"But you were sick... just a few hours ago."

"I told you she'd be fine," Jacosa said from Mack's worktable, not looking up from stuffing her spare plants into her pouch. "It takes about this long for the treatment to work."

Clarion still wasn't convinced. "But you were *sicker* when I left."

"She was probably groaning, throwing off the last of my floating spell." Jacosa stood and nodded, placing her hands on the small of her back in order to stretch. "Okay. I got what I needed. Let's go."

"Wait." Clarion held a finger up toward Jacosa without looking away from Elena. "But that still doesn't explain what you're doing here. Like *that*."

Jacosa threw her hands up. "She obviously had some of my tarragon, same as you."

"Is that what it was?" asked Elena. "I knew right

209

away when they told me you'd run off again where you'd be. I knew you couldn't just leave me without saying goodbye, not when Mariah had panicked and made you think I was sick. I knew you had to be trying to save me." She smiled and tucked a strand of her hair behind her ears. Seeing Elena, as lovely as ever without her cap on, reminded Clarion of how she'd often looked as they'd enjoyed each other's kisses when no one was around to spy on them. Elena usually tossed her cap off then. She wasn't sure Elena had ever seen her much without her own cap on. Both of them removing their caps in private might have led to something more... And Clarion wasn't sure she'd been ready for that back then. "You may not love me anymore, but I know you still care."

Clarion embraced her. "Of course I still care. I'll always care about you." She pulled back. "But how...?"

"I asked to be left alone—for some rest." Elena winked. "Like I needed any more of that. Once I was sure everyone had moved from the hallway, I snuck out and headed to Jacosa's. I almost got caught by Gytha and your mother talking in hushed whispers by the kitchen door, but I ducked into the shadows and left when I had the chance."

Clarion supposed Elena hadn't come across the body of Lord Destrian's poor servant at the bottom of the steps, or surely she would have noticed him. Although she hadn't mentioned anything about blood, either, but who would know to look for that when you were sneaking in the darkness?

"But you *grew*."

"So did you!" Elena laughed. "I knew I couldn't climb the stalk without some help, so I looked around to see what was still growing and I picked up the *only* thing still green in that entire place. It was dried already, but it was all I had, so I ate it. And I grew huge." Her face flushed. "And nude. But I found some clothes in that chest there."

"The one stalk of tarragon I dropped! But after what *just* happened to you, why would you even risk ingesting another..." Clarion drifted off. Just looking at Elena, she knew why. Because of her. She cocked her head. "How in the great big sky could you possibly have *found that*, even if it was the only green thing there? It's not like it was bright green and growing."

"I don't know." Elena walked over to the workbench, her hands out to Jacosa. "Maybe I was just... meant to."

"Yes, yes, that's all very nice. Love and destiny and friendship to be sure." Jacosa climbed onto Elena's outstretched palms, stumbling over the cracks between her fingers. "Now can we go back please? Before that mad king knocks this house down too?"

"Wait a minute." Clarion pounded across the room and shook a finger at the little witch standing on Elena's hand. "What did you *do* back there?"

"What do you mean, what did *I* do?" Jacosa crossed her arms. "Did you not notice the more pressing matter of the king stomping his wife and servant to death?"

Elena gasped, but Clarion ignored the interruption. "You *stabbed* Lord Destrian."

"He'll live. Probably."

"You *drank his blood!*"

Shaking her head, Jacosa cradled her forehead as if she had a headache. "Yeah, and I didn't finish the cup, thanks to you." She stood straight. "Listen, it's a very ancient spell and it can only work when the blood is your enemy's, all right? Now I don't go around making a habit of blood drinking, but the man *destroyed virtually all of the magic* I had to my name, and I had to start anew. Luckily, I suppose, by doing so he provided me with a fresh enemy. He came to me the night I brought Elena to her father, railing about wanting to see his son, saying he'd smoke me out of my home if I didn't fix everything. I refused, saying he could pay for his fix like he always had, but he insisted he wouldn't because my memory spell had worn off—years after he'd ingested the herb, mind you, and in traumatic circumstances—and my magic was all *good for nothing*. He

211

started that blaze and then the idiot chickened out and ran inside the burning cottage to get me. I knocked him out, dragged him out back, and waited some distance away for the fire to stop and another stalk to grow, knowing you'd notice me absent someday." She sniffed. "There were more beans in the cottage, but I figured saving my magic by saving that fool until I could bleed him was more important than trying to scour around and find them before we were all engulfed in flames. I tied him up, and once it appeared, I fed him the same bean Elena took to get him up there."

Clarion decided not to comment on how Jacosa had insisted that spell wasn't for living things. "You met Lord Destrian before. Years ago." Clarion wasn't sure why it mattered, but she was starting to have mixed feelings about leaving this all behind without knowing the full story. "You made him into a giant, and he conceived Mack with a giant woman..."

Jacosa shrugged. "He told me he was tired of traveling the lands looking for a wife and finding nothing but the same, boring type of lady. I promised him he'd find someone much, much more interesting if he climbed up with me."

Clarion practically groaned. "Why would you do that?"

"Why not? He was a client. He had money to spare. I sold him something from my garden, same as I do for anyone."

"But then you helped him take Mack back to the ground, and made it so they wouldn't remember?"

"Again," said Jacosa, running her fingers over her lips and pulling them back to reveal some of the blood that was still there, "he was paying for my goods. He didn't lose his land and title when he absconded to the sky. It was simply a matter of showing up to reclaim it all."

"But why would you even come here to begin with?"

Jacosa sighed. "The women in my family always knew to come here, from years and years and years ago. Our

212

magic is tied to it. It probably grew from this place, or this place grew from our magic. Who knows."

"*Who knows?* Why are you so cavalier about a kingdom of giants in the sky?"

Jacosa's voice grew sharp. "Enough! Is this really the time to be asking these questions?" She pointed a thumb behind her. "Elena's safe. That's why you came up here this time, isn't it? Now can we go?"

"Clarion," said Elena, who craned her neck and jutted an ear sideways. "She may have a point."

With a thunderous roar, the cloud kingdom shook again.

"FEE, FI, FO FUM!" echoed over the air.

"He's destroying Lorica's cottage by now, surely," said Jacosa, as if reporting on nothing more than a storm. "I wonder what the poor woman did to enjoy his ire. He'll have no women left, except Norma and... the two of you, I suppose. Unless you want to wind up a mad king's wife, I'd..." Jacosa's mouth kept moving, but Clarion couldn't hear what she was saying.

"What?" said Clarion, bending her ear closer.

Jacosa jumped, falling onto her back on Elena's palm. She pointed at her throat desperately, shaking her head. Clarion pulled back and Elena shrugged.

"I think the spell of aloe wore off," said Clarion, and as if to verify that, Jacosa's eyes squeezed tight as she placed her hands over her ears. Clarion remembered how disorienting being a small person without the stabilization of the plant was.

"The spell of what?" asked Elena.

Jacosa cringed again.

"There wasn't any left in that stash?" asked Clarion, bending down toward the old woman.

Her eyes were watering as she shook her head.

"Never mind," said Clarion, and she turned toward the door. Opening it slowly, she peeked her head out. "There's no sign of them. Not yet."

"The 'mad king'?" asked Elena, peeking over her shoulder toward the castle. "The one causing all that noise?"

"Yes, and death and destruction besides." Clarion grabbed Elena by the arm and dragged her out of the house. "Take Jacosa back down. Hopefully in that stash she grabbed she's got some tarragon..." She looked at the little witch until the woman opened one watery eye and then the other. "Tarragon?" Clarion pointed at her.

Jacosa cringed but nodded, putting a hand on her satchel.

Clarion let out a sigh of relief, accidentally knocking Jacosa flat on her back again and causing Jacosa's frizzy hair to blow even wilder.

Clarion cringed. "Sorry. But okay. She'll give you what you need to shrink when you reach the bottom. Hopefully before anyone sees you at that size, but even if not, it doesn't matter."

"I think it actually might matter quite a bit," said Elena, pinching her lips. "That would take quite a bit of explaining—"

"Who cares?" Clarion looked over her shoulder. "We're destroying the beanstalk. No one's going to come back here, and no one's going to follow you."

"Follow *me*?" asked Elena. "Don't you mean 'us'?"

Clarion gently lay a hand on Elena's cheek. "Just give me twenty minutes. If I don't come down—or if you hear a lot of noise—destroy the beanstalk."

"Clarion!"

But Clarion had already turned on her heel, determined to bring Mack and his parents with her or she knew she'd always regret it.

Chapter 26

For about a minute, Clarion almost felt like a savior. Like someone whom other people could rely on instead of someone who always relied on other people. Like someone who was strong and willful and full of courage instead of someone who shrank back and cried and clung to the past.

She knew it was ridiculous that she risked everything to save a man she'd started falling in love with, only to risk everything to save the woman she'd left for him, only to risk everything to save him again. It wasn't that her heart was fickle, but that there was room in there for both of them in some form. And that both of them kept needing her. She was so unused to being needed.

Her papa had made her feel needed. But even that was more like it was because he knew she *needed* to feel needed. At the end of the day, he'd liked nothing more than to watch her play his family's harp.

"No, little one. Like this." Her papa leaned beside the harp and picked up her chubby child fingers, pressing the tips of them to a different spot on the strings. He beamed. "Now try it."

She did. The sounds the instrument made were no

longer the sounds of dissonant notes without a purpose. They came together into the start of a song, something that made her heart want to sing.

It'd been too long since Clarion had played just for herself. Too long since she'd played at all. Even though she'd just played for the king at his ball... This place had changed so much since then. The change made the ball feel like so much longer ago than it was.

But she was surprised to find she thought fondly of playing the harp Mack had made, that the awkward construction had still felt like magic beneath her fingertips. Mack had said she could make magic out of any harp, but she was certain he'd made magic in his craftsmanship, too.

It still was hard to reconcile Wilkin with Mack. To put the pieces of the puzzle together and get a whole person.

But she knew if she went back without him, it'd be a puzzle she could never solve.

"I WILL NOT STOP! I WILL NOT LISTEN TO WHAT YOU HAVE TO SAY! YOU WILL SPEAK NO MORE!"

Clarion stopped, her mind brought swiftly to her surroundings. She looked around for something to hide behind, but there were no trees or bushes in this kingdom. The rubble from most of the houses was nearly gone, but she'd arrived at the ruins of the second-to-last standing cottage, and although it was close to the source of the voice, she'd just have to risk using it for cover.

"Your Grace." Mack's mother stood beside Mack, her arm across his abdomen to keep him a little behind her. "You *need* rest."

"I *need* nothing!" The king jumped once, causing Clarion to fall back. She scrambled back to her knees in order to peek through a small hole in the side of the home. He pointed behind him. "Lorica *tried to tell me* I needed rest. Now she's as flat as her house!"

Clarion couldn't believe how quickly the giant town was losing its residents—and that no one seemed poised to do anything other than cower and soothe this giant red-faced baby.

"All right. All right." Mack's mother took a step back. Mack had his palm out and there was a small prostrated figure on his hand. Whether it was his father or his father's body, Clarion wasn't sure. "My son and I will just get out of your way..."

"No!" The king thundered toward her and jabbed a finger at her chest. "You both promised me we could grow more people to live here—to serve me! Then that little witch appears, saying she's run out of magic, and she doesn't have enough plants to do that for me! Then the little harpist—the *one thing I wanted to stay little*—runs off as a giant with my witch!" He screamed and jumped in place again. "Fix this for me!"

"We will," said Mack's mother, her voice trembling. "So excuse us while we—"

The mad king whacked her across the chest, sending her backward into Mack. The both of them went flying several feet before crashing to the ground against a large piece of rubble. Clarion had to cover her mouth to keep from screaming.

The mad king looked on, breathing in and out as if each breath caused him pain he was determined to overcome.

Clarion measured the distance in her head between where she was and where Mack and his mother lay. She heard a groan from their direction, and she knew there was hope for them yet.

But the mad king kept staring at them. Clarion looked around and found a small piece of the cottage that fit in her grip. She had to stop herself from laughing—what madness would lead her to laugh now?—as she palmed it and figured it was probably bigger than her true size. She stood a little more, making sure her head didn't peek over the top, drew her arm back, and threw it. It hit a broken cupboard with a clunk.

The king turned his head to look for the sound. But he stood in place, and Clarion wondered if he even cared what had made it. Still, she placed one foot behind the other and poised her arms to prepare to sprint.

"Witch?" he said at last, clomping over toward the source.

Clarion moved the second the king turned his head. "Mack!" she hissed, as she drew up beside him.

Mack groaned, a streak of red flowing down his cheek. Clarion noticed at once how the hand that had been holding his father was beneath his mother's prone body. She reached a hand out toward his mother, pulling back when she noticed the way her neck bent. She couldn't be all right. The mad king had killed another one of his subjects.

Still, if Mack's father could be saved, despite everything the man had done... She had to try. Clarion took a deep breath, trying not to look at the woman who'd caused her such misery, and pulled her on her side to roll her off of Mack's arm.

She had to cover her mouth to keep herself from vomiting.

Mack groaned again, his head lolling. He blinked. "Clarion...?"

He tried to get up, but Clarion lay a hand on his shoulder. "Don't!" She almost pulled back when she looked down again at the mess that was once his small father in his hand, but she did her best to focus on Mack's face. "Your father... Your mother..."

Mack's eyes widened and he looked over at his hand, at his mother's form beside him, and screamed.

The king, many feet away searching the rubble for the tiny witch, stood and turned. "You live?" he roared. "You're nothing but a useless traitor! You turned your back on your people, on *my* people!" He started running toward them. "Be gone with you! With both of you!"

They were right in the path of his rampage. "Get up!" said Clarion, ignoring the mess in Mack's hand and sliding an arm around him. "We have to go!"

But Mack was heavy, too heavy for her to lift. He seemed to be trying to help her, trying to stand on his own, but his trembling legs kept sliding across the cloud and rubble and his head kept lolling to the side.

"Clarion!"

Clarion froze halfway through another attempt to get Mack standing, the muscles in her back and thighs straining. "Elena...?" She turned. "I told you—"

Elena's palm pressed hard against Clarion's open mouth. She felt something sweet hit her tongue as Elena's hand pressed harder and harder against her lips. She tried to speak, tried to fall back, but with Mack's weight already dragging her down, she could only step back and swallow.

Before she felt herself fall back against the cloud and rubble, there was a burning throughout her body as Mack, Elena, and the advancing king all grew a hundred times bigger around her.

She realized, once she settled into the folds of the giant dress she'd been wearing, that she was the one who had shrunk.

Chapter 27

The sounds were thunderous. Clarion felt as if her head might split. She cradled her hands over her ears and shut her eyes, not even prying them open to look as she felt herself lifted and carried away. The movement of whoever carried her was too overwhelming. She felt as if she might dissolve into pieces from all of the shaking.

Elena did this to me, she thought. *But why? Why would she stay behind, and why did she shrink me right then? When I needed all of my strength?*

She didn't even realize the movement had stopped, or that her cheek was pressed against a hard, warm surface, until she felt something soft placed over her and she heard Jacosa speak.

"Lucky for you, there was this dress on the mantel, where she dropped us off."

Clarion opened first one eye and then the other. She heard a whooshing sound like the air was being sucked out from all around her and then realized it was the sound of her own ragged breaths.

She felt for the soft thing that had been placed atop her and realized it was the makeshift dress Mack's mother had made for her for the giant ball, the one she'd left behind. It should have been somewhere on the ballroom floor, but she supposed a servant might have found it and placed it beside the harp after the party, remembering she had been wearing it earlier. She sat up, almost keeling back over thanks to the worsening of her headache, but pulled the dress over her head anyway. The torn seam meant that it stayed secured over only one of her shoulders, the other tiny sleeve useless.

"I should probably get us both some aloe. We'll need it until we get out of here." Jacosa bent over that basket with the "Eat Me" note, frowning. "It's all gone?"

"We hid it," croaked Clarion, cradling her head in her hands. "So the king would think we'd run out of it. Under the pin cushion chair by the harp." She closed her eyes while she tried to ease her breaths, not opening them again until Jacosa shoved a handful of aloe under her nose.

She grabbed the entire bunch and ate it.

"Good to see your appetite isn't affected." Jacosa sniffed. "Not that aloe is generally something people look forward to eating."

Clarion swallowed and glared up at her before looking around the ballroom, searching for a sign of Elena, Mack, or the king. "What happened? Why didn't you and Elena go back? Why did she..." She gestured to her small body. "Why did she shrink me?"

Jacosa rolled her eyes and let out a breath that made her frizzy hair fly up. Her hair had grown less wild since she'd first drunk the blood. "She was certain you couldn't handle whatever it was you attempted to handle alone. She refused to go back without you. Sound familiar?" She shrugged. "I tried to stop her, although it's quite difficult convincing a giant of anything when your voice is no more than a mouse's squeak, let me tell you, but she muttered something about 'keeping you safe' in that booming, echoing voice and once she shrank you, she scooped you up and bolted for this place."

Tucking her legs beneath her, Clarion placed a palm on the warm tile. The fire was still burning in the fireplace.

"But you'd know all about just scooping up unsuspecting small people, wouldn't you?" Jacosa scoffed and then looked around. "But at least I got to come back here one more time. Where is that goblet?"

Clarion stared out toward the doorway, waiting for Elena or Mack—anyone—to come in. "But where did she go?"

"She figured you wouldn't leave unless she tried to save that boy, so that's what she did. Where *is* that confounded thing? It had to have dropped when you grabbed me..."

"Hand over the tarragon," said Clarion.

Jacosa was searching all over the mantel, weaving her way between unlit candlesticks and a platter. "What tarragon?"

"The tarragon you made me think you had in that satchel..."

"Oh, is that what you asked? If I really had extras, do you think I'd still be small myself? I found exactly two stalks of it in my stash at Norma's, and they were even giant-sized. Perfect for shrinking anyone who wanted to go back to the world below. I'm sure you figured out that Elena took one of them to use on you—grabbed my pouch right out from under me and pulled out the piece. It was all I could to do keep the other from her along with the rest of my herbs. Best save the last one for one of your friends. Only one can take it, though, naturally." She peeked out from around some of the décor on the mantel. "Do you remember if the goblet spilled when you grabbed me?"

Clarion felt so helpless. So small. So powerless. It was like everyone was right all along, that she wasn't a savior. She was just someone to be saved. Someone to be told what to do. Someone to be quiet and meek in the corner, losing herself to her dark thoughts.

"*You play wonderfully,*" *said her papa, beaming. "It*

was like you were born to run your fingers across those strings." He bent forward to kiss her forehead. *"You're better than I ever was. This is your gift to give, Clarion. This is what you were meant to give others."*

Clarion felt a pang of guilt at the thought. She'd rarely truly played for others, even when others had asked her to.

She played for that feeling she got from the music and the movement of her fingers across the strings. This time, maybe it'd be enough to distract the king, to save Mack and Elena—if it wasn't too late.

A roar reverberated throughout the ballroom, and Clarion realized the sound was close. Close enough to echo off the inside of the castle. She bolted up, running toward the pin cushion and the fallen harp Mack had made her. She grabbed the harp and heaved it upright, straining against her weak muscles.

"There it is!" said Jacosa from the edge of the mantel, pointing toward the ground beneath them, but Clarion ignored her as she put her hands on the large funnel and dragged it toward her harp. "It's even sitting upright. There might be some left! Now that I can't get any more from him in any case..."

Clarion dropped the funnel and let out a breath. Jacosa dashed past her toward the staircase that decorated the side of the mantel.

"FEE, FI, FO FUM!"

It was the king. Clarion tried not to think of what it would mean, of how likely it was that either Mack or Elena was gone now—or even both.

She just played.

"They told me you had left for the land above. I told them you would never leave me, my love. But when I looked for you, you had gone. I couldn't give up; I searched all over 'til dawn. Were you stolen away by the kings of old? Or did I know ye not, so I've been told? I'd like to have faith that I knew ye well. That you love me still, and in the land above

you dwell."

Clarion looked up for the first time since her song began and saw the sharp nose, the pale-colored eyes of Wilkin gazing down at her—of Mack.

CHAPTER 28

"**M**ack!" Clarion's fingers stopped.

"Keep playing!" said Mack, his breathing haggard. He sounded so like the king had, so... frightening.

Clarion stood, knocking the pin cushion over, revealing that there was no aloe left after all. Jacosa had given her the last of it or had taken it all. "Where's Elena?" she asked. "The king?"

Mack shook his gigantic head. "She led him away from the castle. I needed to make sure you were okay. I didn't know what she'd done to you—"

"And you abandoned her to him?"

Mack's face paled. "I was worried she'd done something to you."

"Elena wouldn't have hurt me!" Clarion clenched her fists at her sides, pushing down thoughts of the unintentional hurt Elena had done her by not trusting her to save herself. "She needs your help! You're the only one large enough to do anything!" She felt bad even as she said it—she couldn't help but notice the trickle of blood running down his cheek still—but it was true. She felt so helpless.

Mack's expression grew stern. "I wanted to check on

you!"

Clarion pointed to her chest with both hands, her arms trembling, tears threatening to spill down her cheeks. "*I'm* fine! I can't believe you'd leave Elena to that madman alone!"

"She had a decent lead," he spat, reaching a hand toward her. "Now let's go. We can *both* go after her. We can both leave this wretched kingdom."

Clarion stepped back, out of reach, not sure at first why. She stared up at Mack, warped though he appeared to her, no longer either Mack or Wilkin, but something more. His face was reddening and his lips were trembling. "LET'S GO!"

"What's wrong with you?" Clarion stumbled backward, tripping over the length of her loose dress.

"What's wrong with me? Fee!" Mack's shoulders tightened as he fought to restrain himself, and he began pacing back and forth before the hearth, waving his hands about. "Fi! I've lost everything! Fo! That madman has killed my mother and father both—but neither would have been in danger if it hadn't been for that witch—"

He stopped abruptly, looking down at his feet.

Clarion scrambled to the edge of the mantel. "What's wrong? What have you done?"

Mack lifted one of his giant bare feet as the little gold-laying chicken squawked and flapped its wings, disappearing under the table. Clarion staggered back at the sight of the bloody and broken body that was squished tight against his sole.

The dead body of Jacosa.

Clarion clutched the golden goblet in both hands against

her chest as her thigh bumped the harp beside her on Mack's outstretched hand.

She'd insisted on taking his harp along with them—the one good memory she had of this place.

He'd insisted on taking Jacosa's golden cup, red-stained and practically empty though it was. He'd tried to peel her pouch from her abdomen but had nearly retched and thrown Jacosa—pouch and all—into the dying fire.

Clarion hadn't been pleased with that reaction at all, not just for what disservice it did to a woman who was once sort of a friend, but because it burned the very last of whatever magic plants there were with her. Including the last piece of Jacosa's tarragon. She'd never felt so hopeless, so helpless before.

"I killed him," Mack had said, staring down at the fire and resting both hands on the mantel after throwing the witch's body. "Father's servant. Back at your mayor's house. He didn't fall when the earth shook. I got so mad at what he'd done—what they'd all done—that I didn't save him. I let go. I... pushed him."

Clarion hadn't known what to say to that. She'd already asked him to take the harp with them, but now she was certain it would bring no happy memories, not now that the man she'd fallen in love with had truly gone mad.

Like the mad king. Was he ever a saner man—albeit a giant one? What was it about this place?

But he had the last of the tarragon, surely—the blades he'd brought with him when they'd both first grown. She needed it for Elena. She needed it... even for him. They could sort out the madness later. He probably didn't even mean... He couldn't have pushed the man on purpose, and it truly was neither here nor there at this very moment.

As they neared where the beanstalk grew, a woman's scream and a growl tore through the skies.

"Elena!" Clarion exclaimed.

She felt Mack's pace slow, and she worried it was because she had dared to show concern for a person he knew was in a way his rival for her heart.

But just as Mack drew to a complete stop, a hole tore open in his mother's cottage and Elena went flying through it right in front of them.

"Elena!" Clarion screamed again as Mack ran over to her. She was bleeding from her arm and abdomen, and the loose dress was ripped and practically falling off one of her shoulders. But she was breathing, hard, her eyes narrowed with purpose.

Clarion looked to the hole at the sound of a man's roar, as the clouds shook beneath them and the mad king knocked down the last cottage in his kingdom, punching it brick by brick by brick into rubble.

"Elena, you're all right!" said Clarion, grateful there was something else that had at last earned the king's attention.

"We should go." Mack's lips drew into a thin line and he tugged on Elena's arm—the bleeding one.

Elena gasped in pain and Mack dropped it. She glared at him but then looked down in his hand. "You brought her here? I put her in the castle to keep her safe!"

"She wasn't going to be *safe* there," spat Mack. "Not until he's dead."

"Elena, you shouldn't have done that to me," said Clarion, but no one heeded her. "I would have been more help as a giant."

"What do you think I was trying to do?" Elena stood up quickly, grunting and clutching her abdomen as she did. "We could have gotten her *after* I killed him!"

Clarion's jaw dropped. Elena had been here all of half an hour, if that, and already she'd turned bloodthirsty. It had to be this place. The madness clung to the air, rose from the clouds, in this place.

"Better to go now, while we can, rather than risk it." Mack stood, peering his nose down at Elena, and Clarion tumbled over on his hand. He nodded toward the rampaging king. "Besides, you obviously weren't having much luck."

Elena jutted a finger toward his chest. "Better than *you*, who ran off at the first opportunity! The only reason I haven't been flattened yet is because that perverted madman said I'd have to be his wife now! I couldn't get him to stop asking until he finally sent me flying through the wall." Her eyes flicked down toward Clarion, and Clarion opened her mouth to speak, but Elena wasn't interested in what she had to say. "And we can't go! You've forgotten Jacosa!"

"The witch is dead," said Mack. He grabbed Elena by her bleeding arm again. "So let's go!"

"Don't touch me!" Elena tore her arm away, even though the effort caused her to wince and groan. "How did Jacosa die? How do I know *you* didn't do it?"

"Why would I have killed her?" demanded Mack. "On purpose?"

"So you *did* kill her!" cried Elena.

"Stop it!" said Clarion, scrambling to her feet on Mack's palm. "The both of you—just stop it! Now's not the time!" She needed to know, needed to be sure before they left. "Mack, do you still have those strands of tarragon?"

Mack's face went pale. He patted his chest pocket with his free hand and stuck his fingers into the fabric but came up empty. "I gave them to Mother. She never took one. We were going to wait until we got down below—"

Elena ground her teeth. "Are *you telling me* there's no way to get smaller again? And you killed the one person who might have been able to help us?"

Mack's hand shot up, as if coming up with an idea. "They might still be on Mother." He licked his lips. "We'll have to go back—"

Clarion thought of the way the rubble sank into the clouds, the way the waste disappeared into fog beneath their feet. "We have to hurry!"

"What about—" began Elena, but the king jumped up and cut her off with a mighty roar.

"Elena, toward the stalk!" Clarion screamed, hoping her voice could be heard over the cries of "fee, fi, fo, fum" coming from the madman's mouth. "The hole there! Lead him to it!"

"You *want* the king to fall down to your town?" asked Mack. His foot lifted and he seemed stretched in two directions, one toward the king chasing Elena in the direction of the beanstalk, the other toward where his mother's body lay nearer the castle.

"I don't know," said Clarion. "Mack, please. Save her!" She looked up at him. "For me!"

Mack took a deep breath and bent down, dumping the harp onto the cloud ground and sending Clarion lightly stumbling off his fingers. "All right," he said. "For you."

He ran after the king, his own mouth roaring, "FEE, FI, FO FUM! I smell the blood of my one true foe!"

The king had pounced on Elena and Elena struggled to fight him off with her one good arm, screaming and moaning and roaring in her own anger. Mack charged at them, winding his fist back and punching the king right off of Elena, sending him flying.

The king crumpled, his legs and arms bent forward like sticks, his back hitting the top of the beanstalk and his eyes rolling back into his head.

A great thunderous movement shook the clouds beneath Clarion's feet as a spray of red flew off in all directions. The king bled at the impact—his neck had bent as he hit the stalk at just the right angle—his blood dotting the white clouds around where the beanstalk stood. The spray reached as far back as Clarion—covering her in blood, filling the golden cup still in her hands halfway up.

The ruins of Mack's cottage started shaking, the pieces vanishing into the cloud beneath—faster than before, like it was someone else besides the king determining what was unwanted here, and his anger blazed hotter.

Instinct told Clarion to turn around, to look back at the castle, and she noticed it at once—the wreckage of the other cottage was gone. There was nothing between where she stood and the great big castle, not a single thing to dot the white clouds as far as she could see.

Which meant that Mack's mother's body had vanished, along with those last few strands of tarragon.

Neither Mack nor Elena could return to the world below. Not like that. Not so big.

A great crack echoed and the beanstalk again drew Clarion's attention. The king's body was already sinking into the ground, as if the magic holding the kingdom together knew immediately what was not wanted, what was no longer a part of this world above.

And the beanstalk itself was shifting, falling down, vanishing entirely out of sight.

The sound went on for ages, the echo even longer. Only when it dissolved to quiet did anyone move. Elena dragged herself over to the hole where the beanstalk top had been. "It's gone," she said, panting. "Even the hole is closing."

"We'll have to jump!" said Mack, shaking his bloodied fist. Clarion had to close her eyes, shrinking back as a drop or two headed toward her. "We'll have to run and get the tarragon and Clarion and—"

He stopped, at last noticing what she held.

The golden goblet shook in her hands. *The blood of an enemy grants magical power. If I can take up Jacosa's mantle, imbibe her magic, then maybe I can grow more magical tarragon somehow. Even if it's on this strange cloud ground. It has to be possible.*

"Clarion?" said Mack, but Clarion just stared at the ripple of the blood in her cup.

"What's she—" began Elena.

But Clarion didn't hear her. Leaning against the harp behind her, she drew the cup to her lips and wished, *Please give me the power to save the both of them.*

"NO!"

"Clarion!"

The oozing warmth down her throat, the sharp tang on her tongue. But she fought her instinct to spit it back up, she took a deep breath, and she swallowed.

Epilogue

larion had a difficult time keeping track of how many days had passed.

It was easier to pick up on feelings. Snatches of conversations. Glimpses of what went on around her.

"What is this slop?" A bowl clattered against a table. "You call this food, woman? Did you ever learn to cook?"

"No, I *did not*. I had people to do that for me. Starve, for all I care! What do I care if you eat anything? I'd be better off if you didn't! Do you know how hard it is to grow *anything* up here? Do you even care if we starve?"

Clarion knew those voices. Part of her would always flower at the sound of those voices, and she'd remember: Mack and Elena. She'd done something, wished something... For both of them. But then part of her would slowly come to understand what they said and how they said it, and her cognizance would wither again.

A deafening pound, pound, pound and Clarion tried to see—see through her golden eyes that only sometimes felt real—Mack roaring and waving his arms around. "I'd be better off without *you*! How could you lose that hen?"

"*I* lost it?" Elena appeared beside the hearth and whapped Mack with a giant wooden spoon. "I wasn't the animal's keeper! Besides, what good did that hen do you? Where are you going to spend golden eggs?"

"Fi!" Mack waved a hand dismissively and sat down in his chair near the fire. Clarion didn't remember when it'd happened, but the ballroom had become filthy and cluttered. She remembered there were no more guests to be had here. That hurt something in her. She didn't know, though, if she still had a heart.

Elena snorted and left the room. Clarion tried to watch her leave, but she couldn't turn, and besides, it was often hard to see out of her golden eyes.

"Play," said Mack, after a while.

That word she always knew. That word, she always awoke for.

She didn't need to strum fingers across strings anymore. It was enough to think the melody, to feel the strings behind her as if a part of her body.

She sang, but the words didn't come out like words anymore. They were pure melody, pure song.

She wasn't even sure what song it was, or if she made it up herself entirely. She just sang. She just moved the strings. And she kept singing even when she heard the snores of Mack breathing from behind her.

She was saving him right then, she knew it. And it worked on Elena, too, when they could stand to be in the same room together. Her song calmed them. Soothed them. Saved them. Part of her knew that wasn't quite what she wanted, but most of her felt she was meant to do this. That it was her gift to give. That it was what allowed her to offer something to them, instead of always being given something by them.

She kept singing and playing until she noticed the boy, crouched even as he walked, appear at the top of the mantel from the staircase.

Her voice softened somewhat, although she kept singing. She'd seen the boy before. He looked like Jackin, but the closer he got, the more she thought she was looking at Krea. But either was impossible. It was a young boy.

And she'd seen him before.

Her golden mind was slower to remember, slower to think. But it wasn't that she recognized both Jackin and Krea in the boy. She'd seen *this boy* in *this place* before.

He'd been dressed more ragged then. With patches all over his pants and shirt and dirt smudged all over his face.

Now he dressed more cleanly. Even finely, although he was missing a cap.

He took Jacosa's gold-laying hen with him.

That was why Mack was upset. The little squawking creature was gone, and this tiny boy—this not-giant boy— had taken it with him.

There were more beans out there somewhere. More beans that had the magic to grow a beanstalk to the kingdom in the clouds.

The boy approached steadily, one hand out in front of him, his knees bent, as if standing straight would draw too much attention. The sounds of Mack's snoring began to drown out her voice.

She didn't have need for air anymore for her lungs, but she needed air for her song.

The boy held one finger to his lips and covered her mouth with the other.

No! she wanted to scream. The sound came out like a note, but even that was muffled beneath the boy's hand.

He grabbed her by the front of her instrument and lifted her up.

I have to stay! she thought. It came out as a frenzied little melody.

The boy tucked her beneath his arm, grunted, and walked quickly to the staircase. He shifted his fingers to keep covering her mouth, but she kept crying out in one note after another, and he struggled as they descended the stairs to keep her quiet and not drop her.

When they reached the bottom, she finally

235

summoned enough strength from her golden heart to scream a song as loud as she could.

The snoring stopped.

"FEE, FI, FO FUM! I SMELL THE BLOOD OF AN ENGLISHMAN!"

About the Author

my McNulty is a freelance writer and editor from Wisconsin with an honors degree in English. She was first published in a national scholarly journal (*The Concord Review*) while in high school and currently writes professionally about everything from business marketing to anime. In her down time, you can find her crafting stories with dastardly villains and antiheroes set in fantastical medieval settings.

Find Amy at amymcnulty.com and on social media as McNultyAmy (Twitter), Amy McNulty, Author (Facebook), McNulty.Amy (Instagram), AuthorAmyMc (Pinterest), AmyMcNulty (Wattpad), and AuthorAmyMcNulty (Tumblr). Sign up for her monthly newsletter to receive news and exclusive information about her current and upcoming projects. Please visit her Goodreads and Amazon author pages and leave a review!

Prologue from Nobody's Goddess
The Never Veil, Book One

WHEN I HAD REAL FRIENDS, I was the long-lost queen of the elves.

A warrior queen who hitched up her skirt and wielded a blade. Who held her retainers in thrall. Until they left me for their goddesses.

Love. A curse that snatches friends away.

One day, when only two of my retainers remained, the old crone who lived on the northern outskirts of the village was our prey. It was twenty points if you spotted her. Fifty points if you got her to look at you. A hundred points if she started screaming at you.

You won for life if you got close enough to touch her.

"Noll, please don't do this," whispered Jurij from behind the wooden kitten mask covering his face. Really, his mother still put him in kitten masks, even though eleven was too old for a boy to be wearing kittens and bunnies. Especially ones that looked likely to get eaten for breakfast by as much as a weasel.

"Shut up, I want to see this!" cried Darwyn. Never a kitten, Darwyn always wore a wolf mask. Yet behind the nasty tooth-bearing wolf grin—one of my father's better masks—he was very much a fraidycat.

Darwyn shoved Jurij aside so he could crouch behind the bush that was our threadbare cover. Jurij nearly toppled over, but I caught him and set him gently upright. Sometimes I didn't know if Jurij realized who was supposed to be serving whom. Queens shouldn't have to keep retainers from falling.

"Quiet, both of you." I scanned the horizon. Nothing. All was still against the northern mountains save for the old crone's musty shack with its weakly smoking chimney. The edges of my skirt had grazed the dusty road behind us, and I hitched it up some more so my mother wouldn't notice later. If she didn't want me to get the blasted thing dirty, she should have let me wear Jurij's trousers, like I had been that morning. That got me a rap on the back of the head with a wooden spoon, a common occurrence when I was queen. It made me look too much like a boy, she scolded, and that would cause a panic.

"Are you going or not?" Darwyn was not one for patience.

"If you're so eager, why don't *you* go?" I snapped back.

Darwyn shook his wolf-head. "Oh, no, not me."

I grinned. "That's because you're scared."

Darwyn's muffled voice grew louder. He stood beside me and puffed out his chest. "I am not! *I've* been in the commune."

I poked toward his chest with Elgar, my trusty elf-blade. "Liar! You have not."

Darwyn jumped back, evading my blow. "I have too! My uncle lives there!" He swatted his hand at Elgar. "Get that stick away from me."

"It's not a stick!" Darwyn never believed me when I said that Elgar was the blade of a warrior. It just happened to resemble a tree branch.

Jurij's quiet voice entered the fray. "Your uncle lives there? That's awful." I was afraid he might cry and the tears would get caught up in the black material that covered his eyes. I didn't want him to drown behind the wooden kitty face. He'd vanish into thin air like everyone else did when they died, and then we'd be staring down at Jurij's clothes and the little kitten mask on the ground, and I was afraid I wouldn't be able to stop myself from giggling. Some death for a warrior.

Darwyn shrugged and ran a hand over his elbow. "He moved in there before I was born. I think a weaver lady was his goddess. It's not so strange. Didn't your aunt send her man there, Jurij?"

Jurij was sniffling. *Sniffling.* He tried to rub at his nose, but every time he moved the back of his hand up to his face, it just clunked against the button that represented the kitten's nose.

I sighed and patted Jurij on the back. "A queen's retainer must never cry, Jurij."

Darwyn laughed. "Are you still playing that? You're no queen, Noll!"

I stopped patting Jurij and balled my hands into fists. "Be quiet, Darwyn! You used to play it, too!"

Darwyn put two fingers over his wolf-mask mouth, a gesture we had long ago decided would stand for the boys sticking out their tongues. Although Darwyn was the only one who ever did it as of late. "Like I'd want to do what some *girl* tells me! Girls aren't even blessed by love!"

"Of course they are!" It was my turn to put the two fingers over my mouth. I had a tongue, but a traitorous retainer like Darwyn wasn't worthy of the effort it took to

240

stick it out. "Just wait until you find your goddess, and then we'll see! If she turns out to be me, I'll make sure you rot away in the commune with the rest of the unloved men."

Darwyn lunged forward and tackled me. My head dragged against the bush before it hit the ground, but it still hurt; I could feel the swelling underneath the tangled knots in my hair. Elgar snapped as I tried to get a grip on my attacker. I kicked and shoved him, and for a moment, I won the upper hand and rolled on top of him, almost punching him in the face. Remembering the mask, I settled for giving him a good smack in the side, but then he kicked upward and caught me in the chest, sending me backward.

"Stop!" pleaded Jurij. He was standing between us now, the little timid kitten watching first one friend and then the other, like we were a dangling string in motion.

"Stay out of this!" Darwyn jumped to his feet and pointed at me. "She thinks she's so high and mighty, and she's not even someone's goddess yet!"

"I'm only twelve, idiot! How many goddesses are younger than thirteen?" A few, but not many. I scrambled to my feet and sent my tongue out at him. It felt good knowing he couldn't do the same to me, after all. My head ached. I didn't want him to see the tears forming in my eyes, though, so I ground my teeth once I drew my tongue inward.

"Yeah, well, it'll be horrible for whoever finds the goddess in you!" Darwyn made to lunge at me again, but this time Jurij shoved both his hands at Darwyn's chest to stop him.

"Just stop," commanded Jurij. Finally. That was a good retainer.

My eyes wandered to the old crone's cottage. No sign of her. How could she fail to hear the epic struggle outside her door? Maybe she wasn't real. Maybe just seeing her was worth twenty points after all.

"Get out of my way, you baby!" shouted Darwyn. "So what happens if I pull off your mask when your *queen* is looking, huh? Will you die?"

His greedy fingers reached toward Jurij's wooden animal face. Even from behind, I could see the mask tip dangerously to one side, the strap holding it tightly against Jurij's dark curls shifting. The strap broke free, flying up over his head.

My mouth opened to scream. My hands reached up to cover my eyes. My eyelids strained to close, but it felt as if the moment had slowed and I could never save him in time. Such simple things. Close your eyes. Cover your eyes. Scream.

"DO NOT FOOL WITH SUCH THINGS, CHILD!"

A dark, dirty shawl went flying onto the bush that we had ruined during our fight.

I came back to life. My head and Darwyn's wolf mask spun toward the source of the sound. As my head turned, I saw—even though I knew better than to look—Jurij crumple to the ground, clinging both arms across his face desperately because his life depended on it.

"Your eyes better be closed, girl!" The old crone bellowed. Her own eyes were squeezed together.

I jumped and shut my eyes tightly.

"Hold that shawl tightly over your face, boy, until you can wear your mask properly!" screamed the old crone. "Off with you both, boys! Now! Off with you!"

I heard Jurij and Darwyn scrambling, the rustle of the bush and the stomps of their boots as they fled, panting. I thought I heard a scream—not from Jurij, but from Darwyn. He was the real fraidycat. An old crone was no match for the elf queen's retainers. But the queen herself was far braver. So I told myself over and over in my head.

When the last of their footsteps faded away, and I was sure that Jurij was safe from my stare, I looked.

Eyes. Huge, bulbous, dark brown eyes. Staring directly into mine.

The crone's face was so close I could smell the shriveled decay from her mouth. She grabbed me by the shoulders, shaking me. "What were you thinking? You held that boy's life in your hands! Yet you stood there like a fool, just starin' as his mask came off."

My heart beat faster, and I gasped for more air, but I wanted to avoid inhaling her stench. "I'm sorry, Ingrith," I mumbled. I thought if I used her real name, if I let her lecture me like all the other adults, it would help me break free from her grasp. I twisted and pulled, but I couldn't bring myself to touch her. I had this notion that if I touched her, my fingers would decay.

"Sorry is just a word. Sorry changes nothing."

"Let me go." I could still feel her dirty nails on my skin.

"You watch yourself, girl."

"Let me go!"

The crone's lips grew tight and puckered. Her fingers relaxed ever so slightly. "You children don't realize. The lord is watching. Always watching—"

I knew what she was going to say, the words so familiar to me that I knew them as well as if they were my own. "And he will not abide villagers who forget the first goddess's teachings." The sentence seemed to loosen the crone's fingers. She opened her mouth to speak, but I broke free and ran.

My eyes fell to the grass below my feet as I cut across the fields to get away from the monster. On the borders of the eastern woods was a lone cottage, home of Gideon the woodcarver, a warm and comfortable place so much fuller of life than the shack I left behind me. When I was near the woods, I could look up freely since the trees blocked the eastern mountains from view. But until I got closer ...

"Noll! Wait up!"

My eyes snapped upward on instinct. I saw the upper boughs of the trees and almost screamed, my gaze falling back to the grass beneath my feet. I stopped running and let the gentle rustlings of footsteps behind me catch up.

"Jurij, please." I sighed and turned around to face him, my eyes still on the grass and the pair of small dark boots that covered his feet. Somehow he managed to step delicately through the grass, not disturbing a single one of the lilies that covered the hilltops. "Don't scare me like that. I almost looked at the castle."

The toe of Jurij's boot dug a little into the dirt. "Oh. Sorry."

"Is your mask on?"

The boot stopped moving, and the tip of a black shawl dropped into my view. "Oh. Yeah."

I shook my head and raised my eyes. There was no need to fear looking up to the west. In the distance, the mountains that encircled our village soared far beyond the western fields of crops. I liked the mountains. From the north, the south, and the west, they embraced our village with their jagged peaks. In the south, they watched over our fields of livestock. In the north, they towered above a quarry for copper and stone. And in the east, they led home and to the woods. But no girl or woman could ever look up when facing the east. Like the faces of men and boys before their Returnings, just a glance at the castle that lay beyond the woods against the eastern mountains spelled doom. The earth would shake and threaten to consume whoever broke the commandment not to look.

It made walking home a bit of a pain, to say the least.

"Tell me something important like that before you sneak up on me."

Jurij's kitten mask was once again tight against his face, if askew. The strap was a bit tangled in his dark curls and the pointed tip of one of his ears. "Right. Sorry."

He held out the broken pieces of Elgar wrapped in the dirty black shawl. He seemed very retainer-like. I liked that. "I went to give this back to the—the lady. She wasn't there, but you left Elgar."

I snatched the pieces from Jurij's hands. "You went back to the shack? What were you going to say? 'Sorry we were spying on you pretending you were a monster, thanks for the dirty old rag?'"

"No." Jurij crumpled up the shawl and tucked it under his belt. A long trail of black cloth tumbled out immediately, making Jurij look like he had on half a skirt.

I laughed. "Where's Darwyn?"

"Home."

Of course. I found out later that Darwyn had whined straight to his mother that "nasty old Noll" almost knocked *his* mask off. It was a great way to get noticed when you had countless brothers and a smitten mother and father standing between you and any form of attention. But it didn't have the intended effect on me. I was used to lectures, and besides, there was something more important bothering me by then.

I picked up my feet to carry me back home.

Jurij skipped forward to join me. One of his boots stumbled as we left the grasses behind and hit the dirt path. "What happened with you and the crone?"

I gripped the pieces of Elgar tighter in my fist. "Nothing." I stopped, relieved that we'd finally gotten close enough to the woods that I could face forward. I put an arm on Jurij's shoulder to stop him. "But I touched her." Or she touched me. "That means I win forever."

The kitten face cocked a little sideways. "You always win."

"Of course. I'm the queen." I tucked the broken pieces of Elgar into my apron sash. Elgar was more of a title, bestowed on an endless number of worthy sticks, but in those days I wouldn't have admitted that to Jurij. "Come on. I'll give you a head start. Race you to the cavern!"

"The cavern? But it's—"

"Too late! Your head start's over!" I kicked my feet up and ran as if that was all my legs knew how to do. The cool breeze slapping across my face felt lovely as it flew inside my nostrils and mouth. I rushed past my home, not bothering to look inside the open door.

"Stop! Stop! Noll, you stop this instant!"

The words were something that could easily come out of a mother's mouth, but Mother had a little more patience than that. And her voice didn't sound like a fragile little bird chirping at the sun's rising. "Noll!"

I was just an arm's length from the start of the trees, but I stopped, clutching the sharp pain that kicked me in the side.

"Oh dear!" Elfriede walked out of our house, the needle and thread she was no doubt using to embroider some useless pattern on one of the aprons still pinched between two fingers. My sister was a little less than a year older than me, but to my parents' delight (and disappointment with me), she was a hundred times more responsible.

"Boy, your mask!" Elfriede never did learn any of my friends' names. Not that I could tell her Roslyn from her

Marden, either. One giggling, delicate bird was much like another.

She walked up to Jurij, who had just caught up behind me. She covered her eyes with her needle-less hand, but I could see her peeking between her fingers. I didn't think that would actually protect him if the situation were as dire as she seemed to think.

"It's crooked." Elfriede's voice was hoarse, almost trembling. I rolled my eyes.

Jurij patted his head with both hands until he found the bit of the strap stuck on one of his ears. He pulled it down and twisted the mask until it lined up evenly.

I could hear Elfriede's sigh of relief from where I was standing. She let her fingers fall from her face. "Thank the goddess." She considered Jurij for a moment. "There's a little tear in your strap."

Without asking, she closed the distance between them and began sewing the small tear even as the mask sat on his head. From how tall she stood above him, she might have been ten years older instead of only two.

I walked back toward them, letting my hands fall. "Don't you think that's a little stupid? What if the mask slips while you're doing that?"

Elfriede's cheeks darkened and she yanked the needle up, pulling her instrument free of the thread and tucking the extra bit into the mask strap. She stood back and glared at me. "Don't you talk to me about being stupid, Noll. All that running isn't safe when you're with boys. Look how his mask was moving."

His mask had moved for even more dangerous reasons than a little run, but I knew better than to tell tattletale Elfriede that. "How would you know what's safe when you're with boys? You're already thirteen, and no one has found the goddess in you!" Darwyn's taunt was worth reusing, especially since I knew my sister would be more upset about it than I ever was.

Elfriede bit her lip. "Go ahead and kill your friends, then, for all I care!" The bird wasn't so beautiful and fragile where I was concerned.

She retreated into the house and slammed the door behind her. I wrapped my hand around Jurij's arm, pulling him eastward. "Come on. Let's go. There're bound to be more monsters in the cavern."

Jurij didn't give beneath my pull. He wouldn't move. "Jurij?"

I knew right then, somewhere in my mind, what had happened. But I was twelve. And Jurij was my last real friend. I knew he'd leave me one day like the others, but on some level, I didn't really believe it yet.

Jurij stood stock still, even as I wrenched my arm harder and harder to get him to move.

"Oh for—*Jurij!*" I yelled, dropping my hands from his arm in frustration. "Ugh. I wish I was your goddess just so I could get you to obey me. Even if that means I'd have to put up with all that—*yuck*—smooching." I shivered at the thought.

At last Jurij moved, if only to lift his other arm, to run his fingers across the strap that Elfriede had mended. She was gone from my sight, but Jurij would never see another.

It struck them all. Sometime around Jurij's age, the boys' voices cracked, shifting from high to deep and back again in a matter of a few words. They went from little wooden-faced animals always shorter than you to young men on their way to towering over you. And one day, at one moment, at some age, earlier for some and later for others, they looked at a girl they'd probably seen thousands of times before and simply ceased to be. At least, they weren't who I knew them to be ever again.

And as with so many of my friends before Jurij, in that moment all other girls ceased to matter. I was nothing to him now, an afterthought, a shadow, a memory.

No.

Not him.

My dearest, my most special friend of all, now doomed to live or die by the choice of the fragile little bird who'd stopped to mend his strap.

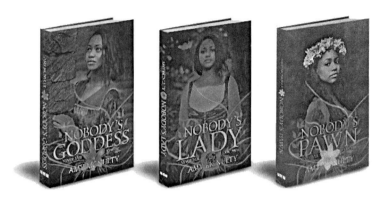

Nobody's Goddess, winner of The Romance Reviews Summer 2016 Readers' Choice Award for Young Adult Romance:

In a village of masked men, each man is compelled to love only one woman and to follow the commands of his "goddess" without question. A woman may reject the only man who will love her if she pleases, but she will be alone forever. A man must stay masked until his goddess returns his love—and if she can't or won't, he remains masked forever.

Seventeen-year-old Noll's childhood friends have paired off and her closest companion, Jurij, found his goddess in Noll's own sister. Desperate to find a way to break this ancient spell, Noll instead discovers why no man has ever chosen her. She is in fact the goddess of the mysterious lord of the village, a man who refuses to let Noll have her right as a woman to spurn him.

Thus begins a dangerous game between the choice of woman and the magic of man. The stakes are no less than freedom and happiness, life and death—and neither Noll nor the veiled lord is willing to lose.

All three books in The Never Veil Series are out now!

FALL FAR FROM THE TREE PREVIEW

I'D LIVED ONLY FIVE WINTERS the first time I saw an infant drowned.

Father's hand lay lightly on my shoulder as the horse jostled us slightly, shaking her head and whipping the tips of her silky black mane across my eyes. Father noticed the instinct that took over, the mere moment my eyelids closed despite how hard I'd fought to keep them open. "Watch, Rohesia. Burn the moment into your mind."

The shrieking woman held aloft by two soldiers kicked her legs, sending her skirt upward. I noticed the mud that collected along the hem, the strands of straw-colored hair that escaped her kerchief and swung wildly across her mouth. The hair billowed with each shriek like curtains in the breeze, the skirt a gale that tore through a field of wheat, the woman the only source of movement beyond the scuffing hooves of the horses beside me.

"The child, Rohesia. Not the mother."

The soldier by the river tossed the tattered cloth that had wrapped the baby to the ground and held the crying infant as far out in front of him as his stocky arms would allow. One gauntlet supported the baby's head and neck, the other gripped the child's body loosely, and I saw one impossibly small leg kick upward vainly.

The horse tossed her mane again, whipping the black hair across my eyes, but I leaned sideways and turned my head away so I wouldn't close them. Father let go of the reins with one hand and ran his fingers through the horse's mane gently, his voice almost a whisper. "Settle down, Sunset." He placed the same fingers atop my head, patting my scalp as he tugged on Sunset's reins, leading her sideways so my gaze was forced again to fall upon the soldier and the infant at the side of the river. "Can you see? Can you see the child?"

I tried to speak, but my voice caught in my throat. I swallowed and forced the sound out, the word I knew he wanted to hear. "Yes." I did not say that Sunset's ears flickered across my view, sometimes blocking what the soldier held in his hands. I wasn't allowed to be comforted by such a thing.

"What do you see?"

I clenched my teeth. There could only be one answer. "Black hair. Golden skin." I took a deep breath. "The eyes..." I couldn't see them clearly from Sunset's back, but there could be no other reason Father would show me the scene.

"Black," Father finished for me. He pulled too hard on my hair, causing my scalp to twinge slightly. He didn't say the rest, what I knew he would only imply: *Like yours. Hair, skin and eyes that you and no one else on this island shares. You and no one else but that baby.*

"Please! Have mercy! She's just a child!" The woman still kicked, forcing the words out between shrieks.

From behind me, Father's composed voice answered the woman. "There is no mercy for traitors." He spoke louder. "Send the outsider back where it came from."

I couldn't blink, but part of me prayed that Sunset would whip her mane across my face to shield me, to comfort me. But I learned long ago there was no one who would ever comfort me. No one but Father. That's what he told me. That's what I knew.

The soldier bent to the river and placed the screaming bundle atop it. The current tore the bundle from his gauntlets, and I watched as the mess of black hair floated further and further away, as if the river were as eager to rid our isle of the child as Father was. For a moment, I thought perhaps it would make its way back home. The child was too far for me to hear its screaming. Perhaps it kept crying. Perhaps it would cry all the way home. But it was the kicking leg, the tiny kicking leg, that brought me back to the truth of what I'd witnessed. Just as the baby reached the horizon, just as I was sure it would drown far beyond where I could ever see it, the tiny leg stopped and faltered, descended and vanished from view.

"Apparently the outsiders don't want it, either." Father gripped Sunset's reins with both hands and pulled her back to face the shrieking woman. I blinked, giving my eyes relief at last from the sting.

The woman slumped at the side of the river, the soldiers stepping back to mount their own horses. "Demon!" she sobbed quietly. "Bastard!"

"This is what happens when you shelter an outsider," said Father. "When you let him into your home, shelter him in your heart." I looked up at Father and saw his gaze turned up to the sky, at the moon that appeared against the blue, the moon that had come out even before the sun had finished setting.

He pulled Sunset's reins, turning her back, back to the heart of the duchy, back to the castle. I slipped my fingers through her mane and gripped tightly, afraid that if I

253

fell into the river then, the waters would sweep me up to join the child who was just like me.

Father nodded at the soldier who'd placed the baby in the river as the man stepped beside us. "If she has nothing more to say about the outsider who left that child within her, let her join it."

The soldier said nothing. I couldn't tell if there was any life at all in his eyes.

Father whipped the reins and Sunset was off. I exhaled as we put the river behind us.

"Demon!" I heard the woman scream behind us. "Your rule is hypocrisy!"

Hypocrisy. The other words I knew, but that was one I'd never heard before. I turned my head, trying to lean around Father to get one last look—

As if he'd heard my thoughts, Father answered the question I'd never dare ask. "She means she doesn't think it's right that I killed her baby and let you live."

I swallowed, faced forward, and stared at the castle. I focused on the rapid clopping of Sunset's hooves, straining to put the muffled screaming far, far behind me.

ᵛᵛᵛ

"Lady Rohesia. His lordship wouldn't approve of you taking this rather, uh, *scenic* route."

Leave it to the sniveling swine to refer to streets covered in fish guts and dog shit as 'scenic.' Sherrod ran his knobby fingers through his limp straw hair, somehow managing to stain his grease-covered fingertips with yet another layer of grime with the gesture. Father often warned me to stay a good few feet in front of the man unless I hoped to wake up with a coating of white flakes and scabs on my scalp the next morning. He had his uses, but companionship was not one of them. Nor was stealth.

I stuck my right hand out to stop Sherrod from overtaking me, my left wrapping around my sword hilt.

"We're not here to pick posies, Sherrod." I nudged the tip of my steel-toed boot forward so I could lean around the corner for a better look. "Father won't care how I got here, so long as I get the job done."

I didn't have to turn around to imagine the pinched look on Sherrod's face, the way he ran his tongue across his protruding front tooth whenever something bothered him. "But may I ask why the stealth was so necessary?" he asked. "Why couldn't we take a band of soldiers and just march right up to the dock, swords extended—"

"Quiet," I hissed, leaning back and retreating to the safety of the alley. I drew my blade out slightly. A sailor pulling on one of the ropes that rolled the barrels down the plank had stopped to wipe his brow, and his gaze had wandered too close to our alley for my liking.

"My lady," Sherrod tried to speak softly, but the best he could manage was sounding like a man told to whisper while screaming, "you've seen only seventeen winters, and are perhaps not quite as familiar with the, uh, position of leadership as you may think, and the duke's guard is at your command—"

"As are you," I reminded him. "And your sole command now is to refrain from speaking."

Sherrod's tongue whipped out and smeared saliva all across his upper lip. Even with his mouth shut, his tooth bulged out, as if it couldn't be contained behind his lips, like most of the refuse the steward felt compelled to tell me. Satisfied he'd keep his tongue occupied with his lips for the time being, I leaned back around the corner for a better view of the newly-arrived ship.

The Duke's Favor was an old ship with golden sails, marking it as a trading vessel under the protection of the duchy's lordship. I'd read up on it before I left that morning, although I'd been familiar with its most recent captain, who'd often dined with Father. It was supposed to supply the duchy with rice, opium and spices, and had done so faithfully for decades, since the time of my father's father.

But Father had received word by pigeon that Captain Tierny had died of fever after they made port, and the ship was late. Too late. Families had gone hungry, and divans had started demanding more gold for their opium, causing a bit of a problem with inflation. Father had put an end to it all by hanging a few divan owners in the market, a reminder to the people that greed would not be tolerated when others go hungry. He'd had to ration the rice, too, and supplement what was left with some of the grain from our fields, but there was never enough wheat to feed the people.

I counted the men pulling the barrels and watched the one who seemed to be shouting the orders. The new captain. Father said the man was softer than Tierny, and younger, too. That wouldn't bode well for what I was there to do. At least, it wouldn't bode well for the new captain.

There were forty-two men on and around the ship that I could see. The rest of the fifty—forty-nine, I suppose, disregarding Tierny—could be below decks or dead at sea. Or if they were too loyal to Tierny, to the duchy... Dead by mutiny.

"My lady," scream-whispered Sherrod from behind me. The simple command of keeping his mouth shut was never bound to last long. "What's the point of skulking in the shadows? Do you even know what to look for?"

"Yes, I do." I smiled, watching as a row of the barrels broke free of the ropes, rolling freely off the side of the plank and thudding to the ground. There was one that bounced and rolled further than the others, causing the captain and a few of the men pulling the barrels to panic and chase it down before it could fall into the harbor.

I straightened my back and slid my sword all the way back into its scabbard. I took a step forward, noticed a bit of dirt on my shoulder plate and stopped to flick it away. I felt Sherrod slam into the back of me, his nose crunching against my cape and jingling the mail beneath my chest plate. I turned, grabbing my cape and inspecting it for a

Sherrod-shaped dirt imprint. Finding a dark spot, I glared down at the steward as he took a step back.

He ran his tongue over his tooth twice. "I'm so sorry, Lady Rohesia." He bent his head and averted his eyes to the shit beneath our feet, as if willing himself to sink into the muck. "I thought we were going—"

"Four feet."

Sherrod wrung his hands together, pausing to wipe the sweat that accumulated on them across the front of his tunic. "Pardon?" He dared to look up.

I let my cape fall, and it swished, blowing air back and rustling Sherrod's greasy hair. I leaned forward, sticking a gloved finger toward his chest, too repulsed to touch it. "You stay four feet behind me at all times. Or is that a problem?"

Sherrod took four exaggerated steps back, his eyes back on the grime below us. "No! Of course not. I mean, of course. I'm so sorry. I have no excuse—"

"Enough." I turned back, my cape swishing once more behind me. "I better not hear you speak. I don't even want to realize you're there."

To emphasize the point, I paused, daring Sherrod to speak in acquiescence. He didn't. A shame. I'd have liked to remind him that I'd outgrown him, in more ways than one.

I stepped forward toward the docking bay, my head held high, my feet slamming into the cobblestones and wood with more force than necessary. I turned a few heads as I weaved my way through the men still attending the remainder of the barrels, stepping over the taut rope a few of them held without acknowledging them or letting my back or shoulders slouch in the slightest. By the time I'd made my way across the crowd of sailors, only the crew and captain attending to the lighter barrel hadn't noticed me. They finished tilting it upward, a few stopping to wipe their brows. The captain crouched beside it, his lips moving.

"Does opium often talk back to you, Captain? That is, when you're not inhaling it?"

The captain's shoulders stiffened. Unfortunately, I didn't hold the advantage long. The captain rolled his shoulders, relaxing as he stood. His face—weather-worn and caked in lines, but not entirely displeasing—lit up with a grin that slithered its way across his features.

"I wouldn't know about opium," he said, placing his right hand on his waist, not-so-subtly close to his blade's hilt. "I never mix business with pleasure." He laid his left hand on the barrel casually. "And besides, this here's spices that's doing the talking."

I sniffed the air, searching for the telltale giveaway of cinnamon and nutmeg, but the air smelled like nothing but rotten fish and sea salt. A gust of wind that changed direction and a flicker of movement out of the corner of my eye demanded my attention. "Seems to me like your spices are bobbing in the sea, Captain."

Like sheep, the captain and the crew looked at once into the harbor. I watched, pleased as the grin dropped off the captain's face and he shouted orders to retrieve the barrel that they hadn't bothered to save from rolling into the waters. The captain was the only one left attending the barrel atop which he still rested his forearm. He smiled again, moving his other hand from his belt to wipe his brow of excess moisture. He laughed. "Two squalls on the return trip, and not a scratch on 'em. Two minutes with this lot, and we lose two barrels." He pointed at the men scrambling to throw a rope down to the floating barrel, but I refused to follow his gesture.

"I don't recall ever having this problem when Captain Tierny led 'the lot.'" I jutted my chin toward him. "I don't think we've had the pleasure."

"I was about to say the same myself. Captain Hann of the Duke's Favor, at your service." The captain bowed deeply, removing his hat and revealing the thinning dark hair clinging to his scalp. He fastened his hat back on his head, careful to leave his left arm on the barrel all the while. His eyes drifted over my head to somewhere behind me.

"And you. I'd have thought to call the soldiers over immediately, but I know that fellow, and I can't imagine him trailing behind an outsider dressed to battle an army."

I clenched my jaw and waited for Sherrod to confirm the acquaintance. But of course, I'd warned him not to speak, and he had chosen this one inopportune moment to decide to follow my commands. Whatever it took for him to make my life more difficult.

I gave up and spoke his name. "Sherrod." Silence. This was getting ridiculous. The captain's grin twisted, resembling something closer to a genuine smirk. I turned and saw the useless man face first on the ground, one foot in the air dangling from the taut rope above him. The remaining sailors holding the rope were frozen in what was probably confusion, neither continuing to pull down the barrels or offering at all to help the steward. I couldn't say I blamed them.

"He's been that way a few minutes," said the captain coolly. "You might want to see if he conked his head in the fall."

The captain still leaned on the barrel, scuffing his boot on the dock and examining his boot toe. If he thought I was going to turn my back on him long enough to help someone who would be no use to me whatsoever, he was grossly underestimating me. "He doesn't have much there to injure."

The captain raised an eyebrow. "Is this how the duke rewards such ardent devotion?"

I smiled, doing my best to echo the sculptured grin Hann had. "There's no reason for the duke to reward what's expected of all men. And I'm not my father." I nodded toward the barrel as I let my left hand pull my sword a little out of its sheath, calling attention to gesture. "Open the barrel, Captain."

Hann laughed, letting his forearm fall from the top of the barrel at last as he threw his hands in the air and then crossed his arms, trying a bit too hard to seem casual. "The duke is so hard up for soldiers, he sends his own daughter to pick up the delivery? Is he that eager to get his first cut of opium and spices?"

"No, the duke, as you phrased it, never 'mixes business with pleasure.'" I pulled my sword out further, knowing the sun would gleam off the metal and draw the captain's eyes toward it. "You're late, Captain. Too late. And smuggling outsiders."

Before I could fully pull the sword from its scabbard, I flicked my right hand. The small dagger I kept there slipped out, and I wrapped my fingers around its hilt. The captain fumbled for a moment but drew his sword in time to cross with mine, but by then, my dagger had already slipped into his arm. He shouted and his sword faltered, drooping slightly. He gritted his teeth and raised the sword back upward to move more in tune with mine. "You missed."

I grabbed my sword with both hands and spun, tearing it free from his weakened resistance and bringing it down toward his shoulder. He dodged, rolling out of the way but grunting as the dagger hit the deck and slid further into his arm, and my sword reached its intended target: the barrel. The wood that chipped off was no bigger than the size of my hand, but I didn't need to see more to recognize the eye that stared back out at me. The dark brown, almost black iris.

The captain scrambled to his feet, sweat pouring down his brow, his hat crooked and in shambles on his head. His arms shook as he struggled to lift his sword out in front of him, his boots slipping on the wood dampened by blowing seawater. "How could you let your father do this?" The words were difficult for him to get past his purpling lips. "You're one of them."

I let myself look one more time at the eye that peeked out from the chip I'd made in the barrel. It darted from me to the captain and back again. I wondered, not for the first time, what an outsider found so appealing about the duchy, knowing what fate would likely have in store for them there. But Father could be generous to his people. Perhaps the risk was worth it to them.

"Captain, you're mistaken." I swapped my sword into my weaker hand, reaching into the pouch at my waist and sliding out the thin silver tool I kept hidden there. Hann flinched but dragged himself protectively in front of the barrel, draping that same elbow on the top, no longer from some futile effort to appear casual but because every step he took was enough to send a weaker man sprawling headfirst to the deck, where he would never get up again. I watched his struggle, thinking of how pathetically he'd tried to fool me with wide grins and teasing. "My feet have never touched soil outside of the duchy. You're more of an outsider than I am."

I brought the flute to my mouth and blew three notes. The notes hung in the air for a moment, reverberating into silence. And then the hooves began to echo on the stones leading to the docks, the clomp of foot soldiers stomping in time to an unsung melody.

"You... bitch..." Hann's legs gave way, and he struggled in vain to stand as his weight collapsed down on top of them. His sword fell numbly from his fingers, clattering to the ground.

I slid the flute back into my pouch and bent forward, ripping the dagger out of the captain's shoulder. "If Ytoile exists, perhaps you'll give Her my regards. Unless you're sent flying into the flame kingdom." I wiped what remained of the blood and poison from the dagger's blade against the top of the barrel.

Hann's eyes fluttered shut and his shoulders slumped forward. "Hypo... crisy..."

Yes, yes. It was sort of a death cry for these types. The whole line was left unsaid: "Your whole existence is hypocrisy."

I straightened my shoulders and turned, sparing one last look for the quaking eyeball seen through the hole in the barrel. The soldiers I'd summoned from the town square were engaged in battle with the remaining sailors, although their armor put them in little danger from the ragtag attack of whittling knives and daggers. I walked back in the direction I'd come, paying no attention to the cries of anger and pain that erupted all around me.

I gazed at the tip of my sword and the scratch in the metal the barrel had put there. The blade was lined with such scratches, the metal almost dangerously close to cracking into pieces. I slid the blade into its scabbard and reached down toward Sherrod, grabbing him roughly under the armpit and dragging him to his feet, feeling his weight tug at the tendons in my arm but determined not to let the strain show on my face. His foot twisted and freed itself from the rope just as his eyelids fluttered open.

"My lady?" His eyes had sort of a glossy look as they darted back and forth wildly, searching my face and what I presumed to be the men gathering behind me. Convenient that he knock himself out while I made my inspection. Too convenient.

"We're done here, Sherrod." I gave him another tug and lurched forward, ignoring the pain in my sword arm. When at last the steward heaved himself up entirely and made a great show of dusting off his tunic, I rolled my eyes and gladly let go of his armpit.

"Was his lordship right about the captain then, my lady?"

I wiped my moistened glove against my cape. "Father is always right, Sherrod."

"Let them take you for a fool, Rohesia," Father had instructed. *"It lowers their guard, and it's more fun to see them act brash before they squirm."*

"It's just a matter of toying with your prey before you slaughter it."

I stepped aside into a puddle to avoid the swinging sword of the nearest soldier, washing away the shit and dirt on my boot in the jumble of blood and sea water.

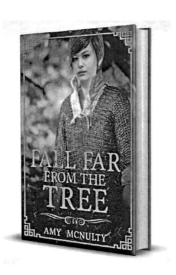

Terror. Callousness. Denial. Rebellion. How the four teenage children of leaders in the duchy and the neighboring empire of Hanaobi choose to adapt to their nefarious parents' whims is a matter of survival.

Rohesia, daughter of the duke, spends her days hunting "outsiders," fugitives who've snuck onto her father's island duchy. That she lives when even children who resemble her are subject to death hardens her heart to tackle the task.

Fastello is the son of the "king" of the raiders who steal from the rich and share with the poor. When aristocrats die in the raids, Fastello questions what his peoples' increasingly wicked methods of survival have cost them.

An orphan raised by a convent of mothers, Cateline can think of no higher aim in life than to serve her religion, even if it means turning a blind eye to the suffering of other orphans under the mothers' care.

Kojiro, new heir to the Hanaobi empire, must avenge his people against the "barbarians" who live in the duchy, terrified the empress, his own mother, might rather see him die than succeed.

When the paths of these four young adults cross, they must rely on one another for survival—but the love of even a malevolent guardian is hard to leave behind.

Add FALL FAR FROM THE TREE to your Goodreads to-read list or order it on Amazon or Barnes & Noble today!

CPSIA information can be obtained
at www.ICGtesting.com
Printed in the USA
LVOW10s1720090518

576572LV00012B/657/P

9 781927 940853